DECEIVED BY MAGIC

A BAINE CHRONICLES NOVEL

JASMINE WALT

DYNAMO PRESS

Cover illustration by Judah Dobin

Cover typography by Rebecca Frank

Edited by Mary Burnett

Electronic edition, 2016. If you want to be notified when Jasmine's next novel is released and get access to exclusive contests, giveaways, and freebies, sign up for her mailing list here. Your email address will never be shared and you can unsubscribe at any time.

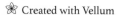 Created with Vellum

AUTHOR'S NOTE

Dear Reader,

If this is the first book you've picked up in the Baine Chronicles series, I've included a glossary in the back of the book to help illuminate the backstory. If you've already read the previous books, this glossary will help reacquaint you to the people, places, and things introduced to you in earlier volumes. You can either read the glossary first to familiarize or re-familiarize yourself with Sunaya's world, or you can plunge into the story and refer to it as needed. The guide is in alphabetical order, and characters are listed last name first.

To the new reader, welcome to the Baine Chronicles! And to those of you who have read the previous books, welcome back and thank you! Your support allows me to continue doing what I love most—writing.

Best,
Jasmine

1

———

"*You're not getting away!*" Rylan's voice echoed in my head. The full moon shimmered above us as we raced across the Palace rooftop in an impromptu game of tag. My claws scraped against the red clay tiles as I bunched my hind legs, then leapt from the edge of the roof and onto a turret that was a good six feet away.

"*Nyah, nyah.*" Peering from around the turret, I let my tongue loll out at him from between my fangs. It felt damn good to be back in beast form—it had been way too long since I'd allowed my animal side to roam free.

Rylan growled playfully at me from across the way, his yellow-orange eyes gleaming in the moonlight. His fur rippled as he crouched—a brownish-yellow with black spots, unlike my inky fur. In human form, he dyed his blond hair black, a habit he'd gotten into as a teen to spite his mother, my aunt Mafiela. But in reality, he shared our family's light coloring, unlike me. He sprang across the divide, landing on the turret as well, then yelped as one of the tiles beneath his paws broke off. He scrabbled up the turret and after me, but he'd been distracted in those crucial seconds, and I was already on the next roof.

"Has old age made you slow?" I taunted, then ducked behind a chimney as he came flying after me. Rylan was only two years older than me, but I never missed a chance to tease him about it.

"Slow!" the ether parrot squawked, materializing by my ear, and I nearly jumped out of my skin. Rylan took advantage of my momentary lapse in concentration and whipped his tail around the corner. It wrapped around my foreleg before I could get clear, and then he quickly retracted it before I could snag it with my claws and tag him back.

"Ha! Who's the slow one now?" Rylan crowed, his voice ringing with laughter. He jumped out of my reach, then over to the next rooftop.

Snarling, I swiped at the ether parrot, but my claws went right through the glowing bird. He was, after all, not a real animal—just a spell made from magic whose only real function seemed to be popping in and out at the damnedest moments. Frustrated, I let out a hiss at being caught, then raced after Rylan. Hopefully the spell would wear off soon, and that pesky parrot would be gone for good.

Rylan and I continued chasing each other across the rooftops for another hour, getting lost in the simple pleasure of a game of tag. It was a lot of fun despite the ether parrot, who continued to pop in and out, antagonizing us both. In fact, I couldn't remember the last time I'd done something like this. I tagged Rylan twice more, but he got me more than I got him— his reflexes were faster, and it was hard to stay away from both his paws *and* his tail.

I was sure Iannis wouldn't appreciate it if he knew Rylan and I were running around on top of the Palace, risking our necks and breaking his roof tiles, but I didn't have much choice. Shifters were compelled to change during the full moon. Since Rylan was pretending to be my tiger-shifter bodyguard, Lanyr, he couldn't be seen walking around the Palace in jaguar form.

So, instead, I'd brought him up here, hoping to keep him away from prying eyes for a bit, as well as work off some of the energy that would be thrumming through his veins. Shifters were bred as a warrior class, so we were physically fearless—the hundred-foot drop from the turrets didn't faze us as we sprang from rooftop to rooftop.

The full moon didn't affect me as strongly as it did Rylan, so shifting wasn't mandatory for me. But that same restless energy still coursed through my veins, demanding an outlet. The full moon heightened our powers, and it was during the night that shifters tended to be most active.

"*Okay,*" Rylan finally said with a sigh, settling down. He rested his chin on his paws and stared out at Firegate Bridge, which glowed a brilliant red as it stretched across Solantha Bay. "*I'm good now.*"

"*You sure?*" I asked, dipping my head to briefly nuzzle his fur. Rylan and I had been very close before he'd joined the Resistance, and I was glad we seemed to be slipping back to the way things used to be between us. We were comrades in arms, the two rebels who could never quite please the Baine Clan matriarch.

Speaking of which, I had a lunch meeting with Aunt Mafiela scheduled for tomorrow. A ripple of apprehension traveled the length of my spine, and my tail whipped to the side. Would we be able to put our differences aside long enough to be peaceable? Or would one of us end up storming from the table?

"*Yeah, I'm fine,*" Rylan insisted, closing his eyes. "*I'll sleep up here tonight. Should be relatively safe—if no one came running when they saw us jumping about up here, they're not going to now. If something does happen, I'll just call for you. Go get laid already.*" He winked at me.

"*Well, when you put it that way.*" I snorted, then turned away and headed down the roof, back toward my open bedroom window in the west wing. Iannis had arrived home from Dara a few hours ago, and he'd promised me a late dinner once he was done dealing with urgent Palace business that had been waiting for him. It was getting close to nine o'clock, so I hoped dinner would be soon. A good thing too, because I was ravenous after all that running around.

As I climbed back into my bedroom, my heart beat a little faster at the thought of seeing Iannis again. He'd been gone three days, and even though we'd only been engaged a short time, I already missed sleeping curled up next to him. But that wasn't the only reason for my beating heart—I was also nervous about what he'd say once I told him what had happened in his absence.

I shifted back into human form, then went to draw a bath so I wouldn't smell of sweat and fur when I saw Iannis. Two days ago, I'd received a letter from my half-sister, Isana, who had apparently noticed a familial resemblance between us from a photograph of me she'd seen in a magazine. She wanted to know whether we were related, and if she could come to the wedding.

A headache started squeezing my temples as I sank into the bath, and I rubbed at them with two fingers, trying to relax. Iannis had urged me to avoid revealing my identity to my father's family at all costs. Doing so could have disastrous conse-quences that would complicate our engagement, amongst other things. I hadn't made any effort to contact them at all, even after discovering who my father was, but apparently being in the public eye was enough to draw their attention. Did I just ignore them? Or should I take the opportunity to find out more about my mage family?

I finished washing, then dried my hair and dressed. I half considered just throwing on a robe, since it was so late, but I wanted to look good for Iannis. So, instead, I pulled out a silver dress and matching earrings. The halter neck and sweetheart bodice did a great job highlighting my assets, and the A-line skirt swept down to just below my knees. I scooped my hair back and twisted it into a high knot, then toyed with the idea of makeup.

By Magorah! I was acting like a schoolgirl going on her first date. But then again, Iannis was worth it. He'd proven time and time again that he loved me and had my back, no matter what, and he'd asked for my hand in marriage despite such a union being unprecedented in the history of the Northia Federation.

The scent of sandalwood and magic drifted to my nose, and I grinned as I heard footsteps in the hall. He was back! The door to his bedroom down the hall opened and closed, and I rushed to the secret door connecting our chambers so I could go to Iannis.

But what if he doesn't want to see you? a doubt-filled voice whispered in my head. *Didn't he say he was going to let you know when he was done with work?*

I hesitated, my hand on the door panel. That was true—he'd said he would call me when he was ready. But I didn't want to wait any longer, and besides, I doubted Iannis was going to complain if I came to him now.

Right?

Stop worrying, I ordered myself as I pushed open the door. I crept down the hall as silently as I could so that he couldn't hear me—which was pretty damn silent. I was cat-footed, you might say.

Okay, that was a bad joke.

His delicious scent grew stronger as I approached, and I took in a slow, greedy breath. Oh yeah, he was definitely here. Warmth began to flow through my veins as my excitement morphed into desire. The full moon made shifters friskier than normal, and I knew just who I wanted to 'frisk' tonight.

I pushed open the door, then greedily drank in the sight of Iannis in front of the fireplace wearing nothing but his bare skin. His blue-and-gold robes were puddled on the floor, and judging by the direction he'd been walking in, he'd been heading to his bathroom for a shower.

"Sunaya!" He froze, and his eyes darkened with lust as he got a good look at me and what I was wearing. I took the opportunity to take in every inch of his body, just as he was doing with mine. The lamplight made his alabaster skin glow, revealing every dip and curve in that lean, muscular body I was itching to get my hands on. I licked my lips as my gaze traveled down his broad shoulders and chest, over abs I could do laundry on all day long, then farther down.

"Well." I gave him an impish grin as heat ignited in my lower belly. "You look happy to see me."

"That's one way to put it," he agreed, closing the distance between us with long, determined strides. The heat spread lower as he pressed me up against the wall, cupping the sides of my face with his long-fingered hands. "I missed you," he growled, feathering kisses over my cheeks, my nose, and my jaw.

I grabbed his head and yanked his mouth to mine, hungry for more. He smelled of sweat and man and magic, and I greedily inhaled his scent in as I kissed him like a woman starved. My fingers twined in his long, dark red hair, the strands sliding against my skin like silk, and his hard body pressed tightly against mine as he kissed me back just as fiercely. My hands roamed over his naked skin, sliding down the plates of muscle layered over his broad back, then molding around his finely toned ass. The muscles flexed in my hands as he growled something in Loranian, and I gasped as his body heat flowed over my suddenly naked skin.

"You've been holding out on me with that trick," I gasped as he picked me up and carried me to the bed.

"Of course," he said roughly, covering my body with his own. His eyes gleamed with wicked intent as he leaned in to nip my earlobe. "I've got to maintain the upper hand between us *somehow.*"

He fused his mouth to mine, driving the pithy comment I was about to make straight out of my mind with his talented tongue and teeth. There was no more talking after that. Our lovemaking was fast and furious, a voracious clash of passion and will as we sought release and completion with one another. There was biting, hair pulling, and maybe a few claw marks. But best of all was the savage satisfaction when we finally reached the edge, when I watched Iannis throw back his head and roar his pleasure as I found mine as well.

I had given him that. Me and no one else. Iannis ar'Sannin, Chief Mage of Canalo, was mine. And soon enough, we would be legally and magically bound unto death.

"So much for dressing up for dinner," I teased, stroking a hand down his sweaty back. His muscles were sleek, smooth, and completely relaxed as he lay atop me, his head nestled in the crook of my shoulder, his warm breath tickling my skin. "I think you ripped my dress."

"That's all right," Iannis said, turning his cheek so he could press a kiss against my neck. "We'll just dine naked."

I chuckled. A few months ago, I never could have imagined dining with the Chief Mage clothed, never mind naked. "I have a feeling we won't get much eating done if we do that," I said, running my fingers through his hair.

He lifted his head to look down at me with those gorgeous violet eyes. "I believe I've proved myself capable of doing more than one thing at a time," he said, a languorous smile coming to his full lips. He reached between our bodies as he lowered his mouth to mine, clearly intending to give me a demonstration.

The scent of steak and potatoes drifted in, and a different

kind of hunger came roaring back. "Let's switch gears for a sec," I said, swatting his hand away so I could sit up. "Our food's arriving."

Despite Iannis's earlier suggestion, he tossed a robe in my direction, then put on one himself and went out in the living-room area of his suite. I waited until the server left, then joined him at the small dining table. Starving now, I attacked my plate of food with the same single-minded devotion that I'd just showed in Iannis's bed, and didn't speak again until I'd cleared my second plate.

"Mmm," I said, sitting back in my chair and resting a hand over my belly. "That was delicious. So, what did you and the Minister talk about while you were in Dara?"

Iannis swallowed his bite of asparagus. "There were various matters of state to discuss, but the main reason he wanted to see me so urgently was the Resistance, as you no doubt have already guessed." He gave me a small smile.

"Yeah, I remember Director Chen said he wanted to discuss 'the Garaian matter' with you," I said. "Was he referring to the lab at Leniang Port? Or the gun running, for that matter?"

"Indeed. It turns out that the Minister was already aware of the facility, and had sent out a mission to destroy it several weeks ago. But the operatives, two men and a woman, have not reported back, and the Minister is beginning to worry that something may have happened to them. Not that he cares so much about them as individuals," he added dryly. "It's more that if their mission was discovered, it might affect our trade with Garai."

"I see." I ran my tongue along my upper teeth. I already knew the Minister was a coldhearted bastard, so his motives didn't surprise me. "Is he suggesting that we go and handle it personally?"

"That possibility was discussed, but it would draw too much

attention for an official of my status to travel to Garai," Iannis said ruefully. "I have no legitimate business in Garai to use as a cover. Besides, the Minister is debating whether it is worth sending another mission—after all, we cannot afford to simply throw our men away."

"Whether it's *worth* it?" I exclaimed, indignant. "Of course it's worth it! He'll just have to figure out what went wrong and find a way around it. We definitely can't tolerate that facility remaining open for long—the Resistance is funneling their guns through there, not to mention those awful diseases."

"I agree, but, ultimately, it is the Minister's decision," Iannis said, though it didn't sound like he meant it, at least not entirely. After all, Iannis, Fenris, and I could think of some way to deal with the problem if the Minister refused to act.

"Is that really all you discussed?" I asked. "You were gone for a few days."

"No, we discussed many tedious subjects like upcoming legislation, and, of course, rounding up the remaining Resistance units," Iannis said dismissively. It was clear he didn't intend on giving me all the details. "And what of you, Sunaya? Has everything been going well in my absence? How are your Loranian lessons with Fenris coming along?"

"Well enough," I muttered, even as my mood turned sour at the very thought. I hated the lessons, mostly because Loranian was so damn hard to learn. I took a deep breath. "I received a letter the other day, from Isana ar'Rhea of Castalis."

"*What*?" Iannis's head jerked upward, and our gazes clashed. There was a short pause, fraught with tension, and then those violet eyes narrowed. "You appear to be fully aware of that name's significance," he said at last. "I take it that, against my advice, you have been digging into your family history?"

"Yes," I said, squaring my shoulders. I wasn't going to let Iannis make me feel guilty about this. "I enlisted Janta's help, and I found out that Haman ar'Rhea is not only my father, but also the High Mage of Castalis." I gave him a dry look. "I also learned their line is directly descended from Resinah. Guess that makes me pretty special."

"Indeed." Iannis sighed, looking resigned. "I suppose you have a right to this knowledge, though I doubt it will do you much good right now. I hope that your investigation is not what drew Ms. ar'Rhea's attention to you."

"No, as a matter of fact, it wasn't." I crossed my arms over my chest. "Apparently, Isana saw my face in the paper and noticed a resemblance. She wants to come to the wedding, probably to see if we really do have a connection."

Iannis pressed his lips together. "Please show me the letter. I would like to read it myself."

I went back to my room to retrieve it, trying not to be annoyed. After all, I knew Iannis would react this way. When I came back, he was sitting on the couch, his face turned toward the empty fireplace. I handed him the letter, then sat down on the opposite side and waited for him to finish reading it. Once he was done, he folded it up, then stared into the empty grate for a long moment.

"Well?" I demanded, unable to stand the silence any longer. "What's going through your head?"

Iannis turned his head toward me slowly, his eyes hard. "It *could* be that this girl—your half-sister—has an unusually enlightened attitude toward shifters, but I suspect that this letter was not young Isana's idea at all. More likely, it was dictated to her by one of her parents."

"Her parents?" I recoiled at that thought. "You mean it's possible that my father told her to write that?" *But why?*

"Yes, or even worse, her grandfather, the former High Mage of Castalis." Worry entered Iannis's gaze, and he reached for my hand, squeezing it hard. "Haman's father-in-law is utterly ruthless, as he amply demonstrated during the century he was High Mage himself. He may have stepped down officially, but I suspect he is still more powerful than Haman. If he knew or suspected that you were related to his daughter's family, he would go to whatever lengths he deemed necessary to remove you as a threat. You may not know this, but Castalians are strongly prejudiced against shifters, and Haman's entire family would be considered disgraced if your existence were discovered."

"Yeah, Janta told me about how one of the previous High Mages drove all the shifters out of their borders." My lip curled in a sneer. "If that's how they still feel about shifters, then I don't want anything to do with them anyway."

"Good," Iannis said firmly, covering my hand with his own. "So long as that's your attitude, you should be perfectly safe. I strongly recommend you avoid contact with them if at all possible. As for Isana's letter, you should write back that the resemblance is simply a coincidence. Sometimes a lie is necessary to save everyone untold trouble. Including Isana herself."

"And what about her request to attend our wedding?" I asked. Was it really wise to snub a member of the ruling family of another country?

"Tell her she is welcome to visit if she likes, but that things are still in an uproar because of our recent troubles with the Resistance, and that it would be safer if she waited until things had calmed down. That should dissuade her."

"True," I said, biting my lip. I'd be dissuaded too, if the country I was planning to visit turned out to be dealing with a huge rebel problem. *Would we ever be free of the Resistance?* I wondered, staring out the window. Or were we forever going to be dealing with them, like a persistent illness that we just couldn't shake?

2

J arrived early for lunch at the Winter Garden, a private dining room in the Palace used to entertain important guests. It was hexagonal-shaped, with a trio of windows toward the back that overlooked the Palace Gardens. A table for two was set near those windows, and one of the servers pulled out the chair as I approached. I had to stop myself from scooting it forward, instead allowing him to push in my chair like a real lady should.

Hopefully this meeting won't be too awkward, I thought as I studied the winter landscape mural that stretched across the walls of the circular room. It was hard to imagine that it might go well, though. I had spent the last ten years hating and resenting the matriarch of the Baine Clan, and with damn good reason. Now we were about to sit down to a civilized meal, and the fluttering in my stomach told me that I wasn't entirely ready for this.

There's no choice but to be ready, I told myself firmly. I'd already committed myself, and it would have been cowardly to back out. I would never show weakness to Mafiela Baine. Vulnerability was something you only showed to people you trusted, and to say that I didn't trust her was the understatement of the century.

I caught Mafiela's daffodil-and-steel scent, and turned my gaze toward the entrance. The double doors opened, a servant announcing the arrival of my aunt, and I stood, careful to keep my expression neutral as I surveyed her.

"Good afternoon," Aunt Mafiela said, inclining her head. My back stiffened in surprise at the respectful gesture—it was as close to a full-on bow as she would come to for anyone except perhaps the Chief Mage. "It is good to see you well."

"And you as well," I said, returning the gesture with a nod of my own. The air crackled with tension as we both stood for a long moment, sizing each other up.

"I can't remember the last time you wore a dress," Aunt Mafiela finally commented, mild bemusement in her yellow eyes as she regarded me. "It, ah, suits you quite well."

"Thanks." I smoothed my hands over the silk skirt of my chartreuse gown, trying not to show my nerves. Unfortunately, Mafiela could smell my anxiety, so it didn't really matter. It did make me feel better to know that she was nervous too—not that you could tell from looking. She was perfectly coiffed and dressed, her blonde hair swept up into a graceful knot, her makeup done tastefully but not over the top, the pearls gleaming at her wrists and throat an indication of wealth without being ostentatious. The Baine Clan owned a large share in the local fishing fleet, and therefore Mafiela was very financially secure. With the way she dressed and acted, no one would ever guess that beneath her pale pink gown and manicured nails still lurked the cunning and savagery of a beast.

But then again, she *was* a shifter. Even though we were part animal, we were also part human. And that manifested itself in different ways.

"Why don't we sit?" I finally asked, gesturing to the table.

"I'm sure you're as famished as I am."

"Yes," Mafiela agreed, finally crossing the rest of the distance to our table. As soon as we were settled into our chairs, the servants brought out the first course—a grilled chicken and arugula salad garnished with nuts and cranberries. My appetite had been dulled by the ball of nerves in my stomach, but the scent of the chicken brought it roaring back again. After all, food was food, and I'd never refused an opportunity to eat in my life.

"I know that you and I have not been on the best of terms in a long time," Mafiela said, her voice subdued. "But I hope we can move past that, and perhaps come to a reconciliation of sorts."

"Is that because you're sorry for how you treated me, or because you want to take advantage of my new position?" I challenged before I could stop myself. I hadn't intended to go down that path—after all, attacking her wouldn't get her to open up about my father—but I just couldn't help it.

Mafiela stiffened, drawing herself upright as if she were about to scold me for being impudent. My fingers clenched around my fork, ready for a fight. But then she let out a breath, as if remembering herself, where we were, and who I was now. With visible effort, she relaxed.

"If I'm being honest, a little bit of both," she admitted. "Watching you survive and prosper, despite the overwhelming odds against you, surprised me. But what convinced me that I have misjudged you was when I watched you go out of your way time and time again to help the shifter community, even though you do not owe Shiftertown your loyalty."

"I owed Roanas my loyalty," I said quietly, and my chest ached with an old, familiar grief as I thought of my dead mentor. "As the Shiftertown inspector, he would have wanted me to help."

"Yes," Mafiela said. Her eyes grew distant as her gaze shifted to the window. "Roanas was a good man. I was sad when he died so suddenly."

Anger burned in my chest as I recalled that Mafiela hadn't even bothered to inform me of his funeral date, but I decided it wasn't worth bringing up. We were finally heading in the right direction, and bringing up every single item on my laundry list of grievances wasn't going to help.

But there was one thought that still niggled on the back of my mind, and I couldn't move on until I had it answered. "Did you really kick me out of your household because you couldn't stand me?" I asked her. "Or was it because I reminded you too much of my father?"

From what I understood, Mafiela had always strongly resented my unknown father for giving my mother a child out of wedlock and then leaving her to deal with the consequences.

Mafiela shook her head. "No," she said. "That has nothing to do with it. I never met the man, so how could you remind me of him? Despite your propensity for getting into mischief with Rylan, you were not a bad child. And it was not your fault that your father did what he did."

"Then why the hell did you do it?" I snapped. To my horror, tears began welling at the corners of my eyes, and I blinked hard to force them back. *That old hurt is done and over with,* I told myself. I was a grown woman now, and a kick-ass one at that.

"It wasn't personal," Mafiela insisted, but I could scent her guilt. "I had to get you away to protect the rest of the clan. As an illegal magic user, you were a liability to us. That constant threat of discovery, coupled with my anger and grief toward your mother for leaving us so soon, drove me to force you from the clan." Shame filled her gaze, and she dropped her eyes to the tablecloth in a submissive gesture that I almost gaped at. The clan matriarch I'd grown up under never would have done such a thing—it amounted to groveling.

"It was wrong of me to banish you from the clan in the manner that I did. I should have ensured you were taken care of, at the very least. I owed you that, as my sister's daughter. I am sorry."

Something in my chest lightened, and I swallowed against the lump in my throat. "Thank you," I said tightly, reaching for my glass of water. "I appreciate you saying that." It wasn't enough to make up for what she'd done, not by a long shot. But it was a start.

I drained my glass, then continued once I'd regained my composure. "What can you tell me about my father?" I asked. "Now that I'm attracting media attention as Iannis's bride, it's only a matter of time until I am forced to deal with my father's side of the family." I chose not to tell her about the letter I'd already received, or the research I'd done. "The more I know, the better prepared I will be."

"I don't know very much," my aunt warned. "Your mother was secretive about the affair from the beginning, and she never brought him home. But she saw him for two months, and I could always tell when she was thinking about him because she would grow dreamy-eyed and was often lost in thought. I warned her not to get involved with a human so close to her Heat, but she did not listen. I believe she was in love with him, or at least she thought she was." Mafiela's voice darkened with anger, and her yellow eyes flashed. "Foolish, and by the time she discovered she was with child, he had already gone."

"Did she ever tell you who he was?" I pressed.

"Yes. She asked for my help in tracking him down, and I was hardly going to refuse her considering the circumstances. It took some time to find him, as your mother had assumed he was human, and knew him only as Haman. By happenstance, we discovered a shifter who had witnessed your father changing his appearance and masking his scent. He followed him for a time, and discovered that he was living with a mage by the name of Ballos—studying under him, in fact." Mafiela's cheeks colored with fury. "It turned out that he was Haman ar'Rhea, a powerful mage from Castalis, and the next in line to become their new High Mage. He was also engaged."

"Yes, I know," I said evenly, though I was angry about that myself. It had been a shock when I'd learned that from Janta. "I had the Palace librarian do some research, and then I went to speak to Ballos myself. But you've confirmed for me, at least, that the affair wasn't just some quick, spur-of-the-moment thing."

"It would have been better if it had been," Mafiela spat. "Then Saranella wouldn't have..." She cleared her throat, realizing what she was about to say. "I apologize."

"No, I get it." And really, I did. It would have been better for the clan if I'd never been born. And yet, here I was. "Did you know that Ballos agreed to bind my magic in exchange for my mother's silence?"

"Yes. That was the only reason I allowed her to stay in the clan with you in the first place," Mafiela admitted. "I loved your mother very much, but I couldn't afford to put the whole clan at risk for a hybrid child. But after her far-too-premature death, your magical episodes got worse. One night, after you turned twelve, you had a terrible nightmare and nearly burned down the house by hurling lightning around in the bedroom."

"Oh." I squinted my eyes as I tried to recall that, but I didn't remember much more than being frightened, along with flashes of Mafiela's angry voice and the rotten-eggs stench of her singed blonde hair. "That was a long time ago."

"That was the final straw. It was all I could do to keep the servants from talking about those incidents, and I couldn't let it get out that you had magic. I had done my best to overlook your previous episodes, but that one had gone too far." Mafiela sighed. "I know the way I handled it was wrong, but I was at my wit's end. And I was still angry at your mother and the choices she made."

So angry you would hold that against her even in death? I wondered. But aloud, I said, "I understand. You were thinking of the clan first, as you should."

The rest of the lunch went smoothly. We discussed my wedding plans, as well as the progress of the Shiftertown rebuilding project. Tensions between Shiftertown and Maintown were still very high, especially now that word was spreading that the Resistance had planned to turn on their shifter members, and the shifter population in general, once they'd overthrown the mage regime. The council was still divided on how to deal with this rift, but they were planning to meet with the Maintown council in a few days in an effort to repair relations between the two sections of town.

I wondered if Iannis was aware of the rift, and if he planned to do anything about it. But then again, he was still busy dealing with the Resistance itself. Besides, for the most part, the Mages Guild had always left the other sections of town to govern themselves. He would step in if it was necessary, but it was probably better to see if the two races could sort themselves out first.

"Lunch was delightful," Mafiela said once our dessert plates were cleared from the table. "Thank you very much for inviting me to the Palace. Next time, you must come to share a meal in my house."

"You're welcome, and I will," I said, and I meant it, though I wasn't planning to do it any time soon. As she made to rise from the table, I held up a hand. "Hang on a moment. I have a surprise for you."

"A surprise?" she echoed, her eyebrows winging up.

"Rylan," I called in mindspeak, turning toward the doors. He was standing just outside, disguised once again as my tiger-shifter bodyguard, and he came in immediately at my signal,

closing the door securely behind him. Mafiela frowned, puzzled, and Rylan touched a pin attached to the lapel of his uniform, which was tied to his illusion. Iannis had decided to allow Rylan to turn it on and off at will, instead of relying on us, since we might not always be at hand.

"Rylan!" Mafiela cried, jumping to her feet as the illusion faded, revealing Rylan's true form. He still wore the same blue uniform, but his long blond hair had turned black again, his face reverting to the same edgy, handsome features he'd been blessed with since childhood, his orange tiger-shifter eyes lightening to jaguar yellow.

"Mother," Rylan said gruffly as he approached. His steps were wary, as if he feared she might rebuke him. I wouldn't be surprised if she did—she'd been furious at him for joining the Resistance over three years ago, and I was pretty sure they hadn't spoken since.

I held my breath as they stared at each other in stunned silence, then let it out silently in relief as Mafiela embraced him. The gesture might have been automatic, judging by the look of glassy shock in her eyes. But at least she had done it.

"You're here. You're alive," she said, pulling back to look at his face. "How is that possible? Last I heard, you had been captured and were awaiting sentence. I thought you might be dead or, at the least, suffering in the mines."

"It's a long story," Rylan began, then broke off as tears began to run down her face. "Oh, Mother, please don't. I'm all right. I'm sorry I made you worry."

I slipped out of the room to give them privacy, a smile on my face. Rylan might not be able to come out of hiding any time soon, but at least he could reunite with his mother and repair their damaged relationship.

Now if only I could do the same with my father's side of the family....

3

"Very good," Fenris said, checking over the worksheet I'd handed him. "You are getting the hang of conjugating your verbs, though you still have a way to go. Verbs are one of the most important aspects of learning Loranian, as spellcasting is almost exclusively done with commands."

"Thanks." I smiled, for once actually pleased with my progress. I'd spent the last two hours with Fenris in my sitting room, where he gave me my Loranian lessons daily. If I was going to become an accomplished mage, I had to master the language—a formidable task considering most mages started early and were fluent by the time they started their apprenticeships. To make matters worse, Loranian was difficult, the words hard to pronounce, and a single mispronounced word or phrase in a spell could result in disastrous consequences.

"Very good!" the ether parrot squawked as he materialized on my shoulder, and I sighed. The parrot was a constant reminder of that very problem—I had incorrectly pronounced a word when trying to conjure an ether pigeon, and instead got a parrot, who insisted on popping in and out of my life at odd moments, and repeating whatever words and phrases were being spoken at the time.

"You're a real nuisance, you know that?" I scolded, reaching for him. I mimed scratching the top of his head with my fingers, and even though they passed through his glowing head, he closed his eyes and bobbed his head against my hand. Could it be that he actually enjoyed it? How strange. I didn't think he could feel it when I touched him, considering he'd been unruffled when I'd thrown pillows at him or swiped at him with my claws.

The phone on my side table rang, and I jumped, then glared at the thing. Who could possibly be calling me? I'd only recently had the phone installed, and I wasn't aware that anyone other than Iannis, Fenris, Director Chen, and my social secretary had the number. None of them would think to bother me in the middle of a lesson, so it had to be someone else.

Maybe getting a phone in my suite was a mistake.

"Oh, go on," Fenris said with a sigh, closing the textbook on his lap. "We're about done for the day anyway."

Nodding, I picked up the phone. "Hello?"

"Naya." Comenius's voice sounded strained as it came through the line. "Can you please come to the shop as soon as you have a free moment? There is something urgent I must speak to you about in person."

"Sure." I blinked, wondering what could be so important that Com couldn't just tell me over the phone. "You're not in danger or anything, are you? Do I need to bring help?"

"No, no," Comenius assured me hastily. "Just bring yourself."

"All right. Be there in a few." Frowning, I hung up the phone, then glanced over at Fenris. "Guess it's a good thing we're ending off now."

"Do you need me to come with you?" Fenris asked, concern in his yellow wolf-shifter eyes. "Comenius has been a great help recently. If there is anything I can do to return the favor, I would be glad to assist."

I hesitated, then shook my head. "He said to just come on my own. I think it'll be fine, but if I do need you, I'll call."

I grabbed Rylan, who was once again Lanyr, and we headed for Witches End on my steam bike. Anxious to know what Comenius needed, I put on a little more speed, the steam engine shrieking behind me and belching out clouds of smoke into the summery late-afternoon air.

"*Thanks for arranging that reunion with my mother,*" Rylan said, using mindspeak as it was impossible to talk around our helmets or over the roaring wind. "*I've wanted to let her know I was all right, but I couldn't figure out how to do it without the risk of compromising my identity. I really appreciate you giving me the chance to reconnect with her.*"

"You're welcome," I said. "*I know that if it was my mother, I would want to.*"

Rylan was silent for a moment. "*Aunt Saranella would be proud if she could see how far you've come, Naya. It's really quite incredible, the strides you've made despite society's disdain toward hybrids.*"

"Yeah. Thanks." My throat tightened at the mention of my mother, and I swallowed hard. It had been so long since she'd passed away, over a decade, but it was still difficult not to ache when I was reminded of the loss. She'd been my champion, my protector, and my best friend. When she'd died, my life had become hell. At least until Roanas had taken me in, and even then, it was still tough. If not for his kindness, as well as the kindness of our neighbors, I wasn't sure what would have become of me.

At least you're not alone, I told myself. Roanas and my mother might be gone, but I had Iannis and my friends. The circle of people I could trust and rely on had grown quite a bit lately, and I really didn't want for anything at this point in my life.

But that wasn't enough. It wasn't right that so many others still suffered under the unjust laws regarding magic. How many magic users were forced to hide their talents and live in constant fear for the rest of their lives? The system Chief Mage Logar was testing in Parabas was a good start, but it was far from perfect. I'd been thinking on this problem for a while, and I had some ideas on how to improve on the system, if only I could get the chance.

I made a mental note to remind Iannis about the issue and insist on having my say. If I wanted change, I was going to need to start on my own turf.

Speaking of change, Mafiela definitely seemed to be softening up. I was glad she had made up with Rylan and was trying to fix her relationship with me. But how long would that last? The three of us were equally stubborn, and Mafiela was used to having everybody bow to her will. It was only a matter of time before heads butted again. Even so, she did love Rylan, and had promised to keep his identity a secret. Revealing it would be dangerous right now, as Resistance supporters, and Resistance members still at large, would resent him for changing sides. He would become a target, as I had when I'd publicly defied them, and they would want to make an example of him.

My grip tightened on the handlebars as a wave of protectiveness surged through me. I would not lose another family member, not for any reason. If there were any other threats from the Resistance, I would personally make sure to wipe them out. No matter the cost.

I turned a corner and found myself on Market Street, a wide boulevard where vendors set up tents on either side and offered their wares. I slowed my speed a little due to the increased foot traffic, and waved to a shifter child who was staring at my steam bike with stars in his big blue eyes. I remembered my own awe and envy when I'd first seen an enforcer tearing down the street on a steam bike. As soon as I was old enough, I'd scraped and saved every last penny to buy my own.

"Sunaya, watch out!"

Rylan's sharp voice jerked me from my memories. I whipped my head back around to see a flaming object the size of my fist hurtling directly toward us. The wards on my bike flared to life, creating a red shield that enveloped us, and it sent the object careening toward one of the tents. Citizens screamed, and I slammed on my brakes and flung my hand out at the same time. Water gushed from my palm as I shouted a Word, extinguishing the fiery missile before it could hit the tents—they were close enough together that if one caught on fire, the whole street would burst into flames.

Unfortunately, the speed at which I'd stopped made it impossible for me to stay on my bike and control the spell, and I went flying over my handlebars. Instinct took over, and I tucked and rolled across the asphalt, saving myself from broken bones. The impact of my body against the hard ground still hurt like hell though, and I knew I'd have some colorful bruises if I'd been human.

"Got ya!" a man crowed as he hurled himself at me. My eyes widened at the sight of the silver dagger in his hand, and I rolled to the side before he could impale me with the nasty object.

"Like hell you do!" Rylan snarled, grabbing the man by his collar and hauling him back. The guy was tall, beefy, and had a good fifty pounds on Rylan, but Rylan's superior shifter strength allowed him to fling my attacker into a wall. The paint cracked beneath the force of the blow, and the man sagged to the ground with a groan, his head lolling forward.

"Are you all right?" Rylan asked, helping me to my feet.

"I'm fine." My heart was jackhammering in my chest, and my shoulder was a bit sore, but the pain would pass quickly enough. Once I was on my feet, I yanked my helmet off so I could suck in a good breath, and get a better look at my assailant. When I did, my mouth dropped open.

"Manson?" I asked. "Is that you?"

The man struggled to lift his head. His eyes were glazed, and blood was seeping from his hairline and down over his brow—he must have cracked the back of his head open against the wall.

"How d'you know my name?" he slurred, squinting at me as the blood began to trickle into his eyes. He wiped at it with the sleeve of his work shirt, and I felt a twinge of pity.

"We worked—" I cut myself off, remembering that Manson wouldn't know me. He and I had volunteered at the Maintown hospital together for a brief time during the Uprising, and it had been he who'd invited me along to see Father Calmias preach at the Maintown Ur-God temple. But he had known me as Brandt, the name I'd given myself since I'd been disguised as a human male at the time. He hadn't known he was actually working with Sunaya Baine.

"Never mind." I dragged a hand through my hair and looked around. The street had completely cleared, aside from the vendors huddled underneath their tents who were glancing fearfully toward us. "What the *fuck* do you think you're doing, attacking me in a public place like this? You could have hurt a lot of innocent people!"

"I would have killed only you, if not for your filthy magic," Manson growled as Rylan approached him. He grabbed another knife from his boot and tried to stab Rylan, but the strike was unsteady, and Rylan didn't have much trouble knocking the knife away. He let it clatter to the ground, untouched, as he pushed the man facedown onto the hard surface.

I approached with my handcuffs. "That's real comforting," I said, sarcasm thick in my voice as I helped Rylan restrain him. "I don't remember your name coming up on the list of known Resistance members, so what the hell is this about? You can't mean to tell me the Resistance put you up to such a foolish attack. Even they're not *that* stupid."

"No, but clearly *you* are," he said. I tightened the restraints in response to the insult, and Manson grunted. "Word is that you're the reason Father Calmias is locked up on Prison Isle. Did you really think you could get away with defying the will of the Ur-God?"

"If this is the best the Ur-God could do, then I don't have anything to fear at all," I sneered, pressing my boot into Manson's back to keep him down. I tapped my enforcer bracelet to activate it, then called for backup so Manson could be hauled away. Hopefully they'd get here fast, because I couldn't go anywhere until they'd detained the homicidal bastard.

"Bitch!" Manson struggled beneath my boot, but it was no use. Blood matted the back of his head, and from the way he moved, I could tell at least one rib was broken. He wasn't going anywhere. "I may not have succeeded today, but there are plenty more who will come after you. Your blasphemy will not go unpunished."

I sighed. "What else is new?"

4

*B*y the time Rylan and I delivered Manson and made our way down to Comenius's shop, it was close to four o'clock. Witches End was bustling with activity, so I was surprised to see the *Closed* sign up in the glass storefront.

"Does he usually close up this early?" Rylan asked as I peered through the window.

"No." Frowning, I trotted around to the side of the building, then up the steps that led to Comenius's second-floor apartment. Comenius and Elania's voices drifted through the door. Though they were talking too quietly for me to pick out what they were saying, it sounded like they were having an argument.

I knocked loudly on the door, and the voices ceased. A moment later, Com opened the door. The lines in his face were taut with strain, and I was alarmed to see circles beneath his cornflower-blue eyes.

"Finally," he said, holding the door open so Rylan and I could come inside. "I was beginning to worry you wouldn't be coming."

My eyes went straight to Elania, who sat on the couch with her hands folded in her lap. She gave me a strained smile, and an uneasy feeling settled in my gut as I noticed her ramrod posture and the lack of warmth in her eyes. She usually exhibited an easy grace and had never once seemed ruffled.

"Sorry," I said as Com closed the door behind us. "We were attacked by some kind of religious fanatic on the way here."

"Are you all right?" Elania asked, rising from the couch. Concern softened the look in her dark eyes as she approached us. "You're not hurt, either of you?"

"I'm fine." I waved her hands away as tactfully as I could, then skirted Comenius and took a seat before he, too, could flutter over me like a concerned mother hen. Rylan joined me on the couch opposite Elania. "Why don't you tell me what's going on between the two of you? It's clear something's got you both upset."

"Very well." Comenius and Elania both sat down, and my eyebrows winged up as I noticed how far apart they sat from each other. That, plus the fact that Elania hadn't offered tea or snacks like she usually did, told me something was very, *very* wrong.

"As you know, Elania and I have been busy with wedding preparations. Well, mostly Elania," Comenius clarified when Elania gave him a pointed look. "She wants a big wedding in early autumn, and there is much to do."

"I have many relatives all over the Federation, and autumn is the best time for them to travel," Elania said, as though she felt the need to explain.

"Okay," I said cautiously. "Is there anything you guys need help with, regarding the wedding? I'm not really good at planning stuff like that, but...."

"No, it isn't that." Comenius let out a hefty sigh. "I just received news from Pernia that my Rusalia's mother has died."

"Your daughter?" I exclaimed, sitting up. Comenius had told me, back when we had first started dating, that he had a young daughter living in Pernia who he helped support. It had been after a couple of drinks, when he was in a melancholy mood, and he had never spoken of her again after that. I had a feeling his daughter was a very sore subject for him, so I'd made a point to avoid bringing her up. "Isn't she still a child?"

"Only eleven years old," Comenius said, nodding. "Her mother died in a magical accident, and unless I come to get her immediately, the officials will have her placed at an orphanage or in a foster home. I must bring her back with me to Solantha," he declared, and though his voice rang with conviction, I could scent that he was conflicted about the decision. But why? Surely his daughter would be better off with him than overseas with strangers.

"I would like to come as well, but I must look after my shop, as well as Comenius's since he will be gone for some time," Elania said. Her full lips curved into another tight smile. "I wasn't expecting to end up with a family so soon, but Rusalia is most welcome. I hope she'll agree to be the flower girl in our wedding party."

I didn't need my shifter senses to tell that Elania wasn't being entirely truthful. But then again, I could hardly blame her. If Iannis had sprung something like this on me, I'd be pissed too. Now that I thought about it, *did* he have any children? He was several hundred years old, after all. A strange feeling went through me at the idea that he might have progeny older than I was. How could I possibly be a stepmother to someone who might be old enough to be my grandmother? I would have to ask him about it at some point. I'd be shocked if Iannis hadn't mentioned to me by now if he was a father, but he was so long lived that it seemed strange that he didn't have any children.

"Does your daughter know you very well, Comenius?" Rylan asked, speaking up for the first time.

"No," Comenius said. His voice darkened with anger and sadness. "Her mother would never let me see her."

"Why?" I scowled, outraged on his behalf. No wonder his daughter was such a sore subject for him! "Don't you have just as much right to her?"

"You would think so, but Hiltraud didn't see it that way," Comenius said. "She and I engaged in a foolish affair when I was young, and Rusalia was the result. I offered to marry her, of course, but she would hear none of it. She claimed that she was too free spirited to tie herself down to the likes of me, that it would ruin her life. But, of course, she was happy to accept my financial support." His fingers dug into his thighs.

"How absurd." Elania took one of his hands before he gouged a hole through his tunic pants. Her eyes sparked with the same outrage I felt. "You are a wonderful man, Comenius Genhard, and that silly strumpet did not deserve you."

Comenius smiled, some of the tension easing from his strong-boned features. "Thank you." He leaned in and brushed his lips against her temple before turning back to Rylan and me. "I have not seen Rusalia since I moved to the Northia Federation. Hiltraud's refusal to co-parent with me, and her efforts to turn our daughter against me at every turn, ultimately drove me to emigrate—I could not take the constant struggle any more, and I wanted a clean break. Now that this has happened, I only hope I'll be able to undo the years of damage I let her mother inflict upon our relationship."

"Man, that's tough." I wanted to get up and give Comenius a hug, but I was reluctant to come between him and Elania now that the two of them seemed to be cozying up to each other again. "Is there anything I can do to help?"

"I'd like you to help Elania out if she gets into any trouble while I'm away," Comenius said. "It would put me at ease if I knew she had someone to turn to, especially since she is running my shop on top of her own."

Elania huffed a little at that. "I did get on quite well before I met you, you know," she said, though her dark eyes sparkled with amusement rather than annoyance.

"Even so, please let us know if you do need anything," I told her. "Rylan and I are happy to come and help out with whatever you need."

"Thank you." Elania smiled warmly at me, looking much more like her usual self. "I've hired a new employee to help me run Comenius's shop, so I shouldn't need assistance. And you ought not to trouble yourself further, Comenius," she added, turning back to him. "You'd be better served focusing on yourself, and your daughter."

"Have you heard any news from Noria?" I asked, mostly to distract Comenius from his worries.

"No." His eyes turned dull. "I assume she'll be in the mines by now. I sent a letter there, but I haven't received a response. I'm not sure if she is ignoring me, or if she hasn't received it."

There was a long moment of depressed silence, and I bit my lip. Maybe Noria wasn't the best choice of subject... but I felt like it was wrong to go on as if she'd ceased to exist. At least not so soon after she'd been sentenced.

"I have not heard or seen anything of Annia, either," Com finally said. "I was going to check on her, but now, with this new problem, there is no time."

"I can do that," I said. Guilt squeezed my chest—I shouldn't have needed Comenius to prompt me to look in on my best friend. "I'll go right now." If it had been tough for me to watch Noria be sent off to the mines, it had to be ten times worse for Annia. If anyone needed a shoulder right now, it was she.

∼

"YOUR FRIEND ANNIA seems to be pretty well-off," Rylan commented as I parked my bike on the curb outside a large, two-story granite brick home. The manicured front lawn boasted an impressive flower garden, and the scents of marigolds and dahlias leant a pleasant fragrance to the warm summer evening. The property was situated on the side of one of the many hills in Solantha, and it offered a great view of the sun setting over the western sea.

"The house belongs to her mother," I told him as we disembarked. "Annia lives in the guest suite out back."

I intended to head around to the back of the house, when the sound of Annia and her mother shouting gave me pause. I stood on the front path, debating whether or not to risk interrupting the argument by knocking on the front door. But the decision was made for me when the birch door flew open, and Annia stormed out.

"Fine, blame me if you think that will help anything!" she snapped over her shoulder, auburn hair flying out behind her. She wore a pair of jeans, brown leather boots, and a button-down green shirt instead of her usual mercenary leathers, which was strange because she should have just recently gotten off her shift. "But don't expect me to stick around if this is how you're going to be all the time!"

She froze on the top step of the porch at the sight of us, her hand on the railing. "Naya? What are you doing here?"

"I certainly don't expect you to stick around!" Mrs. Melcott declared, striding out onto the porch before I could reply. She was a striking woman in her forties, with fine-boned features and a willowy figure. Her chestnut-colored hair was done up in an elegant braid that wrapped around her head, and she wore a black and white knee-length dress and matching shoes. Her dark eyes, identical to her daughter's, narrowed as she caught sight of me, and her pale cheeks colored.

"How *dare* you show up on my property," she railed, pointing an accusing finger at me. "After all you've done!"

"Mother," Annia said tightly, turning back to face Mrs. Melcott. "Sunaya has nothing to do with this."

"She has *everything* to do with it," Mrs. Melcott insisted, her voice trembling. Her eyes filled with angry tears as they focused in on me. "My Noria looked up to you and Annia, and it was you who filled her head with foolish, rebellious thoughts! She should be at the academy now, taking her engineering classes and inventing things, not toiling away in the salt mines where you sent her!"

A pang of guilt hit me hard in the gut. "Mrs. Melcott, I didn't—"

"Don't bother," Annia snarled, striding toward me. She grabbed me by the arm, a little harder than necessary. "My mother isn't interested in listening to reason. She just wants someone to blame, and she's become very good at finding targets." Annia's voice rose as she shot a furious glare at her mother and pulled me along. "I'll be out of your hair soon enough."

"Annia—" Mrs. Melcott called, a desperate edge in her voice now, but Annia ignored her. I had to lengthen my stride to keep up with her as she dragged me to the back of the house—Annia was a little taller than me, and her legs were longer. I kept my mouth shut until she'd ushered us into the one-bedroom guesthouse she'd used as an apartment for as long as I'd known her, then wisely decided to hold my tongue when she slammed the door shut, snatched a vase off a side table next to the leather couch, and smashed it into the wall.

"The Ur-God take it!" she snarled, then seemed to remember she was not alone. Her shoulders slumped a little, and she leaned her arm against the low wall separating the living room from the entry way and looked at us. "I'm sorry you had to see all that, but I wasn't really expecting you. Who is this?" She gestured to Rylan.

"You don't have to apologize. And this is Rylan." I glanced toward him, and he tapped the pin on his chest, undoing the illusion spell. "Iannis and I thought it would be best to keep him disguised until things have calmed down."

"It's harder to impress the ladies smelling like a tiger, but I have to make do in these troubled times," Rylan said, giving Annia a lopsided grin. "I'm posing as Sunaya's bodyguard, Lanyr."

Annia's lips twitched, but the bleak look in her eyes didn't change. "That's smart," she said, heading into the kitchen so she could grab a bottle of wine from a cupboard. There was a loud pop as she opened it using a corkscrew, and I arched a brow as she took a swig directly from the bottle. "Considering that people tend to play the blame game whenever shit doesn't go their way, I had a feeling you'd be a target." I knew she wasn't just talking about me with that statement.

"Pretty much." I decided not to mention that we'd been attacked earlier today—there was no point in distressing her further. "So what was that all about? Are you really moving out?"

"I don't see that I have a choice." Annia brought her bottle of wine into the living room, and we made ourselves comfortable on the couches. Black, cream, and burgundy were the dominating colors in her décor scheme, and her family wealth showed in the expensive furnishings. The sword hanging over the mantel, and the sheathed, ornate-looking knives adorning the walls, leant an edge to the elegance that I'd always admired.

"Your mother isn't kicking you out, is she?" I asked. Another stab of guilt pierced my gut at the idea that I had contributed to this. "I know how much you like living here."

"Those days are over," Annia said, her eyes softening as they filled with sadness. "Noria was Mother's pride and joy, and she's inconsolable now that she's gone. It'll be a long time before Mother can accept that what happened to my sister was no one's fault but her own. It doesn't help that the so-called friends she played cards with four times a week have snubbed her since they found out Noria was sentenced to hard labor in the mines. She has no one to take her frustrations out on but me now, and I can't put up with it anymore."

"I know how that is," I said softly. I'd often felt Mafiela had been taking out her grief and anger over my mother's death on me. Once I'd found shelter with Roanas, it had been a relief to escape all that. "Do you want to come and stay at the Palace while you find a new place?"

"It would be nice to have another friendly face around," Rylan added. "It's hard to make friends when no one is allowed to know who you really are."

Annia shook her head. "That would only anger Mother more. Besides, I need to bury myself in work, or I'll get depressed. Mother doesn't realize it, but she's not the only one grieving over Noria right now." Her voice broke a little, and she took another swig from the bottle.

"Oh, Annia." I shifted over to the other couch and wrapped an arm around her. "I feel like such a horrible friend for leaving you alone at a time like this."

"Don't," Annia said, leaning into me. "You have your own troubles, and I've been busy at the Guild anyway. We all have, what with the city trying to adjust. It's just that Noria, Mother, and I used to have breakfast up in the main house every morning, and we used to hang out in the back garden for an hour before bed most nights. We spent less time together as she got busy with her academy classes, but we were still close up until a few months ago. I didn't realize just how important those little rituals we had were, and how much our family needed them, until she was gone."

Her voice choked with tears then, and the room fell silent. Rylan averted his gaze, and I said nothing, just holding her tight as Annia struggled for composure. Eventually, she let out a breath, then eased herself from my arms.

"How rude of me," she said as her fingers curled around the neck of the wine bottle. "I've been sitting here guzzling wine like a lush, and I haven't offered you anything. Are you two hungry? I can probably throw something together."

"No, that's fine," I said, standing up. Rylan and Annia got to their feet as well. "I have to meet Iannis for dinner. Do you want to come back to the Palace with us for tonight at least?"

"No, I need to pack. I'm leaving the day after tomorrow."

"You're *what*?"

"Not permanently," Annia said hastily as she noticed my eyes nearly pop out of my head. "Just for a few months. I've accepted a guard position for some sensitive equipment being transported to Southia, and once I'm there, I plan to take on some local gigs. Like I said, I need to bury myself in work. A change of environment and routine is for the best, at least right now."

"Well, I'll miss the hell out of you." My throat tightened, and I threw my arms around Annia and squeezed her tight. "Don't be gone too long, okay? I am getting married at some point, you know."

Annia laughed. "Oh, don't worry. I've spent way too much time saving both yours and Lord Iannis's asses to miss the wedding. I'll make sure to send you my address down there, so you can contact me if you need anything."

It was clear from the look in Annia's eyes, and the set of her shoulders, that there was no use in convincing her to stay. So Rylan and I said our goodbyes, then went back to the front of the house, where my bike was parked. My shoulders tightened as I felt Mrs. Melcott's accusing gaze from the window, but I didn't turn to look. There was no point in getting into another confrontation with her. Best to just let her be.

"I understand how Annia feels," Rylan commented as we sped back to the Palace. *"I remember how relieved I felt when I moved further north with the Resistance, away from Mother and the clan."*

"Yeah, I just hope she doesn't end up staying down there permanently. I've heard that Southia's laws are a lot looser, and there's more crime." Then again, that meant plenty of work for an enforcer. Maybe she *would* be down there for a while.

"True, but Annia's a rolling stone. She'll bulldoze through any opposition in her way, and she seems smart enough not to land herself into anything she can't get out of. The Resistance compound notwithstanding," he added hastily. *"But I think that was because Noria clouded her judgment. She's strong, and she'll eventually get past this and want to come home."* The admiration in Rylan's voice was clear, and I wondered if he had a crush on Annia.

"I really hope so," I said, trying my best to share his enthusiasm. But it was hard—there were too many changes happening, too fast, and it seemed like for every new friend I gained, I lost another. Hopefully this wouldn't become a regular pattern, because at the rate I was going, my life would be completely unrecognizable before long. And even though I was becoming a mage, I was determined to remain Sunaya Baine, no matter what.

5

The Palace was in an uproar when Rylan and I got back. Canter, the grizzly old receptionist, was frantically answering phone calls, and servants and Mages Guild staff were scurrying about the halls at an uncharacteristically hurried pace. Usually everything was calm and collected around here—but now nervous excitement buzzed in the air.

"Something big must be about to go down," Rylan said as he followed me down to the Mages Guild, located in the south wing of the Palace. My *serapha* charm told me Iannis was down there, and I wanted answers from him. *"Any idea what?"*

"No. I wasn't told anything out of the ordinary was happening."

"Miss Baine," Dira, the Mages Guild receptionist, called from her desk as I entered the lobby. "Lord Iannis needs to speak to you right away. He asked that you come alone." Her eyes briefly flicked to Rylan.

I nodded. "Go have dinner," I told him. "I'll let you know when I need you again."

Rylan looked slightly put out that he was once again being excluded, but he bowed, then left without argument. He might be my bodyguard now, but he was still an ex-Resistance member, and Iannis wasn't about to trust him with confidential information. After all, Rylan was here to serve out his sentence instead of working in the mines—he wasn't a willing volunteer. He might not support the Resistance anymore, but he still wasn't a fan of the mage regime. I had a feeling that if he saw an opportunity to undermine the Guild in any way, he would take it in a heartbeat.

Once, I would have done the same. But now that I was engaged to Iannis, and learning to become a mage myself, that wasn't an option. I needed to learn how to make the system work better, not bring it down entirely. Revolution sounded nice on paper, but I was beginning to understand that the reality was anything but. Violence, much as I loved using it on an individual basis, didn't solve anything. It only left death and destruction in its wake, and the pieces you had to pick up and put together afterward didn't necessarily assemble to give you what you wanted.

"Enter," Iannis called when I knocked on the door. I opened it to see him seated behind his desk, a grave expression on his face. Director Chen stood at his side, resplendent as usual in her silk robes, and Cirin Garidano, the Finance Secretary, sat in one of the guest chairs. Fenris was curled up in front of the fireplace in wolf form, and he rose to greet me, tail wagging.

"Hey," I said, bending down to briefly stroke my hand along Fenris's coarse, dark brown fur. It occurred to me that Fenris had been spending a lot of time in human form recently, and I wondered if last night's full moon had inspired him to go back to his usual manner of skulking around in beast form. "What's going on?"

"We are about to host some very unexpected guests," Iannis said. "Take a seat, so I can explain."

"Unexpected guests?" I sat down next to Cirin. "From where?"

"From Dara. Minister Graning is preparing his departure as we speak, along with several other high officials. The Mage-Emperor of Garai has died at long last, and the Minister is stopping in Solantha on his way to attend the funeral."

"Through here?" I frowned. "But wouldn't it be easier to travel through the Central Continent to get to Garai from Dara?"

"Perhaps, but the Minister wishes for me to attend the funeral as part of his entourage, so he is coming through here to collect me. The difference is only a few days in the end. He intends to stay in Solantha for three days, bringing half the government along, and then we will travel on to Garai by steamboat. Since the Garaians have to wait for the guests from all continents to assemble in their capital, there is just time enough to go that way."

I crinkled my nose at the thought of a corpse waiting for weeks and weeks to be buried, in the summertime, no less. I guessed they'd have to embalm him in the meantime.

"When you say 'we,' who exactly are you referring to?" Director Chen asked. "I would think that just as the Minister is taking an entourage, so would you want one yourself."

"Indeed." Iannis's lips curved as he glanced up at her. "That is why I am taking Sunaya along, and you as well."

"Me!" Director Chen's almond-shaped eyes flashed with surprise, and more than a little dismay. "I am your deputy, meant to rule in your stead while you are gone. We cannot possibly leave at the same time. Who will run things in our place? You remember the fiasco that occurred when the Council seized power in your absence—that cannot be allowed to occur again."

"I am naming Secretary Garidano as the Director pro tempore, and I will meet with the Council before we leave to ensure that they do not attempt to undermine him in any way." Iannis's voice turned ominous. As Director Chen had said, they couldn't be allowed to repeat the same mistakes they had made the last time Iannis had been gone. It was largely their fault that the Uprising had started to begin with, and the city was still recovering. Half of them had resigned in the last couple of weeks, so I didn't think Iannis would have any trouble cowing the remainder into submission.

Cirin started at this announcement, as surprised as Chen. "Fenris will be here to advise you, Cirin," Iannis continued. "I will also sit down with you and go over everything you will need to know before we depart."

"Yes, sir." Cirin's deep voice was smooth, but the slight pause before his words told me Iannis had shocked the hell out of him. "Thank you for the honor, Lord Iannis." His dark blue eyes gleamed with anticipation, and despite his shock, I knew Cirin had been waiting for an opportunity like this. He was ambitious, and I knew that he intended to take the Chief Mage position the moment Iannis vacated it. I resolved then and there to keep an eye on him—he'd proved his loyalty in the past, but that didn't mean he would always be that way. Roanas used to say to me that the lust for power could warp even the purest heart, and Cirin was no exception.

"But Lord Iannis," Director Chen protested, apparently not at all satisfied at his choice of replacement. "A trip to Garai is not a short affair. I assume we will be staying for the new Mage-Emperor's testing and coronation as well as the funeral? With the boat ride each way, we may be gone for as long as three months!"

"Indeed," Iannis said. "However, it cannot be helped. It is absolutely essential that you accompany us, Director. As for the duration of our absence, until airships become safe enough to cross the big oceans, there is no alternative. We have requisitioned the fastest steamer available."

There was a pregnant pause, and I remembered learning in

school about several attempts to fly dirigibles across the ocean. Over half the voyages had ended in disaster, and further attempts were outlawed until such a time as dirigibles were made safe for these long distances.

"It would be madness to try flying," Chen finally said. "Especially now, during typhoon season."

"So we're leaving three days after the Minister gets here?" I asked, not sure if I should be excited or apprehensive. After all, I'd always wanted to travel outside the Federation, but I'd only just gotten back to Solantha. Was this what my life was going to be like from now on, hopping about from state to state, and now continent to continent, at the beck and call of Minister Graning? Adventure was all well and good, but there was something to be said for 'home sweet home,' too.

"Yes," Iannis said. "You are coming along as my fiancée and the junior member of the delegation, but there will be plenty of opportunities to advance your apprenticeship as well. The voyage is long, and we should be able to fit in quite a few extra lessons."

"I must say I am surprised to learn that Fenris will be my advisor," Cirin said, glancing toward Fenris, who was standing near my elbow. "But I realize his counsel will be an asset, considering how much time he has spent at your side. It is very impressive that a shifter can become a scholar of magic history, law, and Loranian as Fenris has done. Indeed, his accomplishments have quite changed my perception of shifter nature and limitations."

"If only he knew," Fenris told me dryly, the words for my ears only, and I stifled a laugh. I was glad that he was taking the compliment in stride rather than getting defensive, as he had every reason to be. The real reason Fenris knew all these things was because he used to be a Chief Mage, before he was forced into hiding and Iannis changed him into a shifter with an

ancient and highly illegal spell. It was a little worrying that Cirin had made such keen observations about Fenris, and I wondered how many other mages wondered about Fenris's strange knowledge. But Cirin didn't seem to suspect the unlikely truth, and hopefully the others wouldn't think anything of it either.

The Finance Secretary thanked Iannis once more for the opportunity and assured him he'd do his best to deserve his confidence, then took his leave. After Cirin was gone, Fenris shifted back into human form in a flash of white light. One moment, he was a wolf, the next a stocky man with short dark hair and a beard covering his square jaw. He wore a simple dark tunic, his usual dress, and I wondered if his decision not to wear modern clothes stemmed from the fact that in his former life he was accustomed to mage robes. Since he couldn't wear them anymore, tunics were the next best thing.

"While I'm sure the next few days will be very exciting, I will not be around to help entertain your important visitors," Fenris told Iannis. "I have business in the south that must be seen to without delay."

"Of course—that Resistance camp down near the border," Iannis said smoothly, catching on. Fenris obviously didn't want to be anywhere near the Minister and his delegation when they arrived, and I privately agreed. "But you will be back soon, correct?"

"I did agree to advise the Finance Secretary, after all." The hint of humor in Fenris's voice told me he was ribbing Iannis, because Iannis hadn't asked his consent before assigning him the job. "I need to prepare for the trip, though, so I will take my leave now."

"So," I said, once Fenris was gone. "You gonna tell us the real reason the Minister wants us to come to Garai? Because I get the feeling there aren't any other Chief Mages being asked to come along."

Iannis gave me a small smile. "You are quite right." His expression sobered, and he gestured for Director Chen to have a seat. "The reason we need you there," he told her once she was seated next to me, "is that we are to undertake a secret mission once we arrive in Garai. The Minister has ordered us to seek out and destroy the Resistance lab in Leniang Port."

"A Resistance lab in Leniang Port?" Chen frowned. "This is the first I've heard of it. Surely they have not spread to Garai too? I have not heard of Garai forming its own Resistance."

"We don't know how closely they might be affiliated, and I only learned of it recently myself," Iannis said. "The scientists we captured in Osero told the Minister's interrogators about the lab, though it took considerable time to drag the information out of them." Iannis's lip curled briefly at that. "We are not sure exactly what goes on there, but it is highly likely they are manufacturing the same diseases specifically targeted at mages and shifters. We also know for certain that the illegal firearms smuggled in for the Resistance soldiers here in the Federation came from Leniang Port."

"By the Lady!" Chen exclaimed, an expression I'd heard once or twice. Apparently, it was in direct reference to Resinah, though mages rarely used it. "I am certainly willing to help, Lord Iannis, but I must warn you that as a native Garaian, my diplomatic immunity may not be respected. Things could get difficult if I am caught engaging in illegal activity so far from the capital, and I would be subject to Garaian law even though I am a Northian citizen now. 'Once a Garaian, always a Garaian' is very much the national view." Her delicate eyebrows pulled into a frown.

"I will do my best to ensure that you are not caught in such a compromising position," Iannis assured her. "But as you are the only one here who speaks the Southern Garaian dialect, you are very much needed. I cannot risk taking a mere translator on such a delicate mission, and I am only fluent in the main northern dialect."

She nodded, acknowledging the argument. I dimly recalled from my geography lessons that many languages were spoken in Garai, though, oddly, they all used the same complicated script. What else had I learned about Garai? I'd never thought to hold onto the knowledge, since I hadn't in my wildest dreams imagined getting the chance to visit.

Better brush up on those lessons now, I thought to myself. I didn't want to come across like an ignorant hick when we got there!

We talked about the trip for a few more minutes, then Chen took her leave as well, saying that she had much to do to prepare. I was about to follow her, but Iannis held up a hand, a silent command for me to remain.

"So you've saved the best for last, eh?" I said, trying for levity. In truth, I was nervous. What other bomb was Iannis about to drop on me?

"Of course." Iannis's stern features softened into a real smile, and he flicked his hand toward the door. The lock clicked behind me, and he pushed his chair back. "Come and sit with me for a moment. I missed you."

I did as he asked, curling into his arms as I settled onto his lap. Tucking my head beneath his chin, I pressed my ear to his chest and listened to his heartbeat.

"Did you really not know about any of this?" I asked as he stroked my hair.

"No," he said. "The Minister only learned of the Mage-Emperor's passing today—we didn't discuss this at all when I was in Dara. I know it is very sudden, but we cannot pass up this opportunity."

"No, of course not," I murmured, staring out the window behind Iannis's desk. Darkness had settled over Solantha Bay, and the Firegate Bridge blazed red, a beacon in the night. "We have to destroy the source of those diseases and cut off the Resistance's weapons supply." Things might be peaceful here now, but every day that we delayed meant more death and destruction somewhere else. I suppressed a shudder at the thought—I couldn't have those deaths on my conscience.

"Before we go, I have an assignment that I need you to take care of," Iannis said. "It involves the magic testing in the schools. I had planned to assign the task to you anyway, but now, unfortunately, time is very short. You'll have to work fast."

I jerked my head up, narrowly missing Iannis's triangular chin. "We're still doing that?" I demanded. "I thought you put that program on hold."

"We did," Iannis said. "But I have been getting reports that there have been... incidents... occurring in the public schools that indicate budding magical talents. We have not yet come up with a proper system for dealing with them, and we must make time to do so when we return. But for now, it would be unwise to leave for three months knowing that the problem is growing. Since nobody else cares as much about this as you, I've decided to entrust you with the job."

"Makes sense. What do you want me to do?"

"I need you to go around the schools and administer the testing, then make recommendations to the Guild as to how to handle the children that do show magical aptitude." He hesitated, then added, "I'll personally make sure that nobody is permanently harmed, if we do have to perform wipes on some."

"All right." My dread evaporated as I realized this was an opportunity to set a new precedent. Instead of recommending them all for magic wipes, perhaps I could convince the Guild to explore other options instead. "I don't know how to test them, though."

"It's very simple." Iannis taught me the Word, then demonstrated the spell by placing his hands on my head and speaking it. A strange tingle went through me, and the old anxiety I'd felt when I'd been tested as a child kicked in before I remembered that it didn't matter. The world knew I had magic, and I wasn't hiding anymore. I was thriving.

"Now you try it," Iannis said softly, taking my hands in his and placing them atop his head.

I let my finger sink into his soft, dark red hair for a moment, enjoying the way the silky strands slid against my skin. Desire lit my nerves aflame, as it always did whenever we were in close proximity, but I pushed it aside and spoke the Word.

"By Magorah," I gasped as I sensed the enormity of Iannis's power. It was like a flea standing before the might of an elephant —vast, almost incomprehensible. "You're downright scary."

Iannis laughed, pushing my hands away. "You've nothing to fear from me," he said, wrapping his arms around me. "I could never turn my power against you."

"I know."

He pressed his lips against mine, and I forgot all about the testing and the upcoming trip. Who could possibly think about those problems, when I had the most delicious man in the world under my hands?

6

The next day, Rylan and I went to the Records Department and obtained a list of all the junior high schools in Solantha, then made phone calls to each one to find out how many ten-year-olds they had. After calculating the number—around five thousand children, total—I realized there was no way I could get all the testing done on my own before the Minister arrived with his delegation. I needed reinforcements.

There was some muttering as I went around the Guild recruiting apprentices, and dark looks from the mages who used to be in charge of administering the magic wipes. They were not pleased that I was taking over this duty, especially since I was a mere apprentice myself. But since I was acting in the Chief Mage's name, there was nothing they could do. Their displeasure and skepticism only made me resolve to do an excellent job, so they would have nothing to criticize in the end.

"There really aren't very many, are there?" Rylan asked as we headed back to the Palace on my steam bike. We'd just finished the first round of testing, and we wanted to grab lunch before we interviewed more children. *"We've visited sixteen schools and only found two magic users so far."*

"*Yeah,*" I agreed, though my heart was heavy all the same. The teachers of those two children, and the children themselves, had been stricken when I told them the news, but I'd done my best to assure them that no action would be taken at this time. Even so, one of the teachers had fainted dead away when I'd told her that she needed to inform the parents of her student to escort the child to Solantha Palace after lunch to be interviewed. I'd been forced to use my own magic to revive and then calm her.

"*Do you think some of them are going to try to bolt from the city with their children?*" Rylan asked as I parked my bike in the Palace garage. "*That's what I would do, in their stead.*"

"*They won't be able to escape the tracking spell I put on each of them,*" I told him as we made our way toward the dining hall. Iannis had taught me the spell last night, and while I regretted having to use it, I knew it was necessary. "*If any of them fail to show, I will find them.*"

After lunch, I met with a few of the other apprentices in a small conference room in the Mages Guild. I'd recruited fourteen, and I had chosen them for their skill level as well as their temperament. They were all young looking, with calm dispositions, and I'd sent them off in pairs to help with the testing.

"We found three today," Sarai, a female apprentice, told me and handed me a sheet of paper with the names and salient details of the children. She tossed her mane of long, straight black hair over her shoulder as she settled back into her seat. "All Maintowners."

"Two from us—one in Maintown, one in Rowanville," Gorad, the male apprentice from another team, added as he handed me his list as well. "Our partners are keeping watch on the parents and children in the other room."

"Have they all arrived?" I asked as I scanned the names.

"Surprisingly, yes," Sarai said. "Though that might have had something to do with the fact that I sent guards to collect them."

"I didn't tell you to do that," I said sharply. "Did the guards use force? I told you not to scare them."

"They're going to be scared no matter what," Sarai said boldly, pinning me with her dark blue gaze. "They think that you're about to turn their children's brains into mush. I simply ensured that we wouldn't have to go chasing after them, which we really don't have time to do. None of the children are sporting any signs of injury. You can check yourself if you want."

"I will be," I said, trying not to sound too annoyed. Sarai hadn't really done anything wrong—I just didn't like that she'd done this without my approval. "Go and join the others, then send one of the children in. I want to get these interviews done quickly."

The two apprentices bowed, then left. Sighing, I leaned back in my chair and perused the names on the lists once more, going over the details. Ten and sixteen were the typical ages that the tests were done, and I was very glad that we were only doing ten-year-olds right now. If they were wiped at this age, it would leave little-to-no effects on their personality. Iannis had explained that in children, only a small area of the brain was used to control magic, and therefore magic wipes were less dangerous to perform on them. This area grew from a small point in infancy and gradually spread until it was entwined with the entire brain. By the time a mage reached the age of seventeen, the procedure was considered too risky to perform without harmful side effects.

Besides, I wasn't sure I wanted to handle rebellious teenagers just yet.

The door opened, and a young human woman, wearing a clean but faded yellow dress, came in with her son. They both shared the same curly blond hair, though the boy's was a messy mop as opposed to the mother's tamed locks. He gripped her hand tightly as she led him over to the chairs on the table opposite me.

"Good afternoon," I said, rising to greet her with an outstretched hand. I didn't have to, considering my status, but I wanted to make her feel more at ease. "I'm Sunaya Baine."

"Delara Mencham," the woman said, a slight tremor in her voice. She hesitated before shaking my hand. "This is my son, Briar."

"Hello, Briar." I offered him my hand as well, and tried not to be offended when he eyed it like it was a viper. "I really appreciate you coming on such short notice."

"Mom said I didn't have a choice." He glowered at me, but shook my hand anyway when his mother nudged him sharply.

"Do you want anything to drink before we get started?" I asked as we sat down. "I hope you had time to eat lunch."

"He's been taken care of," his mother said sharply. "Let's just get this over with."

"All right." I turned to her and fired the first question off. "How long have you known that your son has magic?"

She stiffened. "I don't know any such thing."

"Mrs. Mencham, I'm sure you're aware that as a shifter, I can smell a lie, correct?" I kept my voice even. "This will go a lot smoother if you're honest with me from the get-go."

"And what will happen to my son once I'm honest?" she demanded. "Are you going to take him away?"

"I won't let her," Briar said, and the air around him shifted. Rylan stiffened as we both caught the scent of magic, and sparks began to rise from the little boy's skin.

"Briar, *stop*," his mother pleaded, her gaze growing frantic. She grabbed his hand, then cried out as her skin sizzled against his.

"Mom!" The magic disappeared immediately, and Briar's

eyes widened with guilt and fear. "Mom, are you okay?" He reached for her, and his mother scooted her chair away instinctively. His face crumpled, and my heart ached.

"Briar," I said, my voice soft but authoritative. He whipped his head around, his dark blue eyes wide with fear. "You need to calm down before someone gets hurt. That's when you lose control of the magic, isn't it?" I asked gently. "When you get upset?"

"I try not to." Tears gleamed in his eyes, and he swallowed. "It hasn't happened in a long time."

"But it happened last month, didn't it?" He was one of the children who had come to Iannis's attention. "You set a boy's pants on fire on the playground, didn't you?"

Briar's eyes flashed. "He deserved it," he insisted, his cheeks coloring. "He was hurting my friend because he wouldn't give up half his sandwich."

"What a total jerk," I said, and Briar blinked, confused at my empathy. "I bet he never bothered you again, did he?"

"Nope." The little boy lifted his chin proudly, and then his shoulders slumped. "But all the other kids are afraid of me now. They won't go near me."

I nodded solemnly. "That's the trouble with our society," I told him. "Since magic is forbidden, everybody's afraid of it. And I can't blame them—you might have only set that boy's pants on fire, but you could have easily set the playground on fire too. And you hurt your mother today," I said, gesturing to her. She was nursing her hand as she watched us, but she dropped it instantly as Briar's gaze turned back to her.

"It's nothing," she said quickly. "He's done this before."

"It's not nothing," I said, and she flinched. "As he gets older, his powers are only going to grow stronger. A small burn today could turn into your house going up in flames tomorrow. He needs to be trained, or he needs to have his magic taken away."

"Trained?" Her eyebrows went up, and for the first time, a hopeful look entered her eyes. "You mean he can be taught to control it?"

"If we can find a mage willing to sponsor him, he could be trained as one in his own right." I turned back to Briar just in time to catch the excitement in his eyes. "You'd like that, wouldn't you?"

He nodded eagerly, then his face fell again. "I would like to learn how to use magic," he said, "but I don't want to leave my mother." He glanced guiltily at her. "If I have to do the magic wipe instead, I guess I will."

"Oh, Briar." She placed a hand on his small shoulder, her expression softening. "I would never take your magic from you if there was a way for you to keep it without hurting people. Do you really think there's someone who can help him?" she asked, her voice going a little high. "I don't want you putting false hopes in my boy's head, but if there's any way...."

"I can't make any promises, but I've been intending to start a program to help train new mages like your son," I told her. "If I can convince the Mages Guild, your son would be one of the first to participate."

The mother looked like she wanted throw her arms around me in gratitude, but she settled for squeezing her son so tightly that he began to protest. Now that the two were calmer, I finished the interview, asking detailed questions about the boy's past. How long had he been exhibiting magical traits and what sort of 'accidents' had happened? I took copious notes, then set the paper aside in a file that I would later present to Iannis and the Council.

Once the interview was done, I sent the mother and son home, promising I would contact them in a few days. I then went through the rest of the interviews, with mixed reactions. One of the parents was adamant that he wanted his daughter to have nothing to do with magic, and eagerly offered her up for the magic wipe once I assured him that it would be done by a qualified expert and no harm would come to his child. The girl readily agreed, but I was conflicted about the decision. How could a ten-year-old, so strongly influenced by her father, make such a choice? The magic wipe wouldn't just take away her magic—it would also shorten her lifespan to that of a normal human. Did a parent really have the right to take such a gift away from their child?

But there was nothing I could do about that, so I signed off on it, then made arrangements for them to come back to have the procedure done. Going through the rest of the children, I discovered that another parent was more like Mrs. Mencham, but far more doubtful, and the parents of the last two children were undecided. Good. It troubled me that a parent would make such a momentous decision about their child's future so quickly.

"Do you really think that you'll be able to find mage families willing to help these children?" Rylan asked skeptically as we walked into a Rowanville school the next day. *"They're such snobs, the lot of them. I can't imagine any of them will want to sully their hands with a human child. And if I'm right, aren't you just raising false hopes?"*

"I'm not sure," I admitted. They certainly hadn't been willing to train *me*, though that might have been because I was half-shifter. *"But Iannis encouraged me to find another way, and if he thinks it's possible, it's worth a try. Not all of them are as snobby as you'd think, and if it was done as a favor to Iannis, I think we'll find some willing."*

It was ten-thirty in the morning, recess time, and after meeting with the principal, we went to the empty classroom that was set aside for us to use for the testing. One by one, the children were brought in, many of them with their parents, but some without. I tried to put them at ease, but they were all quiet and tense, and I couldn't blame them. Children who had never once exhibited magic had been found to be magical in the past —none of them could be truly confident.

A girl with short, glossy sable hair wearing a pale blue dress and shiny black shoes entered next. Her face was pale and pinched, and the expression on her mother's face was cold and haughty. A shiver went down my spine as I looked at her—she didn't look like the type who'd take well to the news that her daughter was a mage.

"Let's get this over with," she said, herding her daughter into the chair in front of me. "I have things to do."

"We'll be quick," I promised, deciding to ignore her rude behavior. Her daughter was clearly terrified, and a confrontation wouldn't help things. "What is your name?" I asked the child, gentling my voice.

"Tinari Schaun," she said in a small voice. She bit her lip and looked down, unwilling to meet my gaze.

"Nice to meet you, Tinari. My name is Sunaya." I smiled at her, then asked the same question I'd asked all the other children. "Have you ever used magic in the past, Tinari?"

"What an asinine question!" her mother snapped. "My daughter is incapable of such a thing, and your tests will show that."

"I wasn't asking you," I said, my voice hard. Rylan angled his body toward the mother a little, his hand drifting closer to the sword. The woman stepped back, her cheeks coloring. "I was talking to your daughter."

"N-no," Tinari stammered, and I could smell the lie a mile off.

"All right." I placed my hands atop her head and spoke the Word aloud, already knowing what I would find. The pulse of magic inside this little girl was strong, nearly ready to come to the surface. If she hadn't had a real episode yet, she would have one soon.

I removed my hands, then looked her in the eye. "Tinari Shaun, you do have magic. How long have you known?"

"*No*," the mother shrieked, her eyes wild. To my astonishment, she pulled a kitchen knife from her purse, then lunged at her daughter. "I won't have it!"

In a flash, Rylan had the woman up against the wall, her wrist pinned straight up over her head so that she couldn't get any leverage with the knife. I grabbed the child and gathered her up in my arms as a teacher rushed into the room.

"What *is* the meaning of this?" the teacher cried. "I won't have any violence on these premises!"

"She's an *abomination*," the mother howled, struggling as Rylan restrained her. The kitchen knife clattered to the floor, and the teacher flinched. Tinari let out a sob, curling her face into my shirt, and I held her tightly. "And so are *you*," Mrs. Shaun snarled at me, her eyes flashing with a zealous light. "Father Calmias told us of your wicked ways! He has shown us the light, and we will not go back now that we know the truth!"

We cancelled the rest of the interviews for that day, then took the girl home with us to the Palace. Her mother spent the night in a cell at the Enforcer's Guild, and Tinari slept in my bed with me that night, too frightened and sad to be left alone with anyone else. Careful questions elicited the information that her father was also adamantly opposed to magic and mages, and she was afraid to go home.

"It's terrible, what's happened here," I said quietly to Iannis the next morning over breakfast. We ate in my sitting room for a change—Tinari was still asleep in my bed, and I didn't want to stray far in case she woke up. "That a mother would go so far as to want to kill her own daughter."

"An unfortunate side effect of religious fanaticism," Iannis said over his cup of tea. His violet eyes were sad. "Father Calmias has managed to fan the flames even higher since his imprisonment. Something really must be done about him. But never mind that. What have you and the apprentices discovered?"

"Aside from Tinari, we've found fifteen magically talented children in total," I told him. I'd had the apprentices finish up at the school I'd left, as well as the other ones. "I interviewed all of them last night. Three of them want training, two of them have such feeble magic that it's not worth dealing with, and ten want nothing to do with their powers at all." That fact made me sad, because I'd sensed a lot of potential in one of them in particular. But it wasn't my place to force them. "I'd planned to recommend wiping those ten, leaving the two alone, and placing the final three with families who are willing to train them. But now I'm wondering if a biased parent and a young, impressionable child should be allowed to decide on such an important matter so soon." I bit my lip as I thought back to my own ten-year old self. "At that age, I probably would have agreed to be wiped if I'd thought it would help me fit in with the Baine Clan. But now that I'm older and I don't care about that, I can see that it would have been a horrible mistake. What if the child goes through with this, and then regrets it for the rest of her life?"

"That would be terrible," Iannis said, his expression turning thoughtful as he regarded me. "I'm very glad the tests missed you," he said with feeling.

I nodded. "I am too, in the end. But the only reason I survived so long without causing trouble was because of the spell Ballos put on me, and the charms and training Roanas gave me later on to help control my outbursts." I bit my lip. "But if we wait until the children are older and they decide they don't want their magic, there's an increased risk that the wipe will damage them mentally. And if they're allowed to remain unchecked in the meantime, they could cause harm."

Iannis raised an eyebrow. "It sounds like you are convincing yourself of what you already know must be done."

I let out a gusty sigh. "Yeah. But it really pisses me off that it has to be this way." I took a sip of my cooling coffee, focusing on the bittersweet flavor of the beans and sugar. "I guess if they don't want to be trained, there's no alternative."

"No, there isn't," Iannis agreed solemnly, reaching over the table to grasp my hand. "Sometimes, Sunaya, there is no perfect solution. One of the hardest things about being a leader is having to choose between the lesser of two evils."

I gnashed my teeth at that. I didn't want to choose between the lesser of two evils! "Just why *did* they miss me?" I demanded, frustration simmering in my voice. "Why was I passed over, when so many others were not? And if Ballos was strong enough to bind my magic, why didn't he just wipe it altogether?"

Iannis put down his cup. "He probably would have wiped it if he could," he said to my surprise. "Being a half-shifter protected you. Shifters all have some magic too, in order to be able to change form—that is also what makes their lifespans longer than humans'. To attempt to wipe a shifter infant's magic would make him or her unable to shift, drastically shorten their lives, and very possibly kill them."

"Oh." I let out a surprised breath. I hadn't really considered how being a shifter would affect the magic wipe. Did that mean the mages couldn't have wiped me at all? Or did it just mean that they would have killed me straight off? Ballos probably wouldn't have cared about the risk of wiping me if not for fear of inciting my mother's wrath, so I wondered if the mages would have tried to wipe me anyway.

"Anyway," Iannis went on, "binding is very difficult at such a young age, as the brain must be allowed to grow and develop. If the binding is too tight, it leads to lethal complications—too loose and it could fail. Ballos had to make the binding elastic enough to accommodate your growth, which is why your magic sometimes escaped."

"That's interesting," I said, and I truly meant it. "But none of this is helpful for our current dilemma. What about the children who do want to become mages? Are we going to be able to find mages willing to train them? If we can't resolve that, then we may as well wipe the lot of them." I pushed my coffee cup away in disgust. What was the point in all this work I was doing, if in the end, these kids still didn't have a choice?

"Of course we will find mages to foster them," Iannis said with a reassuring smile. "I've discussed the matter with Cirin already, while you've been out. We are setting up a program with incentives for the mage community, presenting it as a scientific experiment. In fact, he has already signed on two volunteers."

"He has?" My mouth dropped open, and I shook my head. "I don't know why I'm so surprised. You're always one step ahead of me." Relief coursed through me as the heavy weight on my chest melted away, and I snatched up his hand so I could press a kiss against his knuckles.

Iannis chuckled. "I'm always eager to please, when it comes to you." His hand curved along my cheek, his thumb stroking gently across my skin. "I wouldn't leave such an important matter to fate or chance."

"Right." I swallowed against the sudden lump in my throat, pushing away the rising emotion so I could focus. "What about the children whose parents want the magic wipe? Is there anything we can do to safely postpone the decision until they're old enough to truly consider all the pros and cons? What if we could bind them, the way Ballos did to me?"

"Hmm." Iannis tapped his chin, his brows drawing together in thought. "That would be an interesting challenge. It would mean effectively isolating the magic for another decade, not allowing it to emerge at all, and yet do no harm to its possessor.

We could not allow magic to leak out, the way yours did, not with the way the human community is still so afraid of it. Unfortunately, there is no standard spell for what you are suggesting."

"But you know many non-standard spells, don't you?" I coaxed, my veins humming with eagerness. Iannis had that glint in his eyes, the one he always got right before he rolled up his sleeves to tackle an interesting problem.

"There are two different procedures I have learned during my travels that could possibly be combined to that effect," Iannis admitted, and I grinned. There was likely no other mage in Solantha willing or able to attempt such a complicated spell, especially not for ungrateful and half-rebellious humans. But Iannis had proven with Fenris that he was willing to try unusual solutions, and I was thrilled that he would do this for me, when he was so busy with his other duties.

"Before I think on this further, I will have to check your results," Iannis warned as I popped a piece of bacon into my mouth. "And go over your proposal with the Council as well. I am very pleased with how quickly you've worked. I'm certain that between the two of us, we can create a successful program for managing new magic users."

"If we do, then all of this will have been worth it for that alone." I smiled, content for the first time in a while. I was finally tackling this issue, which had made my life hell for so long. Even if I had to deal with scornful looks and death threats for the rest of my life, if I could change the tide for people like me, born with mage talents through no fault of our own, it was a price worth paying.

7

"I'm going to miss the hell out of you," I told Fenris, squeezing him tight. We stood outside the side entrance to the Palace, waiting for the carriage that would take him to the airport.

"I'm going to miss you too." Fenris hugged me back, then stepped away as the carriage came around. "Don't worry about me when you're gone. I will be fine, and I will take good care of our friend here." He slapped Rylan on the shoulder.

Rylan huffed a little, but he smiled. Since Rylan couldn't come with me to Garai, we were leaving him in Fenris's care. Fenris would be able to restore his illusion if it failed for any reason—though Rylan didn't know that—and the protection would be mutual, though I would not have offended Fenris by suggesting so. Rylan would be more useful with him, rather than twiddling his thumbs at the Palace while I was gone.

"We'll make sure to check in on Elania regularly, and on the children, as you requested, once we return," Rylan promised. "I know how important these children are to you."

"Thanks." I smiled, relieved to know someone would be here to make sure things didn't go to hell while I was absent. I wasn't worried about the children who thought they'd been personally "wiped" by the Chief Mage. Upon reaching their majority, they would learn that they still had to make a decision regarding their magic. Iannis had successfully managed to bind it in such a way that wiping would still be safely possible, though it had taken him a bit of time to figure it out. I hoped this would become the new standard for dealing with gifted children across the whole nation someday, and not just in Solantha.

"Around six hundred years ago." The look in Iannis's eyes grew distant. "My career started in Manuc, the country of my birth, but it didn't take me very long to realize that I was not of much use there. I traveled extensively before I eventually ended up as the Chief Mage here."

"Really?" I frowned. "I can't imagine that a mage of your talent and power would be useless anywhere."

Iannis smiled. "Perhaps, but things are very different in Manuc. There is a much higher concentration of strong mages on the island, largely because of the Tua blood mixed into our heritage. Many of the oldest living mages in the world reside in Manuc, and they are vastly more powerful than I. I'm afraid that amongst my own people, I am not very special, Sunaya."

A knock on the carriage door interrupted us before I could ask more questions. "Sir, the Minister is approaching," a guard called.

I glanced out the window, and my mouth fell open in amazement. Three large airships were indeed approaching, and the one in the middle was twice the size of the two that flanked it. I'd never seen such a large airship in my life.

"How many people did you say he was bringing?" I asked faintly as I watched the ships descend, the airport staff scurrying about as they prepared for the landing. "He looks like he's coming with a small army."

"I understand that half the government decided to see him

off at the pier," Iannis explained as we disembarked from the carriage. "There will be only thirteen of us on the boat, counting the five servants. We are not just attending a funeral, but a coronation, and the Federation is expected to bring gifts for the new Mage-Emperor."

"That's a hell of a lot of gifts," I muttered as we all formed a semi-circle near the landing strip—close enough that the Minister wouldn't have to walk far to get to the carriages we'd brought for him, but far enough away that we would be safe. "I have a feeling we're gonna need more carriages."

"We won't be unloading everything now," Director Chen said, sounding slightly amused. "That would be far too much work. But we will have strong protection spells set up around the ship, and mages guarding it day and night." She gestured toward several of the mage guards who had been brought along —large, imposing men who were powerful both magically and physically. I figured they would be supplemented by regular human and shifter guards as well.

It took some time for the ships to make a proper landing—it was a slow, delicate process to make sure they touched down without causing damage. The Minister disembarked from one of the smaller ships, dressed in burgundy robes, his long blond hair tied back from his stern face into a braid. He was accompanied by at least twenty other mages—guards, aides, and high officials—and trying to keep up with all the introductions was impossible. Luckily most of them would not be coming on to Garai with us, but, in the meantime, they were our guests and had to be looked after.

Once we were all back at the Palace and settled, Iannis and I had lunch in the Winter Garden with Minister Graning, Director Chen, and a mage named Garrett Toring, who was introduced to us as the Director of Federal Security. He was tall and handsome, with gilded hair and a charming smile, but there was a cold, calculating edge to his hazel eyes that made me instantly dislike him. I could tell from Iannis's scent that he didn't like Toring, either, though he hid his emotions well with his impeccable manners.

"I thought I would make things expedient by briefing you over lunch," the Minister said after he'd taken a sip from his glass of water.

Well, that explains why the other guests are eating separately, I thought as I piled my plate high with appetizers. The servers had brought out trays of coconut-encrusted shrimp, tiny tarts filled with spinach and goat cheese, and bowls of lobster bisque. I was starving, so it took great effort for me to restrain myself from inhaling the whole table's worth and nibble delicately on my shrimp like a lady.

"That sounds like an excellent idea," Iannis said. "You provided scant details over the phone, so I can only assume you are about to divulge highly sensitive information."

"Director Toring," the Minister said, inclining his head to the Director, who sat at his elbow. "Why don't you take the lead?"

"Of course, sir," Toring said smoothly. To Iannis, Chen, and me, he said, "We will be traveling by steamboat to the port of Maral, which is well north of Leniang Port, in order to attend the funeral. The Garaian government will be sending a troop from the Imperial Guard to meet and escort us, as well as the various other heads of state arriving, to Bilai, the capital." He glanced at me, and the tips of my ears reddened as I realized the geographical explanations were specifically for me. Chen would know where these locations were, as a native Garaian, and Iannis probably did, too, since he was so well traveled. Director Toring obviously assumed I was completely ignorant, when in fact I'd known the capital of Garai since I was eight years old! And despite my schedule being dominated by the school investigations, I'd managed to find time to refresh my knowledge of the country. Not that I was an expert, but still—I wasn't a *total* idiot. Silently, I fumed, curling my hands into fists beneath the table.

"How many days will we be required to remain at the capital?" Iannis asked. "I am not quite familiar with the Garaian custom for state funerals. There have only been two in my lifetime, the last one three hundred years ago, and I was not invited either time."

"Depending on the outcome of the imperial heir's testing, it should be two to three weeks, minimum," Director Chen said before Toring could answer. "I expect we'll be housed in a pavilion specifically set up for our delegation, so we should be relatively safe from snooping, and from any nations who might wish us harm. Even so, I assume you will be employing strict security measures of your own." She inclined her head to Toring.

"Of course," Toring said smoothly, but I caught a hint of annoyance in his steely gaze. I had a feeling he didn't like that Director Chen had answered for him, even though she *would* be the expert on her native country's customs. "After the funeral, there will be eight days of mourning and seclusion, and after that, we will attend the ceremonial testing for the successor, the deceased Mage-Emperor's eldest son. Following that, providing he passes the tests, comes the Coronation, which is marked by an eight-day celebration."

"By Magorah," I complained, drawing all eyes to me. "That's a long time. I'm assuming there's a reason why they like eight days, instead of seven, or say, one?" A hint of sarcasm entered my voice at the end—I mean really, how long did it take to stick a crown on a guy's head?

Toring shrugged. "I am told eight is the most auspicious number in Garai—considered to ensure good fortune. Luckily for us, the long period of mourning means that we should just have enough time to complete our mission before we are due back for the testing ceremony and coronation."

The servers came back in with the next course—grilled salmon, seared scallops, thin noodles in a cream sauce, and green beans—and we ceased talking. The silence went on for a bit longer as we dug into our meals, for which I was grateful. The food was delicious, and I wanted to enjoy it.

Eventually, though, the Director resumed his briefing. "In that enormous airship, amongst other things, we have brought a very special experimental flying machine. It is small, light, and quite unobtrusive. We will be using it to slip away to Leniang Port during the week of mourning. The five "servants" we are bringing are trained mages and operatives, and one of them is a pilot."

"Our objective is to find and shut down the lab in Leniang Port as quickly and quietly as possible," the Minister said. "The mission is not without risk, as the Garaians can be very touchy about their sovereignty. Discretion is of the utmost importance —we do not wish to trigger a diplomatic incident, or worse, a war."

"Certainly not," Iannis agreed. "A war with Garai would be devastating for both countries. And we want to keep our lucrative trade with them intact."

"There is another complication," Toring said, his expression growing serious. "After learning about the gunrunning problem, the Minister and I sent a team of highly trained and powerful mages into Leniang Port to deal with the matter directly. We did not discover the lab's existence until we questioned the doctors from Osero, but managed to transmit the information to the team while they were still *en route*." His words were for Director Chen and I, and I kept my face neutral so I would not betray more foreknowledge. Iannis had already told me about the gunrunning issue, though Toring obviously assumed he wouldn't have bothered my pretty little head with such details. "We lost contact with them awhile ago, after they had faithfully reported in every other night with a special long-range magitech device."

"Where were they when they last reported in?" Chen asked.

"They had just arrived in Leniang Port," Director Toring said. "We have not heard from them for nearly ten days now, so we can only assume that they have been captured or killed, or that they have betrayed us. The latter seems unlikely—they are experienced operatives, handpicked by myself."

"Then it's possible that the lab has been forewarned, and that they might have even relocated now that they know we're onto them," I pointed out.

"Yes, unfortunately." Toring's face was expressionless, but I sensed this was a sore topic for him. It would be for me, too, if I'd sent in a team only to have my mission backfire so badly.

"I surmise that you have not involved the local or national authorities?" Chen asked, her face lined with tension.

"We considered it, but decided not to involve the Garaian authorities, precisely because the problem is in Leniang port," the Minister said. "We fear that the local warlords, who are thoroughly corrupt, would try to get their hands on the disease-causing substances and use them to blackmail everyone else. That, or use them against Garai's enemies, some of which are our allies. And if it ever leaked out that those substances were created by scientists from the Northia Federation, our reputation could be damaged irreparably."

"I see your point," Chen said, sounding resigned. "I suppose this is why I was not aware of any of this. But I'm glad to know and will do anything to help. I have family living in that area, and would not want my younger sister or her children endangered."

"She lives in Leniang City?" Director Toring asked with interest. "Are you close? Will she be willing to help?"

"I have not seen Asu for twenty years, since before she was married," Chen said. "But Garaian families have strong ties, and I am the elder. She will do what she can."

"We are counting on those familial ties to help us with our mission," the Minister said, smiling. "Which is another reason why I am appointing Lord Iannis as the leader of this mission, since you work for him."

"Thank you, sir," Iannis said, not sounding the least bit surprised. Had he expected this? He was the logical choice, so I supposed he would have prepared himself for the possibility.

"Minister, with all due respect, I must protest," Toring said, and the stiffness in his voice made it clear that he had *not* expected this decision. "I am the Director of Federal Security, after all, and my department provided both the airship and the pilot."

"That is true," the Minister acknowledged. "However, your experience with international affairs is not comparable to that of Lord Iannis and Director Chen. Before Lord Iannis came to Northia, he spent a good bit of time in Garai, amongst other countries. Isn't that right?" he asked, turning toward Iannis.

"It is," Iannis agreed, inclining his head. "I speak the northern dialect quite well, and am familiar with many Garaian customs. However, I have not traveled much in the south, which is where Director Chen's experience will come in."

"That is all very well," Toring interjected, "but what about your young fiancée and apprentice?" His cold gaze flicked briefly toward me, and I clenched my fists beneath the table at the disdain in his eyes. "I understand you do not wish to be separated from Miss Baine for months—she is, after all, very pretty —but this is not the sort of mission where one takes a lover along." Noting the dangerous glint in Iannis's eyes, he hastily amended, "An apprentice, I meant to say."

"This is not up for debate," the Minister said firmly, saving me from firing off a scathing response. How dare that pompous bastard try to shut me out! And how were we supposed to work together with this oaf? It was a good thing he hadn't been put in charge, or I would have refused to go. Iannis's fingers found mine beneath the table, and he squeezed my hand—a show of solidarity as well as a warning to hold my temper in check.

"I already put Lord Iannis in charge of the mission, and he is free to bring along whomever he deems essential. If that includes Miss Baine, then so be it." It was obvious from the Minister's tone that he wasn't convinced I was needed either, and I gritted my teeth. Zavian Graning had made it clear the last time I'd been to Dara that he did not hold me in high regard. But Iannis made no bones about the fact that he wouldn't allow the Minister to intimidate or bully me, and it looked like the Minister was taking that to heart.

Whatever, I thought as I finished the last of my meal. The Minister and his Director of Federal Security could think what they wanted. I would use this opportunity to prove them so wrong, they would be begging me for help the next time they needed us to go on another mission.

In the meantime, though, I had to put up with these guys for several weeks, no, *months*. And, boy, was I *not* looking forward to that.

8

To my chagrin, there were no magic lessons for the rest of the day. Sure, I'd expected that, but it would have been nice to have a legitimate excuse to slip away from the guests. Unfortunately, Fenris wasn't here to tutor me in Loranian, and Iannis was busy entertaining the Minister.

If it had been up to me, I would have snuck out of the Palace and gone to help Annia pack or something, since she was about to leave and I had no idea when I'd see her next. But that would have been the coward's way out, and besides, Iannis was having none of it. He roped me, Chen, and Cirin into helping him entertain the delegates, essentially turning us into glorified tour guides. I was assigned to the Federal Secretary of Economic Affairs, Solar ar'Dakis, a lanky mage with jaw-length brown hair and hawkish features.

"It is a pleasure to finally make your acquaintance, Miss Baine," he said in a tone that suggested anything but as we headed for the side entrance of the Palace. "I have heard good things about you."

I glanced sidelong at him. "You know that I can smell lies, right?"

His cheeks flushed, and he looked away. "I was trying to be polite. Something you're clearly not interested in," he added pointedly.

"Oh, I like good manners just fine," I said easily as I held one of the double doors open for him. "But lying to a shifter is downright insulting. Not that you would know that, since you clearly don't interact with our kind." Solar frowned as we descended the steps toward the waiting carriage. I had half a mind to send it away and stick him on the back of my steam bike instead. A good, hard ride up and down Solantha's steep hills and around sharp corners would probably go a long way toward getting that stick out of his ass. But Iannis would kill me, so I held in a sigh and allowed the driver to help me into the carriage after him.

At least I'd changed out of that fancy dress and back into normal clothes again. I wore a dark green top with my leather pants and boots, and my weapons were strapped to my body in clear view. It wasn't safe for me to go around unarmed, even if I did know magic and had a trained mage along for the ride.

Solar's eyes lingered on my crescent knives as the steam carriage rumbled forward, taking the main road that ran through the Mages Quarter and into Rowanville. "I see that despite being an apprentice to the most powerful mage in your state, you insist on dressing like an enforcer."

"I am still an enforcer," I said evenly, meeting his gaze. "Becoming a mage isn't going to change that."

"So you plan on chasing bounties after you're wed to Lord Iannis?" Solar arched a brow. "That doesn't seem very practical."

I forced myself not to react. "I'll cross that bridge when I come to it. In the meantime, Lord Iannis does not object to my enforcer shield. In fact, he continues to call upon my services as an enforcer from time to time."

"Most unusual," Solar murmured, some of the stiffness leaving his voice. He relaxed against the plush seating as he regarded me. "Earlier, you spoke of yourself as though you were just a shifter, and not also a mage. Is that how you regard yourself?"

"It was, for a long time," I admitted, though I wasn't entirely sure why I was telling him this. It wasn't as if we were buddies or anything. "When I first started my apprenticeship, I worried that I was going to have to choose between the two. But Resinah has helped me realize that it's important to maintain both halves of my identity."

"Resinah?" Solar's eyebrows winged up. "You mean to say that you have spoken with the First Mage?"

"Yes." I resisted the urge to clap my hands over my mouth. Should I have not admitted that aloud?

"That is very interesting," Solar said, and to my surprise, he looked mildly impressed. "Resinah very rarely speaks to any of us directly. No wonder you have had such success in combating the Resistance with Lord Iannis, if you have had Resinah to guide you."

I opened my mouth to tell him that, for the most part, Resinah had nothing to do with any of that, but thought better of it. Why ruin the moment, when he was clearly softening up to me?

"Her wisdom has proven very useful for me," I said instead, allowing a smile to come to my lips. Hey, maybe I could actually get along with this guy. It would certainly make my temporary job as a tour guide more bearable.

I took Solar across the Firegate Bridge and up Hawk Hill so that we could visit the secret temple that was hidden from the naked eye by a powerful illusion spell. I spoke the Word that peeled back the illusion, and a little thrill went through me as the temple came into view. The domed building soared above me, constructed of a strange blue stone that sparkled in the afternoon light. Runes were carved into the moldings surrounding the round glass windows, and I wondered when I was going to start learning how to read them.

The heavy, carved entrance door to the temple was open already, so Solar and I quietly stepped through and into the large interior. Sunlight filtered in through the skylight set into the top of the domed ceiling, illuminating the interior and shining a spotlight directly onto the enormous white marble statue of Resinah, the First Mage and the mouthpiece of the Creator. She towered a good thirty feet above the half-dozen mages who knelt in prayer on the stone floor, and my eyebrows rose as I noticed they knelt not on the stone, but on woven rugs.

"Have you come to pray?" an attendant in a white robe asked softly as she stepped from the shadows to my right. She had a rug draped over each forearm, and she offered one to both of us.

"Yes, thank you," Solar said before I could answer. He took one, and I did too, trying to hide how flustered I was. The last two times I had come here, the temple had been empty. I didn't know anything about kneeling or praying, and when I'd spoken to Resinah, she hadn't seemed to expect it.

Solar moved forward without hesitation, finding an open spot on the floor. I mimicked his moves, placing my rug down in a horizontal fashion before kneeling on it. The rugs seemed to be pure gold in color, but as I knelt, I noticed there were actually thousands of tiny runes etched into the fabric that all seemed to run into each other.

Welcome back. Resinah's voice echoed in my head, and I jerked my chin up. The flame in her outstretched hand was dancing, as it had the last time I'd spoken with her.

Hello, My Lady, I replied, bowing my head as I clasped my hands in prayer, which was what the others were doing. Not wanting to look out of place, I kept my head bowed even though I really wanted to look into the statue's face. *It is a pleasure to speak with you again.*

Resinah chuckled a little at that. *Your manners are improving.* She paused, then added, *As is your countenance. You are more balanced since the last time we spoke.*

I've been taking your advice, I told her. *You know, accepting both sides of myself. I'm still working on how to make them a whole.*

Patience, child. You've only just begun on this path.

In case you haven't noticed, shifters aren't very good at patience. I resisted the urge to stick my tongue out at her, because I was a mature, balanced woman. And besides, I was sort of talking to a deity. *I thought I was supposed to embrace both halves.*

Flippant as usual, Resinah said dryly. *There is danger ahead in your near future. You will be tested. When the time comes, do not give in to your emotions. Stay your hand.*

I froze. *What does that mean?* I asked carefully, my mind spinning. I knew I was going into danger—I was on my way to destroy a Resistance lab, after all. *What do you mean 'stay your hand'? I am probably going to have to kill people at some point.*

I do not mean that you should not defend yourself, Resinah said in that calm, distant way of hers. *Only that you should not give in to hate.* Her voice began to fade away. *Let logic guide you, not emotion, when the time comes.*

Is that seriously all you're giving me? I shouted angrily in my head, my hands balling into fists.

"Seriously?" the ether parrot squawked, materializing by my shoulder. Solar and I both jumped, and several other mages let out startled exclamations.

"Miss Baine," the attendant hissed, rushing over. "Performing casual magic is strictly forbidden here!"

"Sorry," I muttered, getting to my feet. I swatted at the parrot, but he evaded the blow easily. "I can't really control him."

"*Sorry,*" he cawed, louder than before, and I glared murderously at him. He disappeared in a flash of blue light, and I sighed.

"That's all right," Solar said smoothly, taking me by the elbow. He pressed a coin into the attendant's palm, then handed her the rugs. "I just finished my prayers. Apologies for the disturbance."

He guided me out of the temple, and I let out a little sigh of relief as the annoyed stares from the other mages receded. "Thanks for that," I told him as I slid my arm from his.

"Not a problem," he said as we approached the carriage. The driver hopped down from his seat and opened the door for us. "It has been some time since I was so thoroughly entertained in a temple." There was a hint of humor in his voice.

We got inside. When the door closed, he spoke again. "I felt Resinah's presence more strongly than usual today. Were you communing with her?"

"You can sense that?" I demanded. "How?" There was a spiritual aura when I'd entered the temple, as there always was when I visited, but then again, I'd felt the same sort of thing whenever I'd visited Magorah's temple in Shiftertown as a teen.

"My great-grandmother was a witch with a talent for reading auras, or so I'm told," Solar said with a shrug, though he sounded a little uncomfortable about the admission. The carriage began to roll along the path winding around the hill, and I shifted in my seat to adjust for the motion. "I seem to have inherited something of her ability."

"Really? That's interesting." I wondered if there were other mages around with 'special' talents like that. Iannis had his super speed, and his extraordinary healing abilities were probably boosted by his Tua heritage. How many mages in the world had other peculiar bits of magic flowing through their bloodlines?

"It comes in handy at times," Solar conceded. "If I didn't believe you before about your connection with Resinah, I certainly do now. I think if the Minister knew, he would respect you more. I could mention it to him, if you'd like."

"I'm not going to go bragging about it to him, or anyone else, just to curry favor," I snapped before I could help myself. "I want to be judged on my merits, not my connections."

"I'm afraid that's not how politics works," Solar said, looking out the window. "But it is an admirable attitude nonetheless."

9

*A*fter I showed Solar around the city, we returned to the Palace for a banquet held in honor of our guests. Back in my rooms, I sighed a little as a maid helped dress my hair and do my makeup—I was already out of my street clothes and stuffed back into a dress. Funnily enough, I'd been reluctant to come back to the Palace—I'd been having a good time playing tour guide for Solar, once we got past the initial unpleasantness.

At least it's not a super-formal outfit, I mused, running my hand along the silky, persimmon-colored fabric my social secretary had selected for the occasion. It was a summery, high-waisted dress, with off-the-shoulder sleeves and a hem that brushed against the tops of my feet. It didn't exactly seem like the type of dress I'd have picked to wear to a fancy banquet, but I wasn't about to argue with Nelia when it was more comfortable than what I'd been wearing this morning.

Just as the maid was leaving, a knock came at the door, and Iannis entered. He too was dressed in lighter robes than usual, though they were still the blue and gold state colors he always wore. There was a gold sash cinched at his waist, and his long, cherry-wood hair was tied at the nape of his neck. He looked grand and stern all at once, but he nodded cordially at the maid as she bowed to him.

"You look beautiful, *a ghra*," he told me once she'd closed the door behind me, using the foreign endearment that meant 'my heart' in his native tongue. His arms encircled my waist, drawing me into him, and I inhaled his sandalwood-and-magic scent greedily, as I always did when we were alone together. Desire stirred in my belly as he lowered his lips to mine, but I held it at bay—we didn't have time.

And besides, I had things on my mind.

"Do you think the Minister would respect me more if he knew I was a direct descendant of Resinah?" I asked, gently pulling my lips from his.

His eyebrows rose. "Where is this coming from?"

I sighed. "The Federal Secretary of Economics suggested it. I wouldn't have thought much of it, except that in the beginning, he was acting like an ass, and then once he found out that Resinah and I are like, best buds, he started acting all impressed."

Iannis frowned. "You shouldn't speak about the Lady so flippantly," he admonished, though he softened the scold by tapping a long finger against the tip of my nose. "You never know when she might be listening, and it would be foolish to risk losing her favor."

"True," I muttered, glancing around. Unlike in the temple, I didn't sense anything spiritual. Then again, I never really had except during the few times Resinah had shown herself to me. I wondered if Solar was able to tell whether she was around or not? That would be a useful talent to have.

"I ran into Mr. ar'Dakis not very long ago," Iannis said, his violet eyes narrowed in thought. "He congratulated me on selecting such a beautiful and intelligent bride, so I gathered you had made a good impression. I hadn't realized it was based solely on your connection to Resinah," he said, his mouth turning down.

"Well, I don't know that it was," I told him. "After I broke the ice with that revelation, he was a lot friendlier, and we had a good time."

"Is that right?" Iannis asked, tracing the outline of my jaw with the pad of his thumb. "Not too good of a time, I hope."

I snorted. "Please. He doesn't hold a candle to you."

Iannis grinned at that. "I should hope not," he said, moving to kiss me again.

I put a hand against his broad chest, stopping him before he made contact. "Uh-uh. You didn't answer my question."

"Does it matter? Zavian Graning does not think highly of anyone besides himself. He owes his life to us, and yet he still plays those little political games, pitting Director Toring and I against each other, and he barely tolerates you. He is an astute politician—most of the time—but as a person, he does not deserve respect, so why should we worry about his esteem? Sunaya, he is not worth worrying over."

Put like that, I had to agree with Iannis. "And what about Toring? Why was he so annoyed that you were put in charge of the mission, and why do you dislike him?"

Iannis sighed. "It's a long story, and we don't have time now. Just be very careful around him, and do not mention Fenris."

We headed down to the banquet hall in relative silence after that, both weighed down by heavy thoughts. But my worries fell away as we arrived, replaced by a sense of awe. The last time I'd attended a banquet in here, the place had been transformed into a jungle, where I'd hid amongst the trees in panther form and listened to a bunch of mages gossip right before Iannis announced that I was going to be his apprentice. This time, the dirt floor and jungle trees had been replaced with palm fronds and white, powdery sand. The walls had disappeared, replaced with a view of the ocean and a cloudless blue sky, both of which seemed to stretch around us for miles, as though we were on a small island in the middle of the sea. And damned if I couldn't smell the salty sea breeze in the air.

"If I'd know this was the theme, I would have left off my shoes," I murmured as Iannis led me to the long table in the center of the room. It was draped in a white linen cloth, and seashell centerpieces had been placed at intervals down its length. Servants stood at the ready, trays of canapés and wineglasses balanced in their well-trained hands, and there were already several members of the delegation seated. I spotted Director Chen close to the head of the table, chatting with Director Toring. The polite smile on her face was at odds with the coolness in her dark eyes, and I sensed she liked the Director of Federal Security about as much as Iannis and I did.

At least that was one thing we could agree on, I thought to myself as we joined them.

The rest of the guests filed in not long after that, and, to my relief, I found myself seated next to Solar. I was glad not to be stuck next to the Minister, or any of the other delegates—I didn't feel like having to go through the whole ordeal of breaking the ice with yet another prejudiced mage.

"So," I asked Solar as we worked our way through a salad. "What can you tell me about the Director of Federal Security? I have never heard of that position before. Just what does he do?"

"Director Toring?" Solar asked, his gaze briefly flickering to the mage in question. Toring was in deep conversation with the woman to his left—Marlis Ugorna, the Federal Secretary of Foreign Relations if I remembered correctly. "The position has been created especially for him. He was instated only a few months ago, but the department is growing at an almost alarming pace."

"What was he before that?" *And how was it that he felt more qualified to lead the mission than Iannis, if he was so new to the position?* I wondered to myself.

"He worked as a deputy in the Secretary of Justice's office." Solar's lips briefly twisted in a sardonic smile, and he kept his voice low so that Toring would not overhear from his side of the table. "In fact, he used to *be* the Secretary of Justice, but was demoted from the position some years ago for mishandling a case—he let a high-profile fugitive escape."

"And yet he's back in a similar position now?" My eyebrows rose so high they probably touched my hairline. "That doesn't seem particularly smart."

Solar shrugged his left shoulder. "That's politics," he said, then took a sip from his glass of white wine. "Garrett has worked hard to climb back up the ladder after his fall, and now that he's back on top, I doubt anything will knock him down again. With his rapidly growing staff and budget, I can only foresee him becoming more powerful." The hint of displeasure in Solar's voice spoke volumes. Perhaps he thought Toring didn't deserve the money or manpower, and could have used some of that extra budget and personnel himself.

The servants arrived with the main course, and the conversation around the table subsided as everyone dug into their food. As I twirled pasta around my fork and studied Director Toring through lowered lashes, I was glad that Fenris had decided to leave. Such a driven and ambitious man would not be able to let it slide if he discovered Fenris was actually Polar ar'Tollis, a mage who had been sentenced to execution for treason against the Federation. He could have Fenris executed, and perhaps even Iannis himself for aiding a traitor.

I remembered Iannis's hint not to mention Fenris. Could it be that Toring had been involved in sentencing Fenris to death, back when he had been the Secretary of Justice? Was that the case he had mishandled, or had he already been demoted by then? My blood boiled at the thought that we might be consorting with Fenris's worst enemy, and I glanced toward Iannis. How could he sit here with Toring so calmly, if that was the case?

"Not all of them are like that, you know. We have a shifter here in Solantha who is a scholar of magic," Cirin said in response to something I hadn't caught. "His name is Fenris, and though, of course, he cannot use magic himself, his interest and breadth of knowledge are most impressive. I have never before seen a shifter so comfortable and fearless around mages. It makes me wonder if our relations with the shifter community might be strengthened if they had a better knowledge of how magic worked, instead of clinging to superstitious fears."

"That's an interesting theory," Toring said, tapping the side of his cheek with his forefinger. My breathing hitched, and I wished that Cirin was closer so that I could give him a good kick in the shins even though he didn't know what he'd just done. "I would love to meet this unusual shifter. I hear he is a good friend of yours, Lord Iannis?"

"Yes, he is," Iannis said smoothly, but I knew he was on his guard now. Fucking hell. Why did Cirin have to bring up Fenris's name?

"How and when did you meet this Fenris? It is most unusual for a shifter to be living at the capitol palace in any state," Toring commented, his gaze turning speculative.

"It certainly is," I interjected loudly before Iannis could answer. "Things were particularly difficult for me in the beginning, when I was first brought to Solantha Palace. But ever since I became the Chief Mage's apprentice, it has become a lot easier to integrate with mage society."

"Yes, and you have done quite well so far," Iannis said warmly, and I could tell he was grateful at my change of subject. To my relief, the conversation turned away from Fenris, and onto my apprenticeship. Even though I didn't like that I was shining a spotlight on myself, it was better that they looked toward me instead of discussing him. We couldn't risk anyone wondering why it was that Fenris had chosen to take a trip right when they were arriving, or for Director Toring to start digging further into the matter.

I could only hope that by the time we got underway with our mission, Toring would have forgotten all about Fenris. The last thing I wanted was for Fenris to go on the run after we'd just convinced him to stay in Solantha.

10

———

*T*he next two days passed far too quickly. Before I knew it, I was staring out a carriage window at the setting sun, the evening before our trip. Everything was packed and ready to go, and the only thing left to do was one last inspection of the flying machine Toring had provided, which we would be using to fly from the capital to Leniang Port.

As the carriage rolled over a pothole, my knees jostled against Toring's. He sat across from Iannis and me, squeezed next to Director Chen and Henning Mogg, the pilot. Our eyes met, hazel against green, and I held that speculative gaze with defiance. Was he going to make this journey difficult for me? I wasn't about to forget that he hadn't wanted me to come along. I wondered if it was because he was prejudiced against me—or maybe shifters in general—or because he didn't think it was wise for Iannis to bring a lover on a dangerous mission, as he'd stated so rudely.

"Are you looking forward to the trip, Miss Baine?" he asked pleasantly, as if there were no tension between us.

"I am," I said, giving him a faint smile. "I've never been to

Garai, and I'm very much looking forward to the experience, even if we are embarking on a dangerous mission."

"I have only been once myself, and that was a good hundred years ago," Toring admitted, breaking his gaze so he could look out the window. We were approaching the docks now, and I easily picked out the red, white, and blue Northia Federation flag flying from the mast of the *Voyager,* the massive steamship we would be traveling on to Garai. "So I'm sure much will have changed."

"Actually, it hasn't," Director Chen said in that voice of hers that was like the smooth, polished surface of a lake. "Garai is much the same today as it was even three hundred years ago, when the late Mage-Emperor ascended his throne. Steeped in tradition and unwelcoming to outsiders unless invited. We should be very careful to mind our manners during this visit." Her dark eyes slid to mine, and I knew that statement was directed more at me than Toring. "Diplomatic immunity will only get you so far."

"I know," I said, trying not to sound annoyed. I couldn't really blame her for being concerned about me—though I'd studied up as best I could about Garaian customs over the past few days, I doubted it was enough for a diplomatic mission, or that I would remember everything. I would have to rely on Director Chen, and Iannis, to guide me as far as what was or was not appropriate. Much as I hated the thought, the best course of action was probably for me to keep my mouth shut, and do a lot of smiling and nodding.

The carriage brought us to the docks, and we headed up the gangway and onto the main deck. The guards on board had already unpacked the flying machine and brought it up to the deck. My eyes widened as I got a good look at it.

"It's so *small*," I exclaimed as we approached the apparatus. It stood barely a foot taller than Iannis, and looked a lot like an overgrown metal beetle, with a stocky, round body, and short wings that looked like they could be folded down and tucked away. "I don't think this can fit more than four people."

"That is supposed to be the maximum passenger load, but since there is no copilot, we can squeeze in a fifth," Toring said confidently as the pilot slid the door open so that we could look inside the cabin. The Director stroked a hand down the shiny green metal paneling covering the machine's side, a look of pride on his face. "We just won't be able to take very many supplies, to compensate for the extra weight."

"Is that accounting for my long legs?" Iannis asked dubiously as he peered inside. "I imagine this will be a very cramped flight."

"Comfort must be sacrificed for economy sometimes," Toring said coolly, with just a hint of annoyance in his voice.

"Of course," Iannis said, and something about the way he said it made me wonder if he was just yanking Toring's chain. I suppressed a smirk at the thought.

"How exactly does this thing work?" I asked, giving the aircraft a critical eye. "It doesn't seem like it's steam-powered, judging by the lack of vents or furnace."

"It is powered by a special magitech battery that cost a small fortune," Toring explained. "The battery powers the wings, which rotate very fast and are almost silent. Human ears would not be able to detect us once we are at full altitude, though perhaps a shifter might if they were paying close attention."

"We've field-tested this aircraft three times now," the pilot said, patting its shiny nose. "And she's performed very well. I've studied and memorized the map of Garai, and, based on my calculations, I believe I can get you from Bilai to Leniang Port in three days, even if we can only fly by the cover of darkness. Since our craft is so small and faster than the average airship, it might even be feasible to use it during the day." He tipped his hat toward me, then added in a more subdued voice, "Those were my colleagues who disappeared out there, and I want to find out what happened to them, more than anyone else. I'm just as invested in the safety of this craft as you are."

"Of course," I said, hiding my surprise as I remembered that he was a mage. I had forgotten, as his demeanor was so different from the other mages, and he was dressed in a white shirt, suspenders, corduroy pants, and boots—quite unlike what a typical mage would wear. Guess he took this whole 'secret agent' thing seriously.

Even so, Iannis and Director Chen insisted that they imbue the craft with their strongest protection spells before embarking on it. Toring seemed slightly insulted, but he agreed—after all, it would be silly to refuse. He needed us to come along, and that meant putting us at ease about flying in a strange country in what amounted to a glorified beetle.

Did life *really* always have to be so exciting?

~

As soon as we returned to the Palace, I made a quick stop at my room, then hurried down to the library to see Janta. I'd yet to return the *gulaya* I had borrowed from her weeks ago, and I wanted to do so now since I wasn't going to see her again for another three months.

Besides, I'd grown fond of the very helpful librarian mage, and she deserved a proper goodbye since I was heading off into danger again. There was always a chance that I wouldn't come back, though I didn't like to dwell on that sort of thing.

The door to the library was locked, but not warded, so I assumed the staff was in there doing after-hours work before they went home. I muttered the Words of an unlocking spell, and after the resulting click, turned the ornate brass handle and entered the room. Two servants were dusting the tables and shelves, and they started as the door swung open.

"Miss Baine!" the one nearest to me, a woman, exclaimed. She dipped into a curtsy, her duster still dangling from her fingertips. "How can I help you?"

I asked her if Janta was here, and after confirming that she was, picked my way through the shelves toward her office at the back of the library. It was a stylish but comfortable space, with birch-wood furniture and paintings of cityscapes, the visitors' chairs fitted with powder-blue cushions that invited the visitor to sit and have a conversation, unlike a certain woman I knew with uncomfortable dragon carvings in her furniture that liked to gouge into one's back.

"I came to return this," I said once we'd exchanged greetings, removing the *gulaya* from one of the pouches on my belt. I felt a twinge of nostalgia as I offered the small, star-shaped object to her. It had saved my life, whisking me to a deserted island an instant before Petros Yantz almost sliced into me with a silver knife. It was on that island I'd made love to Iannis for the first time. Heat flooded my body as the hot, sultry images of that night flitted through my mind, and I cleared my throat, pushing them away. Now was *not* the time to get hot and bothered.

"Oh, thank you," Janta said, surprised and pleased. "I suppose you've no use for this now, since you've used up the charge?" Her eyes twinkled knowingly.

"Umm, yeah." I smiled sheepishly at her. "It came in handy, but I'm not going to be needing it again."

"It's a pity we don't have one that could bring you straight back here, should you run into trouble in Garai," Janta said with a little sigh.

"Maybe we will someday," I said, smiling. "The Chief Mage is looking for an enterprising mage who would be interested in producing and recharging *gulayas*, now that we have discovered a legal method to do it. Hopefully these old ones will become useful once more, and we can have new ones made."

"How interesting! But I don't think we should restrict knowledge of this new method to Canalo. It should be published across the whole Federation."

"Maybe." I shrugged. I had a feeling Iannis had his reasons for not wanting to do so, at least not right away. At another time I would have thought to ask him about it, but there were more important things to think about right now.

"Anyway, I worry about you going on such a long trip, Sunaya," Janta admitted. "I hope that things go smoothly for you."

"I'll be with Lord Iannis and several other highly trained mages," I reassured her, surprised at her concern. "Besides, it's just a funeral. I don't think we're going to run into that much trouble." I felt only a slight twinge of guilt at omitting the rest of our plan—after all, a secret was a secret.

Janta's lips curved into a wry smile. "I may spend my time poring over old manuscripts, but I was not born yesterday, Sunaya," she said, sounding amused. "I doubt the Minister is inviting you and Lord Iannis along just for the pleasure of your company. But in any case, it is not the funeral itself, nor whatever other festivities, that I am concerned about. I am worried because there will be Heads of State from many other countries attending, including, very likely, your father."

Cold shock hit me, like a bucket of ice water dumped on my head. I gripped the arms of my chair as my spine went ramrod straight. "Are you serious?"

"I would be more surprised if he were *not* present, considering that invitations will have been sent out to heads of state across Recca," Janta said. "Such gatherings are considered a good opportunity for rulers to negotiate tricky deals or initiate favorable matches for their offspring and successors, so he might well bring his older children along too."

"By Magorah," I muttered, shaking my head. "Do you think Lord Iannis would know if my father was attending?" I wasn't sure what to do if it turned out he was there. Should I attempt to avoid him? Should I pretend that we were strangers? Or should I confront the elephant in the room head-on, and hope I didn't get impaled on one of its tusks?

"I doubt anyone knows the guest list for certain, not this soon. But I suggest you get hold of it the moment you arrive there," Janta warned. "The better prepared you are, the better armed you will be. Do be careful, and remember what I told you about Castalians and shifters." She cleared her throat. "Don't expect miracles, Sunaya. It might be wisest to simply keep your distance."

I thanked Janta for her advice, then surprised her with a goodbye hug before taking my leave. On a whim, I told her about the talented children, and asked her to check on them now and then in my absence. Yes, Fenris and Rylan were already on that, but as far as I was concerned, I couldn't have too many people looking after the children.

Anxious thoughts about a possible meeting with my unknown father swirled in my head as I walked down the hall. But the anxiety was tempered by an almost overwhelming curiosity about what the future would hold. Was there any connection between Resinah's cryptic warning and the prospect of meeting my unknown father? Was she telling me that I might end up fighting him, and, if so, to hold back from the killing blow? I really hoped not—the last thing I wanted was to end up in a death match with the man who'd unwittingly given me life.

Besides, I told myself, *even if you did end up in a duel, there's no way you'd win against a man as powerful and experienced as the High Mage of Castalis.* No, that couldn't be it. Resinah must have meant something else. I just hoped it wasn't even worse than what my imagination had conjured up.

welve days later, aboard the Voyager.

"Much better," Iannis praised, examining the wooden blade I'd magically sculpted out of a log of wood. "That was a distinct improvement on the last one, Sunaya."

"Thanks," I said, grinning with pride. The knife he held in his hand was a far cry from my first attempt, which had essentially been a pointy wooden plank. This blade was long, with as sharp an edge as one could achieve with wood. I'd even managed to carve a little floral design into it. "Do I really have to change this one back?"

"I suppose not," Iannis said, handing it back to me. We were sitting in an empty room on the main deck that he'd cleared specifically for my training—it held nothing aside from a table, two chairs, and a small shelf with some magical textbooks. "But there is not a large supply of these on the ship, and I promised to return any we took." He pointed to the small pile of logs by the door.

Since there was nothing much to do aboard the ship aside from sleep and eat, Iannis and I had taken the opportunity to catch up on my magic lessons. I'd made good progress with my Loranian, and had mastered the juggling exercise to the point that Iannis felt comfortable with letting me practice spells that required greater control. Transmogrification was one of those, and over the last few days he'd been having me reshape logs of wood into various objects. Technically this barely qualified as transmogrification, as the real purpose was to transform an object into a completely different material, like taking a piece of metal and turning it into marble. But I wasn't advanced enough for that yet.

"Do you think dinner will be ready soon?" I asked, tucking the blade beneath my belt. Performing magic, as always, had left me with a healthy appetite.

Iannis opened his mouth to answer, but he paused as the floor beneath us began to sway, faster than usual. I tensed as the boat shifted in one direction, then the other, then gasped as a huge wave rocked the boat very suddenly. Iannis and I grabbed onto the table, and I was glad it was securely bolted down. The wooden logs rolled across the floor, one of them smacking into my boot.

"By Magorah," I gasped. "What the hell was that?"

"Nothing good," Iannis said, rising from his chair with a worried frown. "It would take a very large wave indeed to rock a steamship of this size."

He opened the door, and I followed him as we climbed the single flight of stairs to the main deck. My mouth dropped open at the sight before me—the sky had turned dark, and the sea around us was very choppy. A cold wind whipped around us, yanking at my curls, and I snatched at my wooden knife as it was almost torn out of my grasp. The crew was rushing about, the first mate barking orders, and I was nearly mowed down by a sailor rushing full speed along the walkway.

"Hey!" I snagged him by the collar and brought him to a screeching halt. "What's going on here?"

"There's a storm coming, miss," the sailor said, his eyes wide. He looked about nineteen, his freckles stark against skin that was pale with worry. "The Captain says it looks to be a typhoon! You and the lord ought to get below decks."

"A typhoon?" Iannis echoed. "We'd best go find the Minister and other mages aboard. From the look of those clouds, it might not be enough to rely on the crew. We may have to use magic to save the ship."

We hurried over to the Minister's cabin, which was above deck and close to the bow of the ship. About halfway there, the clouds opened up, and a heavy rain began to pelt down on us. I conjured a pocket of air around us to keep Iannis and me dry, but by the time I got the spell going, we were already soaked, our hair plastered to the sides of our faces, our clothes clinging to our skin. Iannis could have done the spell himself, but doing such tasks for him was part of my apprenticeship. Though he probably would have done it anyway if he hadn't been distracted.

"Minister!" Iannis shouted, pounding on the door. He didn't wait, but let himself in. "Are you aware of the storm?"

"The Captain just sent a cabin boy to warn me it's going to get rocky," the Minister said. He was seated at the small desk inside the cabin. Malthasius, his private secretary and assistant, was there already, but the other delegates were nowhere to be found. "Rather annoying, considering that we're only a few days away from reaching Maral. But there's nothing for it but to put our trust in the Captain's seamanship."

"Perhaps we can help. There is an anti-storm spell I know from previous sea voyages," Iannis said. "For diverting a typhoon, it requires at least ten mages, the more the better.

Since all the attendants are trained mages, we should be able to do it."

"Very well." The Minister turned to his assistant. "Malthasius, please round up the others, as quickly as possible. Miss Baine, go and help him. We'll meet at the bridge to confer with the Captain."

Malthasius and I did as we were ordered. Several of the delegates and all the pretend "servants" had berths below decks, so Malthasius went down to collect those while I grabbed Director Chen and Solar from their cabins on the main deck. It wasn't hard to find them—they were already on their way toward the Minister's cabin.

"I knew it was a typhoon," Director Chen said as we hurried through the wind and rain toward the bridge. Her teeth chattered despite the air pocket I was using to keep us dry. "I had hoped we would be able to avoid one, but, unfortunately, this is typhoon season."

I guess it was too much to ask the Mage-Emperor to wait until after typhoon season to die, I grumbled to myself as I pushed open the door to the bridge. It was a large room surrounded by windows that offered a three-sixty view of the ocean, with various gadgets, dials, and levers that I couldn't begin to understand. In the center was a raised platform where the helm stood. To the left was a large table with nautical maps spread out. The Captain and another man stood over the table, along with the rest of the delegates and attendants, poring over a map.

"Normally I would tell you not to bother, as this ship is very sound," the Captain was saying. "But I really don't like the look of these yellowish clouds or these giant waves."

"Good, you're here," the Minister said as we entered. "We need to start on the spell right away."

"Lord Iannis, if this is the spell I'm thinking of, I can help direct it," Chen said. "I am familiar with these storms, though the version of the spell I learned is in Garaian."

"Very well," Iannis said. He waited until Malthasius returned with the other mages, then gave us the rundown. The spell had to be performed outdoors, on the deck, and involved the heavy use of elemental magic, specifically air and water. If done properly, the spell would direct the storm away from our ship. But we needed to do it quickly, because the closer the typhoon's center got to us, the more power it would take to turn it away.

After Iannis explained the procedure, and the first mate distributed stout ropes to all participants, he and Director Chen ushered us out and began guiding us to our stations. The deck was slippery now, the gale howling around us, and we had to proceed slowly, gripping the railings tightly. As soon as I got to my position by the starboard beam, I lashed myself to the railing using one of the ropes. Everything on deck had been lashed down or cleared away to reduce the chances of being hit by flying objects or debris, but as I watched the high winds batter the tied-down masts, I knew that our safety was far from assured.

I wished that I could be close to Iannis, but he was at the prow of the ship, with Director Chen at the stern. Instead, I was stuck near Director Toring, the last person I wanted to be close to when facing death. I did my best to ignore him, and focused on the power deep within me. It pulsed to life as I called it to the surface so that it sizzled just beneath my skin, making my fingertips glow in the darkness of the storm. A wave crashed against the ship, soaking me to the skin, and I held onto the rope for dear life as water sluiced over the railing—I'd abandoned my air bubble to conserve power for the more important spell.

A faint tearing sound raised my hackles in alarm. Frantic, I peered through the rain and wind just in time to see Toring flying over the side of the ship, his torn rope flailing out behind him. I sprang forward, my fingers grasping for the rope's jagged end, but it slithered into the abyss before I could get a hold.

"Shit!" I shouted over the howling wind as I watched Toring disappear into the darkness. Though he wasn't exactly my favorite person, I couldn't let him die. I ripped the rope from my body, then flung myself into the sea without a moment's hesitation. There was no time to ponder—if I didn't act now, he'd be lost. But as I started to kick up to the surface, using all my strength against the tumultuous current, I couldn't help but wonder if I'd thrown my life away on a stupid impulse.

"*Iannis!*" I called mentally as I broke the surface, squinting through the foam and rain as I searched for Toring. I caught sight of him being carried by the crest of a wave, and from the utter lack of struggle and his closed eyes, I gathered he was unconscious. "*Toring fell overboard!*"

"*What?*" Iannis shouted in my head. "*Where?*"

Fear lanced through me as I watched the wave drag Toring under, and I dove beneath the surface once more. "*We went over on the starboard side!*" I kicked my legs as hard as I could, reaching out blindly. Hopefully I didn't run into some kind of sea creature, but considering we were in the middle of a storm, I doubted any living thing would willingly be so close to the turbulent surface.

"*WE?*"

My foot bumped against something that felt like a shoulder, and I grabbed hold of Toring. "*Hurry up!*" I snapped, diving below the water so I could drag Toring up with me. He was big and bulky, and it took forever before we broke the surface even though we weren't very far from it. A gust of wind slapped my cheek as I gasped for air, hauling him against me so that he wouldn't sink again. I couldn't tell if he was breathing or not, and the smell of blood near his scalp told me he'd probably hit his head when the rope broke, which explained why he was unconscious.

Magic sizzled around us, and I exhaled a sigh of relief as we began to rise up out of the ocean. Iannis had clearly employed a levitation spell, something I probably could have done myself if not for the crazy winds. Grateful, I focused on clinging to Toring as tightly as I could as we were guided above the huge waves toward the ship. Lightning flashed in the sky above us, and, for an instant, I saw Iannis clearly, standing at the prow. His hair flew about his face, his robes billowing in the wind, and his handsome face was drawn tight in concentration as he made sure the winds didn't knock us out of the air and right back into the stormy sea. Toring's body seized in my arms as I squeezed his chest, and he began coughing up lungfuls of sea water. Thank Magorah. He was alive.

"Thank the Lady you're safe," Iannis shouted as my feet touched down on the ground. My legs felt strangely weak, and I gratefully took the hand he stretched out to steady me. Iannis looked angry and relieved all at once as his violet eyes swept over me, and I knew that under different circumstances, he would have hugged me fiercely. "Take Garrett inside and stay with him."

I opened my mouth to protest, but the words died on my lips as his expression turned thunderous. Instead, I took a deep breath, hefted Toring onto my back, and did as he asked. We didn't have time to argue, and though I wanted to help with the spell, making sure Toring didn't die was more important. Toring moaned a little as I adjusted his weight, his head lolling against my shoulder, but he didn't react otherwise. I hoped his injury wasn't too serious.

Still, there was no way I was going to miss out on this completely, so instead of heading below deck, I climbed the stairs up to the bridge. It was no easy feat to do so, with slippery decks, buffeting winds, and a full-grown man on my back. On top of that, I still had to dodge various members of the crew who were rushing about as the first mate barked orders. Obviously, they weren't going to sit back and hope the mages managed to pull off their spell—not when their lives and the safety of their ship depended on it. Thankfully, someone from inside the bridge saw me coming, and they held the door open.

"By the Ur-God," the sailor exclaimed as he held the door open for me. "What happened? Is he all right?"

I lowered Toring into a chair that was bolted to the floor, then pressed two finger against his neck. "He's got a pulse," I said. "A rather strong one, actually." I sought out the knot on his head, which was sizeable, but my fingers came away clear. The water must have temporarily staunched the blood flow. "One of the mages will heal him after this is over—he'll be fine in the meantime."

The sailor nodded, then went back over to the large station toward the prow of the ship, where the Captain was monitoring the various dials. The Captain grabbed the brass phone on the wall, and I turned back toward the window as he shouted instructions to the engine room down below. My eyes found Iannis, who was still standing at the prow, his hands outstretched to the elements, his entire body glowing incandescently. The other mages were glowing too, I realized as I glanced out at the other windows. I turned my gaze back to Iannis, and my eyes widened as I watched a huge wave crest both sides of the prow, forming a towering wall of frothy water. My breath caught in my chest, but just as I was sure the wave would crash down on the deck and obliterate everything, a magical shield flared to life around the ship, and the wave slapped against it instead. I let out a huge sigh of relief as the water sluiced harmlessly off the sides of the ship, heading back down into the ocean.

"The wind is starting to calm!" the Captain said incredulously, looking at one of his gauges. "The spell is working!"

Sure enough, it was. The rocking gradually began to subside, and the huge waves pummeling the ship grew smaller and smaller. The howl of the wind died down, the torrential rains subsiding to a patter, and I let out a huge sigh of relief. The storm was being turned away from us.

We would live to see another day.

12

"I have never been so glad to see land in my entire life," Garrett Toring proclaimed fervently as we stood on the main deck, watching the steamship dock as we finally arrived at Maral Port.

"I agree." It had been three days since that awful storm. The ship had managed to survive it without much damage, thanks to the powerful spell Iannis and Director Chen had used to protect it. "It'll be nice to finally have solid ground under my feet again." I hadn't suffered seasickness, unlike poor Solar and two of the servants, but it had been very disconcerting how the ground had consistently swayed beneath my feet.

Since learning that I had saved his life, Garrett had slightly warmed to me over the past few days. He'd even thanked me, saying that he regretted ever doubting my usefulness on the mission. It turned out that when he wasn't trying to engage in a pissing contest with Iannis, he could be charming and funny, and I'd even played a few rounds of cards with him and Solar. But though I sensed Garrett wasn't evil, I knew better than to let my guard down around him. He was Iannis's rival after all, driven by ambition, and Fenris's mortal enemy. I could never forget that.

"Are you ready?" Iannis asked, appearing by my side. His arm settled around my waist in what would have been a casual gesture if not for the fact that he rarely touched me affectionately in public, and I hid a smirk. The show was for Garrett, whose hazel eyes cooled significantly at Iannis's presence. "We are going to disembark very soon."

"I've already double checked our quarters," I insisted, refusing to let him pull me away from the railing. Excitement flooded my veins as I watched the hustle and bustle of the port from this vantage—from what Iannis had told me, Maral was the largest port in the world, which was damned impressive considering that Solantha's port was the biggest in all of Northia. I watched large steam-driven machines with gigantic, claw-like arms carefully lift huge colored crates, cages, and boxes from the decks of cargo ships, and then place said crates in a row of hundreds of others like it. Trade was obviously booming in Garai—the country was even wealthier than the Federation. However, I'd learned from Director Chen that Garai's wealth was mostly in the hands of mage traders and high officials, while rural humans lived hand-to-mouth from one harvest to the next.

We headed down the gangway, and were met by a platoon of thirty soldiers, dressed in sturdy metal armor over long, colorful tunics. The combination must have been hot as hell in this humid summer weather, but they all stood at attention, not betraying any sign of discomfort. I was surprised to see that some of them were shifters—tigers and lions, judging by their eye coloring and scents. The largest, most imposing of them, a tiger shifter in a red cape, stepped forward and introduced himself in fluent if slightly accented Northian as Captain Nagi Zhou. He informed us that his platoon would be escorting us to the capital, Bilai, but first we had to wait on two more delegations, which were supposed to be arriving tomorrow.

There was some grumbling about this, especially from the Minister, but we allowed the soldiers to escort us to an extravagant hotel not far from the harbor, where we were to spend the night as guests of the Garaian government. Captain Zhou warned us not to try and tip anyone, as this custom was considered insulting here. We brought some of our bags, but left the bulk of our belongings on the ship. Ten imperial guards stayed behind to ensure our belongings were not stolen, as well as the agents that we brought. They would supervise the transfer of all our gifts and luggage to a barge, hopefully without calling attention to, or betraying the purpose of our odd little flying machine. After all, it *could* have been intended as a present to the new Emperor.

There was time for a quick tour of Maral before our dinner, an experience that took a heavy toll on my ears and nose. At a nighttime marketplace, the bustle and colorful crowds were indescribable. Just crossing a street looked next to impossible, and highly dangerous, given the multitude of vehicles charging at each other with complete recklessness. They ranged from the latest-model steam car or steam bike to rickety contraptions where the passenger essentially sat behind a cyclist, clutching their baskets of live chickens to their chests. Shouts and toots combined into an unharmonious concert.

"Too chaotic for my taste," the Minister said with a slight sniff.

"But fun, when you visit for the first time," I argued. It figured that a stuffy bastard like him would not enjoy such a colorful, exotic place. Iannis smiled at me in silent agreement, his hand briefly brushing against the small of my back as we walked.

"We did not come here to have fun," Garrett said, his voice grim. "Let's keep our minds on the mission."

Scowling, I considered reminding him that Iannis was the boss for the secret mission, but let it go, distracted by a strange vehicle that turned out to be a steam cycle heaped with hundreds of bird cages. The sleeping birds reminded me of my ether parrot, who had remained behind in Solantha. Why hadn't he come along with me to Garai? Had he disappeared for good, or was he simply waiting back in Solantha for my return? Despite his irritating nature, I found myself missing the magical creature. I hoped he'd reappear when I returned. If he did, I'd give him a name, as Rylan and Fenris had suggested more than once.

Our local escorts made sure we stayed at a safe distance from the pickpockets and charlatans said to frequent the city. I was a little disappointed that I wouldn't get a chance to tangle with the criminals here, but then again, I had no jurisdiction in Garai and could claim no bounties for any thieves I might catch.

"Do you have enforcers here, and bounties?" I asked Captain Zhou, unable to keep the wistful tone out of my voice. "I am an enforcer by trade, back home."

His black brows rose in surprise. "Indeed we do, Miss Baine. But it is not an occupation for the squeamish, nor for pretty girls —even shifters."

I opened my mouth to tell him what I thought about *that*, but Garrett interrupted. "I've heard there are powerful criminal gangs operating all over the country, for which all the smaller crooks work. Is this true?"

The Captain's stern face darkened. "Unfortunately so. We are all hoping the new Emperor will get a handle on the problem. Even the local enforcers have to come to some arrangement with the gangs, or they won't last long."

I pressed my lips together at that. If the Garaian enforcers were cooperating with the criminal gangs, then how could the good guys be separated from the bad? Who would protect the innocent, if the enforcers were siding with the criminals?

Zhou then turned the tables on us by quizzing Garrett about the Resistance, wondering aloud, with entirely fake sympathy, how such a scourge could have grown so big under our very noses. I buried a grin as Garrett struggled to remain polite. Outwardly, he appeared perfectly calm, but I could scent his irritation, and I knew Captain Zhou sensed it too.

After our sightseeing tour, we were herded to a restaurant on the top floor of a very tall building for a sumptuous dinner, compliments of the Maral City Council. The fresh seafood was more varied than I'd ever sampled, and mostly delicious. I wasn't too keen on the shavings of gold on some of the finger food, though at least it wasn't silver, or the dish of pickled black sea cucumber. Captain Zhou encouraged us to try the strong local spirits, and even the dour Minister unbent a bit by the end of the long meal.

The next morning, on the massive steam barge, we briefly mingled with the other two delegations aboard. The deputy president and party from Bonara in Faricia were tall, black-skinned mages with strange scars on their cheeks. They were polite, but very much inclined to keep to themselves. By contrast, the King of Belgar was a haughty, vocal bastard, who was visibly miffed at having to share the barge with new-world upstarts like us. Not that he liked the Bonarans any better, going by his sour expression. We ignored him as we admired the various landscapes passing before us, some flat and others mountainous. The Garaian people were dressed in colorful fashions and busily going about their agricultural tasks. Almost all wore something white, if only a ribbon, to join in the state mourning.

"This brings back old memories," Iannis murmured,

standing beside me on deck. "I was traveling alone then, and not in state as we are doing now."

"I bet that was a lot more interesting," I commented, smirking a little. "If I was here with no one watching over my shoulder, I'd definitely have some fun."

"Oh, indeed," Iannis agreed with an enigmatic smile. "I had some misadventures that I'll tell you about when we have nothing better to do." *And in private,* he didn't say aloud, though the sentiment was clear.

"I can't stop thinking about my father," I confessed, crossing my arms against my chest against a sudden chill that swept through me. "He's going to be there, isn't he? What'll I do if I run into him?"

"Whatever we find there, we'll deal with it together, Sunaya," Iannis said gently. He gave my shoulder a reassuring squeeze, and my spine relaxed a little. "Not knowing you is your father's loss. You don't need him."

I bit my lip at that, but before I could ponder Iannis's words much more, Garrett appeared. "Lunch is about to be served, and the Minister has been asking for you," he said stiffly. He didn't seem pleased to be playing messenger, and I hid another smirk.

"We'll be right there," Iannis said, but he did not budge. He and Garrett stared at each other for a long moment, and I held my breath as tension crackled in the air. Nearly a minute passed before Garrett broke the staring contest, settling for shooting a resentful look over his shoulder as he left us.

"I'm wondering when he's going to outright challenge you do a duel," I said once he was out of earshot.

"He wouldn't dare risk the Ministers wrath by doing so, not when his position is still so new." Iannis's hands settled on my shoulders, and he turned me to face him. My breath caught at his simmering gaze, which was not filled with anger, but lust.

Desire surged low in my belly, and I clutched at his arms as he kissed me hungrily. His tongue swept against mine, deep, sure strokes that made my knees weak, and I cursed the sleeping cabins for their thin walls.

"I am growing tired of our unceasing company," he murmured against my mouth, pulling away slightly.

"A deserted island would be nice right about now," I agreed, and he gave me a crooked grin. I considered kissing that gorgeous mouth again, but footsteps sounded, and we reluctantly broke apart. We did have to answer the Minister's summons, even if I was hungry for something other than food at the moment.

As we sat down to dinner, I noticed with some dismay that the portions had been calculated for mage appetites. Resigning myself to the prospect of snacking from our private supplies later on, I ate slowly so I could stretch out the food as much as I could. However, as soon as I'd cleaned my plate, a server appeared at my elbow with another platter piled high with various meats and fish.

"Compliments of Captain Zhou, miss," he said, setting it down in front of me.

I raised my glass in thanks to Captain Zhou, who was sitting at another table, then tucked into my meal with gusto. Director Chen's eyes fixed on me, and after a couple of minutes, I finally glanced up at her with a scowl.

"What? Am I being rude somehow?" Sure, I was eating a little fast, but I wasn't making weird noises or spraying my food everywhere.

"No, of course not," she assured me. "I am simply wondering if the Captain is sweet on you."

"Nah." Huffing out a laugh, I set my fork down. "He just knows that we shifters need more food than most. I've gotta say,

I'm really impressed by Garaian hospitality so far. I'll miss this kind of generosity when we return home." I caught Captain Zhou's eye, and he grinned at the compliment, raising his wineglass to me.

"Hey," I said to Zhou after dinner as we filed out of the dining hall. "I could use some exercise. What do you say to a bout of unarmed combat?"

He gave me a once over, taking in my leather and weapons, then glanced toward Iannis, who was just ahead. "Will your lover have a problem with that?"

"Sunaya is her own woman," Iannis said, looking over his shoulders at us. The expression in his eyes suggested he wasn't particularly thrilled about the idea of watching me fight another man. "But if it's all the same, I will observe during the match."

I met Zhou in the large cabin Iannis and I used for our magic lessons, thankful that, for once, I'd be getting some physical exercise. Iannis took up a spot against the back wall, out of the way but still close enough to interfere should he feel it necessary. I really hoped he didn't—I understood his protective instincts, but I didn't want a shining knight coming to my rescue.

I wanted a brawl.

"I don't usually fight females," Zhou warned as he stripped off his outerwear. Beneath, he wore a sleeveless undershirt that showed off his broad shoulders and the thick, corded muscles in his arms. "I won't use my full strength on you."

"Then you're dead," I said flatly, placing my leather jacket on a nearby table. We'd cleared a space in the center of the room, pushing the sparse furniture against the walls. "Because I won't hold back."

Zhou smirked a little as he watched me lay my weapons on the table. "Without your weapons, you're no match for me."

Refusing to let him rile me, I met him in the center of our

makeshift ring. We locked eyes as we bowed, and I refused to break the gaze as we both sank into fighting stances. Zhou's stance was much looser than mine, leaving his broad chest and throat exposed, and I bit back a grin. He'd never be able to get past my tighter stance, and he was a walking target.

"Begin," Iannis said, and I shot forward, already swinging. But Zhou was much faster than I'd anticipated, and before my fist could connect, he was already behind me. I whirled around, and he swept out his foot, knocking me to the ground. I landed on my ass with a hiss, then rolled backward and onto my feet, avoiding his kick and just barely managing to stay inside the ring. Snarling, I sprang at him sideways and scissored my legs around his hips and knees, sending him slamming to the ground before he could turn.

"Got you!" I crowed, grabbing his legs. But before I could get them into a lock, he twisted out of my grip. Next thing I knew, he was on top of me, driving the breath out of my lungs as he dropped his full weight on my chest. I bucked hard, trying to get him off, but he grabbed my wrist and slid his arm beneath mine, then locked his hands and pulled.

"Okay, okay!" I cried as pain shot up my arm, smacking at his thigh with my free hand. "I give."

Smirking, Zhou got to his feet, then helped me to mine. "You fought well," he said as I gulped in air. "But you've a long way to go if you think to best me in unarmed combat."

We fought twice more, and even though I managed to get him into a lock during one of the bouts, he still beat me easily. By the time we'd finished, I was sweaty and breathless, sore and tired, and my pride was a little bruised. But I was nevertheless satisfied, and we parted on amiable terms before Iannis and I returned to our room.

"Is that enough to tide you over for the rest of the trip?"

Iannis asked, sounding a little amused as I flopped onto the bed. "Or are you still in need of more 'exercise'?"

I stuck my tongue out at him. "I'm not going to let you take me down a peg," I told him as he sat down on the bed next to me. "So what if he kicked my ass? It was still a good workout." Yeah, so I was a little disappointed that I hadn't won a single match. But I couldn't really complain—the guy had forty years of experience on me, and a good deal more muscle. If he hadn't been a shifter, I might have been able to beat him, but shifter males were stronger than females.

"Of course," Iannis said. He pressed a kiss to my sweaty brow, then made a face. "Now why don't we get you cleaned up?"

DESPITE THE AWE-INSPIRING VIEWS, the delicious food, and the magic lessons, I was getting antsy at the ridiculously long time it was taking to get to Bilai. The last leg of our trip we spent aboard an oversized airship. Its golden silk canvas was half covered with white swathes of the same fabric, to signify that we were in mourning. Weighed down as we were, our airship was among the last to arrive, but the Imperial protocol official who received us did not betray the slightest irritation at the delay—he was all smiles, a true professional. He didn't even react at the sight of my shifter eyes.

"Please follow me," he said, and we fell in behind him with the Minister up front and the servants behind us. The Imperial Palace was not far from the open space in which we'd landed, and I gazed around curiously, wondering what exotic sights we were about to behold.

"*Try to look bored,*" Iannis advised me in mindspeak. "*We come from a great country too.*"

I schooled my expression, forcing my wandering eyes

straight ahead. Iannis was right—if I acted overawed, I would appear provincial, even if I had never visited an emperor's palace before. *You're a descendant of Resinah,* I reminded myself, lifting my chin.

As it turned out, the Imperial Palace was not a single structure, as I'd imagined from the name, but a small city set within high walls, consisting of over a dozen buildings of various sizes. Even its spacious halls, however, were not big enough to hold all the heads of state and their parties invited to this shindig. So the Garaians had custom-built another small city on what was normally an empty space used for parades and exercises by the imperial guard. Each delegation was assigned its own pavilion, made of beautifully carved wood, and each one different, incorporating elements from the guests' home countries. It was ridiculously impressive.

"How did they manage to build all this in just a few weeks?" I asked as we approached our own lodgings. The Northian pavilion was decorated by a frieze featuring grizzlies, condors, wolves, and buffalo, and the door was inlaid with semi-precious stones forming a map of our Federation.

"Garaians are very good at organizing," Iannis explained as we inspected our adjoining rooms. They were not overly large, but comfortably furnished with colorful silk hangings, and the canopied beds with a multitude of soft pillows looked most inviting. "I imagine they did the planning and some of the work beforehand, since the late Emperor was ailing and senile for some time."

A pretty Garaian woman rushed in and bowed deeply. "Lord, Lady, the Empress's reception will begin in two hours—may I help you get ready?" From her tone, that was not nearly long enough to prepare. We had arrived in the nick of time.

"I can manage," Iannis said, "but you'd best use her help, Sunaya." He spoke to the servant in Garaian, and I swallowed a little as she advanced on me in a purposeful manner. Steeling my shoulders, I allowed her to guide me into a chair, then held still as she began to work her magic on me.

After all, there was a good chance I might run into my father in two hours. And if I did, I at least wanted to do it in style.

13

*W*ith the skilled help of the maid, I got ready just in time to join the rest of the delegation as we set out. Two guards escorted us to the Hall of Dragons in the Imperial Palace, where the reception was to take place. All the various heads of state, and their accompanying delegates, were expected to be present, so this was my opportunity to make my first impression on the world leaders. For once, I had agreed to dress as a mage, but instead of the ugly apprentice robes, I wore fuchsia and gold, with a matching gold sash around my waist. My hair was piled atop my head, with a gold chain woven through the curls. Matching earrings dangled from my ears.

Like our pavilion, the Hall of Dragons was fashioned of wood, but the twisting columns must have been carved from ancient oak trees, for they were easily five times Iannis's height and as thick as three average men standing close together. The pillars were decorated with winged dragons, a motif repeated on the carvings of the ceiling high above, and the silk embroidered wall hanging. There even was a glass dragon lamp hanging from the ceiling on solid gold chains, glowing from within with magical light. The late Emperor's widow was standing in front of her dais at the far end of the hall. All newly arriving guests approached her in an orderly queue to pay their respects and give their condolences before mingling or partaking of the abundant food and drink.

"Is all this fuss really necessary?" I muttered to Iannis in mindspeak as we joined the queue. *"These earrings are so heavy; I won't be surprised if my earlobes drag on the carpet by the end of the night."*

"This may be hard to believe, but you are dressed rather conservatively for Garai," Iannis replied. He nodded his head toward Director Chen, who was wearing multilayered Garaian robes in subtly contrasting colors, embroidered with magical symbols. Her hair was done even more elaborately than mine, and jewelry dripped from every possible place on her body. *"They love to wear flashy and ostentatious costumes, to display their rank and wealth."*

Finally, it was our turn to bow before our hostess. Her Imperial Majesty Chari Hahn wore robes of spun gold, the color reserved to the Emperor, with diamonds and dark pearls glittering in reckless profusion. "Welcome, Minister Graning," she said in a low monotone as we approached, coached by the Head of Protocol standing at her left side. Two men and three women who bore strong resemblance to her were also present, and as introductions were made, I found out that they were her sons and daughters. It was a little disconcerting seeing as how they all seemed to be of similar age, and I wondered how old they really were.

"So this is the unusual Miss Baine," Chari drawled once Iannis and I were introduced by the Minister, and we'd expressed our condolences at the Mage-Emperor's passing. "The newspaper photographs do not do you justice."

My cheeks colored a little, and I bowed again, pretending to take her remark as a compliment. "You're very kind, Your Majesty."

"We have never had a shifter attend as a guest, not even a half-shifter," Princess Ra-Sai, the middle daughter, observed. Her expression was more reserved than her mother's. "I hope that you have found your stay in Bilai to be pleasant so far."

"We have been very well taken care of, thank you," I assured her, refusing to let her know that I'd noticed the stares that had followed us around the room, specifically me. To make my resemblance to the ar'Rhea family less striking, I had lightened the color of my hair from black to dark brown, but my green shifter eyes were still drawing a lot of attention.

Maybe they've just never met a panther shifter before, I thought as we continued around the room. Despite what Princess Ra-Sai had said, I was not the only shifter present—the Mage-Emperor's famous Lion Guards were patrolling the crowds. They wore red and gold tunics, with a lion's head emblazoned on the backs, and they all dyed their hair gold and wore it long and untamed around their oblong faces, like a lion's mane. Most of them were in human form, but some prowled around as lions as well. A smart choice, since shifter senses were much stronger in animal form, and they could still use mindspeak to communicate with each other.

Servants circulated in the room as well, plying us with strong spirits that burned like fire in my throat, and made some of the guests cough and turn red in the face. Thankfully, I was unaffected, but many of them became quite drunk, and the more they drank, the more freely their words flowed. Others imbibed much less, including Iannis, Director Chen, and the Minister, and they took advantage of the opportunity to prod and pry at their inebriated fellow-guests, gaining useful information. I tried to do the same, but I could not understand most of the languages spoken.

Amongst other things, I learned that many of the guests were speculating, and even placing bets, that Chari would try to sabotage the trials of the potential new Mage-Emperor after the funeral. Apparently, Chari was a second wife—the late Mage-Emperor's first son, Kazu, was born of the first wife, who had died long ago. Chari, of course, wanted her own eldest son, Bu-Sai, to take the throne.

"I don't know why you would bet against Kazu," a black-skinned delegate from Faricia scoffed to her fellow delegate. She wore colorful orange-and-green robes, and her beads clinked as she tossed her braided hair over one shoulder. "I understand he has done an admirable job of defending the Garaian border against desert tribes—he is no pushover."

"Perhaps, but being a good warrior is not enough to make a leader," the other delegate said. "Bu-Sai is more intelligent, from what I have heard, and, alongside his late father, has done much for trade in Garai."

Unable to stand the suspense anymore, I approached one of the assistants to the Head of Protocol. To my relief, she understood Northian. "Do you happen to know if the delegation from Castalis has arrived? Are they present?" I asked, lowering my voice to a discreet murmur.

"Certainly, miss. The High Mage has brought his son and daughter, as well as several advisors. I passed them earlier near one of the pillars."

Excitement and apprehension filled me, and I looked eagerly around the crowded hall, trying to spot my unknown relatives. It took some time, since there were over five hundred people milling around, but eventually I caught sight of the Castilian High Mage, standing over by a refreshment table as he conversed with a caramel-skinned delegate from Southia. I stilled, taking slow, even breaths to quell my suddenly racing heart. I had already seen the High Mage's photograph, but in person, his resemblance to me was even more obvious in his thick, curly black hair, startling green eyes, full mouth, and olive skin tone. His son, Malik, was a lankier version of Haman, and my heart thumped a little harder as I caught sight of Isana, his older daughter, who had sent me that letter. Her thick black hair was straight, unlike my own, and her skin was several shades darker, but the fullness of her mouth, her straight nose, and her bottle-green eyes reminded me of the reflection I saw every time I stared into my bathroom mirror.

Iannis appeared next to me, abandoning a Pernian mage with whom he had renewed an old acquaintanceship. Noticing who I was staring at, he seized my elbow and steered me in the opposite direction. *"If anyone saw you and Isana together, they would see the resemblance instantly,"* he warned, releasing my elbow to settle his hand on the small of my back instead. *"Perhaps we should have done something more drastic about your coloring."*

I held back a snort. *"I don't really think that would matter. And besides, the last thing I need is for Garrett to become suspicious."* I glanced over at the Director of Federal Security, who was across the room chatting with a pretty blonde mage from the Central Continent. The color in his cheeks was high. Judging by the animated gestures he was making, he had not been able to resist temptation like Iannis and the Minister had. But I couldn't count on him being drunk and oblivious for the rest of the trip.

"Lord Iannis. It has been a long time since I last crossed paths with you, back when you were traveling in Castalis," a deep voice said from behind us, and I forced myself not to stiffen at the rolling 'Rs and stretched vowels—hallmarks of a Castalian accent. Slowly, Iannis and I turned to see Haman standing behind us. Trepidation rushed through me, but also relief, as I noticed he had left his children back on the other side of the room.

"Lord Haman." Iannis smiled, and the two shook hands. "Times have certainly changed since then. Your father-in-law was High Mage at the time, and now you rule Castalis yourself. And you have a wife and grown children, too."

"Indeed!" Haman agreed, chuckling. "Rumor has it that you are about to marry yourself." His green eyes turned to mine with open curiosity. "May I have an introduction?"

"Certainly. Allow me to present my fiancée, Miss Sunaya Baine," Iannis said, smiling fondly down at me. There was absolutely zero indication in his expression or voice that this was anything other than an introduction between strangers. "Sunaya, this is Lord Haman ar'Rhea, the High Mage of Castalis."

"Pleased to meet you." I held out my hand for him to shake. Instead, he took it and turned my knuckles up to him. A strange feeling went through me as his lips brushed them—my first physical contact with my father in my entire life. He seemed to pause for a moment, and my breath caught. Did he notice the resemblance? Did he suspect, as Isana did?

"Your fingers are calloused," he said, releasing my hand as he straightened. "Much like someone who wields weapons on a regular basis. I think I remember reading that you are an enforcer?"

"I am," I said, straightening my shoulders. I would not be ashamed that my fingers weren't manicured and that my hands were not butter soft. I'd earned my calluses, and I wore them with pride the way a human might wear scars. "Seven years now."

"That sounds like a thrilling profession." Haman said. He held my gaze a moment longer, a thoughtful expression in his eyes, then turned back to Iannis. "I wanted to congratulate you not just on your engagement, but also on becoming Chief Mage of Canalo. I remember Solantha well from my time there, nearly thirty years ago."

Iannis and Haman launched into a conversation about

Solantha, the Federation, and general politics, and I forced myself to stand there, smiling and nodding politely, and acting as though I hadn't just met my father for the first time. How the hell could Iannis be so calm and unruffled, knowing who this man was? Luckily, Haman didn't notice the resemblance between us, either because he couldn't look past my shifter features, or because he was thick-headed. Judging by the intelligence in his eyes, and the acumen with which he discussed various topics with Iannis, I suspected the former.

"Darling," I said after a while, placing my hand on Iannis's shoulder. "I'm starting to get a little tired. I think I'm going to find somewhere to sit and rest for a bit."

"Of course." Iannis squeezed my hand, understanding in his eyes. "I will come find you as soon as I am done here."

I bid Haman a good evening, then slipped through the crowd, away from his too-curious gaze. My skin prickled, and I didn't relax until I'd made my way into a secluded corner of the room. I snagged a glass of water and a small plate of refreshments, then made myself comfortable on one of the small couches in the corner and ate. The food, plus the lack of stares my way, finally calmed me down, and I settled back against the cushions, content to wait here in relative privacy.

"Miss Baine." I nearly dropped my glass at the sound of a female, Castalian-accented voice to my left. Schooling my expression, I turned to see Isana standing a few feet away, a hesitant smile on her face. "I hoped I might run into you here."

"Miss ar'Rhea." Reluctantly, I stood to greet her, and offered her my hand. "I received your letter not very long ago."

"Oh, good. I was wondering if it had made its way to you before you embarked on your journey to Garai." Isana shook my hand, then settled onto the couch next to me. She wore beautiful green robes embroidered with pink-and-gold flowers. They flattered her curvy figure, which resembled my own, though not quite as fleshed out yet as she was still a teenager. "Have you given much thought to what I wrote?"

"No," I lied, thankful that she did not have my shifter nose. "I'm afraid I can't figure out how we might be related. I didn't know my father very well, but I am almost certain he was Northian."

"I see," Isana said with a smile, but I could tell that she didn't really believe me. "It is curious though, that the resemblance between us is so strong."

"Yes, well, we could share a very distant ancestor," I suggested, doing my best to play it off even though I was well aware of how much we looked alike. "After all, we all share common ancestors from hundreds of thousands of years back, don't we?"

"That's true," Isana said dubiously. Nope, she definitely didn't believe me, and the mixture of curiosity and fear I scented from her left me with a bad feeling. Would she tell her father about her suspicions? Had she done so already? Disappointment surged in my chest, and I fought to keep the emotion from showing on my features. From her letter, Isana had sounded like a sister I might enjoy knowing, but now that we'd met, I wasn't so certain of that anymore. I couldn't trust her—that was for damn sure.

"Sunaya." Iannis materialized out of nowhere at my elbow. He offered his arm to me, and then nodded politely at Isana. "I am sorry to interrupt, but it is time we left. We have had a very long journey."

"Of course." Isana rose. "Good night, Lord Iannis, Miss Baine. I do hope we can speak more tomorrow, at the funeral."

"That was fucking close," I said as Iannis whisked me out of the hall and into the night. I took in a deep lungful of the cool night air, grateful for it—I was far too overheated after being in that crush of a reception, and not to mention that tension-filled conversation with Isana.

"Indeed," Iannis agreed, and a guard escorted us back to our pavilion. We remained silent until we were back inside, the doors closed firmly behind us. "But I would not worry too much. Though Haman seemed curious about you, I did not sense any ill will toward you. If he does suspect, I do not believe that he will be eager to out your relationship. He is no fool, and he stands to lose more than he would gain from such a revelation." He headed toward his bedroom, and I followed.

"I guess so," I said, shoving a hand through my hair. My curls tumbled free, and the gold chain slid to the carpet. "But Isana definitely suspects. What if she makes a big deal about it?" Nervous again, I began pacing back and forth in front of the bed.

"Hush now." Iannis securely locked the door to his room, then snagged me by the sash around my waist and pulled me into his arms. "We will deal with Isana when the time comes. For now..." His eyes darkened, his voice turning sensual, and he slid his hands slowly down my sides. "I suggest we focus on a different topic."

"That's a little difficult, considering that I can't think about anything else," I said, but my breath caught as he tugged off my sash, and my robes began to slide open.

"Oh, I believe we'll be able to solve that problem shortly," Iannis said, cupping the back of my head. He pulled my mouth against his, and all thoughts flew straight out of my head as his tongue slid inside to stroke mine. My own hands tugged at his clothes, and desire surged through me as my fingers met bare skin and hard muscle. When he carried me to the bed, our lips still locked and our clothes in a forgotten puddle on the hardwood floor, I knew that by the time he was done with me tonight, I would be too exhausted and satisfied to worry about anything at all.

14

I meant to sleep in, but my rumbling stomach woke me just as the sun was cresting the horizon outside our window. I rolled over to see the early dawn rays cast a glow over Iannis's sleeping face. He looked so peaceful, with his long, dark lashes fanning against his sharp cheekbones, and his stern mouth unbowed and slightly open. I ran my fingers gently through his long, rumpled hair, and he rumbled a little, then turned into my touch like a big lion seeking a good rub behind the ears.

Part of me wanted to stay there and snuggle with him, but hunger won out. Guess that was what I got for going without a midnight snack, especially after sex. Careful not to wake him, I slipped out of bed and dressed in my normal clothes, then slid the lacquered door open as quietly as I could and stepped out onto the porch.

The cool morning air, and the sound of birds chirping, greeted me along with the rising sun. The blue-grey sky over-head, with tiny white clouds, was the same as back home in Canalo. All I could see were the pretty pavilions and beyond, bits of the higher palace complex. The wall around the Imperial

City prevented me from glimpsing any forests, though my nose told me that a garden with trees must be nearby, and ponds with fish and aquatic birds. Beyond those walls were the private palace grounds, off limits to visitors. A whiff of incense wafted on the air, and my nose twitched. Did Garaian mages also worship the Creator and the First Mage? And what of the Garaian humans and shifters? I'd have to ask Director Chen.

I took my time enjoying the exotic architecture and intriguing smells as I picked my way along a path to a nearby pavilion with a twenty-four-hour buffet. It had been set up to cater to the Empire's guests in between more formal meals, and I was eager to try the many and varied dishes that I was told would be offered.

"Good morning, miss," a female servant greeted me, bowing deeply. She spoke Garaian, but I knew enough by now to recognize greetings and a few other phrases. She was dressed in white, the color of mourning, as I would be soon enough—our hosts had provided stiff, heavy robes for the funeral ceremony that I was very much *not* looking forward to wearing.

"Good morning," I replied in Garaian, one of the first expressions I had picked up. I stepped past her, toward the rows of long tables laden with trays full of strange delicacies, many of which I'd never seen before. Picking up a plate, I made my way up and down the tables and piled it high with almost everything I saw. It might be a long time until I returned to Garai, and I might never get to try these particular dishes again. Every type of meat I had ever tasted was present, as well as some I had not—what *was* that meat in a red pungent sauce?—but quite a few of the dishes were completely meatless. Not a single grain of rice was in sight, which would have surprised me had I not learned in my studies that rice was considered peasant food. I wondered if eating vegetables by themselves was some weird Garaian custom. Definitely not the right diet for a shifter like me.

Going by scent, I decided against trying the dark green "thousand-year-old" eggs. I ended up with three full plates, which I balanced precariously as I took my food to one of the nearby tables and ate. I devoured everything, then went back for seconds, thirds, and fourths, until I was stuffed. Director Chen had mentioned that the buffet would be closing down when the funeral began, and that it would not be opened again during the traditional eight days of mourning. Everyone, even the guests, was supposed to remain secluded and fasting during that period, though we had all brought enough provisions to make the week bearable.

I wonder if fasting applies to the Lion Guard, and shifters in general, I thought. I wasn't sure I'd be able to survive a weeklong fast unless I slept through it, and the guards would have to keep up their strength to be effective. Thank Magorah I wasn't going to be in Bilai for the mourning period. Blowing up another Resistance lab was a small price to pay for being allowed to eat warm meals on a regular basis.

With my belly pleasantly full of roast pork, duck, and a whole bunch of things I couldn't name but had tasted delicious, I headed back to our lodgings in the other pavilion. The path wound past several guest pavilions on the way back to my own, and as I passed between two of them, the back of my neck began to prickle with awareness. Was someone watching me?

A blade hissed through the air, and I ducked in time to avoid a throwing star winging toward me. The multi-pointed blade embedded itself in the wall behind me, and I grabbed a chakram from my pouch as three humans dressed in black, their faces covered by masks and hoods, dropped down from seemingly out of nowhere. I flung my chakram at the first one's head, but he ducked out of the way with impressive speed, then flung another throwing star at my head.

"Dammit!" I ducked, then rolled aside as the other two

attackers charged me with swords. I needed to get out of this narrow alleyway...or did I? Why was I fighting like a street thug? Didn't I have magic?

Grinning, I sprang to my feet, then shouted a spell that activated a shield around me. The first swordsman's blade clashed against the red field of energy, and his eyes widened right before he was thrown back against the pavilion behind him. Screams came from within, but no one came out to check what was going on. Cowards. Fed up, I threw my hands out and blasted the other two attackers with fire before they could run away. They dropped to the ground, shrieking in pain, and began to roll back and forth, trying to extinguish the flames. Furious, I drew my crescent knives, then grabbed them both by their long hair, one by one, and slit their throats. Their blood pooled thick and fast beneath them as I tossed their carcasses to the ground, poisoning the peaceful air with the scent of copper and death.

"You," I growled, turning to the last one, who was struggling to rise. "Who sent you? Why are you trying to kill me?"

A burst of green energy came flying toward me, and the hair along my arms stood on end as the magic barreled straight through my shield, which was only meant to withstand physical weapons. I managed to duck just before it hit me, but the mage who'd thrown the blast stepped from behind one of the pavilions, and blasted me again. He was tall and broad-shouldered, but his voluminous black robes and hood disguised every other feature. Worse, I couldn't even detect his scent, which meant he was disguising it with magic, as I'd often done myself.

"What is this shit?" I shouted, jumping over the blast and closing the distance between myself and the enemy mage. He jerked back, an involuntary reaction, and before he could utter another Word, I drew my fist back and punched him in the face. The force of the blow was compounded by gravity as I landed on my feet, and he went sprawling in the dirt.

"Miss Baine?" Garrett called, and I turned to see him rushing toward me on the path. A mistake, as the remaining human slashed at me with a knife he must have hidden in his sleeve. I hissed as the blade sliced my arm open, then whirled back around and grabbed his knife arm. He screamed as I twisted it back around, and there was a sickening crack as I broke it at the elbow. He fell to his knees, tears streaming from his eyes, and I brought down the crescent knife in my other hand, intending to end him. But out of the corner of my eye, I caught a movement from the other mage and turned to see him throw a small dark sphere to the ground. Purple smoke exploded from it, and I choked as a thick, pungent odor filled the air, clogging my nose and stinging my eyes. My grasp on the wounded assassin slipped, and I stumbled back from the noxious cloud, desperate to get away so I could clear my senses.

"Miss Baine!" Garrett grabbed me by the shoulders and dragged me away from the acrid smoke. He released me, magic crackling at his fingertips, and we both waited for the masked mage to emerge from the artificial fog. But when the smoke cleared, he and the surviving human were gone, leaving behind only the bodies of the two assassins I'd killed.

"Are you all right?" Garrett asked, dropping his hands. The magic at his fingertips faded away. "I was on my way to the buffet when I heard the commotion."

"I would be fine, if not for this stupid scratch." Lifting my left arm, I examined the wound. The flaps of skin were still hanging open, revealing raw flesh underneath, and I grimaced at the pain. Normally, my flesh would have already started pulling itself back together by now—I'd just eaten, and the full moon had recently come and gone. "Why the fuck isn't this healing?"

"Here, let me take care of it." Garrett took my arm, and I hissed as agony exploded up my nerve endings. He held his free hand above the open wound and spoke a few Words, that I recognized from Iannis and his healing spells. Pale green magic spilled over the wound, and we both stiffened and grimaced in pain. I watched in disgust and awe as my ragged skin slowly came back together over my flesh, then fused into an ugly scar.

"Lord Iannis will be able to heal this better," Garrett said, letting out a tired breath as he released my arm. "But this will keep you from bleeding out, for now."

"Are they gone?" a coffee-skinned woman asked in a trembling voice as she came out of the pavilion to the left. Other mages were emerging as well, worried and angry looks on their faces. "What happened?"

"I was attacked," I snapped, stalking over to the burned bodies. "Thanks a lot for the help, by the way."

Three Lion Guards arrived on the scene—late, as far as I was concerned—and after checking on the bodies, approached us. "A thousand pardons, my lady, for allowing this to happen," one of the three guards said in a thick accent. They all crouched down, lowering their brows to the dirt.

"How the hell did these guys manage to get onto the grounds?" Shaking my head, I ignored them and picked up the bloody knife that I'd been sliced with out of the dirt. It had a black handle, and seemed to be made of ordinary steel, but there were runes carved along its edge, and it smelled strongly of magic.

"Let me see that," Garrett said. I handed him the knife reluctantly, and he peered closely at the runes. "This knife has been spelled so that whatever wounds it inflicts will not close," he said grimly. "Anyone cut by it would bleed out and die if not seen to by a mage healer, even a shifter like you."

"This is not a Garaian blade," one of the guards said, his black brows pulled together in a worried scowl. "Whoever attacked you tonight was not one of us."

Great, I thought, looking around at the growing crowd of

delegates who'd come out of their pavilions to investigate. *That really narrows it down.*

"I'VE HALF *a mind to pack you up and send you off on the first ship back to Northia,*" Iannis growled. We sat side by side, along with the rest of our delegation, atop a huge litter, as part of a mile-long procession toward the funeral site.

"*I'm not going to tuck my tail between my legs and run away every time someone tries to kill me,*" I declared. "*Didn't I survive and kill two of them? I'm too tough to be easily picked off.*"

Iannis had been beside himself when he'd learned about the attack and seen my healing wound. He'd blamed himself for allowing me to go to the buffet by myself instead of getting up and coming with me, and since that moment, he had not strayed from my side for an instant.

"*You could have been killed.*" Iannis gently pushed the sleeve of my white robe up and traced the inside of my arm. He'd healed it right away, and there was nothing left, not even the trace of a scar. The knife that had inflicted the wound was in the custody of the Lion Guard, much to my annoyance, but this wasn't my home turf and there was nothing I could do. Hopefully, they had some magical method to trace the owner.

"*But I wasn't,*" I soothed Iannis. "*And now that the guards are hyper-vigilant, I doubt the assassins would dare to attack again.*" The guards had assured me that they were looking into the assassination attempt, and, in the meantime, they would put extra guards outside our pavilion. "*That is going to pose a bit of a problem when we try to sneak out tonight.*"

"*I'm not concerned about that,*" Iannis said. The litter gently bobbed beneath us as the dozens of muscular servants carried us. I couldn't help but feel sorry for them—they didn't even have the benefit of the baldachin that covered our litter and shielded us from the hot summer sun. *"It is not good enough for us to leave this investigation to the Lion Guard. We must find out which delegation is responsible for this attack."*

"Do you think it's the Castalians?" I bit my lip. Haman had seemed friendly enough, but Isana's reaction had been less welcoming. Could she have ordered the attack?

"They are my main suspects," Iannis said grimly. *"Haman didn't act as though he wished you ill, but we mages are very good at hiding our emotions. Even if it wasn't him, one of his children may have orchestrated the attempt on your life. They stand to lose just as much, if not more, than Haman himself, should your connection to their family be revealed."*

I held back a sigh, not wanting to draw the attention of the Minister, who sat behind me, or any of the others. He had questioned me at length about the incident, though he had been more worried that this was an attack against the Northian delegation rather than a personal one on me. Garrett and Solar had argued that perhaps it was my shifter heritage that had prompted the attack—prejudice was alive and well in Recca, stronger in some countries than others. But the Minister had pointed out that if he was going to attack a shifter, he would have made sure the weapons were silver, and none of the ones found at the attack site had been. He surmised that the attackers either did not know enough about shifter weaknesses, or that they were just attacking Northian delegates in general.

"I guess it's a good thing we're leaving tomorrow, then," I finally said. *"The assassin, whoever he is, won't be able to follow us to Leniang Port."*

"True, but we do have to come back here afterward, and there is still the rest of the day and this evening to look forward to." Iannis's voice darkened. *"I doubt they will try a physical attack again so soon, not with the guard on high alert. But that does not mean they*

will not try more subtle methods. I will be checking all food and drink that is given to you from now on, for the duration of our stay."

I frowned. *"Don't you think that will insult our hosts?"*

"If they take offense, then so be it. That is a price I am willing to pay for your safety."

My heart warmed, and I wanted to take his face between my hands and kiss him. But that would be extremely inappropriate during a solemn funeral procession, so I settled for squeezing his hand instead.

During the funeral, I was thankful that Iannis and I could converse by mindspeak, as the next sixteen hours stretched interminably with much sitting, standing, and waiting. We had to listen to recitations of the late Mage-Emperors distinguished lineage and his memorable deeds, in Garaian, and there was no way I could have understood anything without Iannis's explanations. Not that the recitations were very interesting even when he did translate them. I learned more about Garaian history than I ever wanted to, and the never-ending speeches nearly put me to sleep. The only reason I stayed awake was Iannis, who entertained me with some irreverent anecdotes of the Emperor's past that the orators conveniently left out.

After the recitation, a troupe of masked actors came out to perform notable scenes from the Emperor's life. It was difficult to tell which of them were supposed to be male or female, especially since all the parts were played by men, and their voices sounded unnaturally high. After the performance, five long poems chosen out of more than ten thousand submitted by the populace were solemnly read out, each celebrating a different aspect of the dead Mage-Emperor's long rule. By the time it was over, I was thoroughly sick of all the fervent praise. If I never again heard about the great Emperor's exploits, it would be too soon.

After the play, we finally got to the actual burial part of the ceremony. The foreign guests, and a much larger number of distinguished Garaian mages and officials, all dressed in white silk just as we were, were arranged around a large oblong pit in the ground, on one end of which a structure like a temple had been erected. In this gigantic hole, the sarcophagus of the late Mage Emperor was placed and surrounded by statues of his family, his guard, his favorite concubines, his pets and horses, and enough treasure to feed a large Garaian city for several lifetimes. Ceremonial gifts from all the guests and delegations were also included. It seemed a terrible waste to bury priceless books, weapons, and jewels with a dead man who had no use for them any longer, and I knew there were thieves who would think the same. This tomb would have to be guarded very well, once it was closed.

"In the past..." Iannis observed to me in mindspeak. *"Before the First Mage's influence made itself felt in Garai, they did not bury statues, but the real people and animals. They used to kill several hundred or more whenever an Emperor died."*

I suppressed a shiver at that, keeping my face carefully blank as the Emperor was finally buried. This funeral was creepy enough without adding extra bodies to it, and I couldn't wait for it to be over. After all, the sooner we left this ceremony behind, the sooner we could get on with our *real* mission.

15

"By Magorah, I thought the funeral was never going to end." Groaning, I flopped onto the bed face-down, too tired to even bother taking off my stiff, white robes. "Can I just lie here for a little while? I'm not ready to face the world again."

"If you do that, you'll miss our departure, and will be forced to endure the week of fasting." Iannis turned me over, amusement twinkling in his tired eyes, and began to work on the ties of my robe. "Besides, you'll miss all the adventure."

"True." My robe fell open, and I purred as Iannis's warm hands glided over my bare skin. "Oh yeah," I groaned as his fingers slid behind my neck and began to dig into the knots there. The tension headache drumming at the base of my skull began to melt away. "Maybe I'll just hire a Garaian masseur to attend to my needs and stay behind after all."

"You could," Iannis growled, leaning in and nipping my neck. I gasped at the sharp pleasure-pain, arching into him. "But I'm afraid I'd have to gut him when I returned, and you as well."

"How romantic." I pulled open his robe as well, then slid my hand beneath his silk pants. A sharp knock interrupted us just as I closed my fingers around him, and Iannis let out a strangled sound as I squeezed.

"I hope you two are getting ready," Garrett called through the door. "We're leaving in half an hour."

"We'll be ready," Iannis called, his voice completely normal even though I was still massaging him. He held his breath until Garrett's footsteps receded, then let out another low groan of pleasure.

"Much as I'd like to continue this, Garrett is right." Iannis gently removed my hand from his pants, then backed away. "We don't have much time. Let's get ready to leave."

"Fine," I grumbled, but only a little bit, then threw off the remainder of my outfit and dressed in my leathers. I did my best to ignore Iannis as he changed into a set of black robes, knowing that if I spent too much time staring, I'd want to jump his glorious, naked body despite Garrett's warning. Instead, I strapped my weapons on and double-checked my pouches to make sure they were stocked with the charms and snacks I always carried. I pulled the small pack out of our luggage that I'd brought along for the trip south, and double-checked it as well to make sure I had enough clothing and supplies. We were only supposed to be gone a week, but I packed extra just in case—you never knew what might happen.

With our packs tightly secured on our backs, Iannis and I went out to the common area in the center of the pavilion, which was furnished with exquisitely carved furniture, colorful couches, and incredibly soft rugs. The Minister and Garrett stood in the center of the room, conversing in low tones, but they fell silent and turned to us as we approached. Garrett too was dressed in dark robes, but the Minister was still wearing the stiff, white ceremonial garb from the funeral. The pilot, Henning, stood off to the side, waiting patiently. The sight of him wearing a long, double-breasted pilot's jacket and flying goggles sent a bolt of excitement through me, reaffirming that we were truly beginning our adventure.

"Lord Iannis, Miss Baine." The Minister nodded to us both gravely. For once, there was not a hint of censure in his eyes as he looked at me. "You are both ready to depart?"

"Yes. We are just waiting on Director Chen." Iannis nodded toward Chen's room. The door slid open, and Director Chen stepped out. Her long, fine hair was tied back from her face in a high knot, and she looked very inconspicuous in her black robes, which was quite a change from the usual bright-colored silks she liked to wear. She'd even foregone makeup, and I was surprised at how much younger, and less intimidating, she appeared without it.

"All done," she said firmly, her shoulders squared as she adjusted her pack. "Is our transportation ready?" she asked Garrett.

"Yes. It's waiting in the inner courtyard."

We stepped out into the balmy evening air, onto the porch that ringed the small courtyard built in the center of our pavilion. I wasn't entirely certain how the servants had managed to sneak the aircraft in, but there it was, its metal body gleaming in the waning moonlight as it crouched like a giant bug in the center of the courtyard. Two servants stood nearby, and the abandoned crate next to them suggested that they'd hauled it in like that before unpacking it.

"Director," the servant to the left said, stepping forward. "Everything has been prepared."

Garrett and the pilot briefly spoke with them, and then we got into the craft. It wasn't as tight a fit as I'd feared—there were two seats in the front for the pilot and co-pilot, in front of two huge, round windows. Before the seats were an array of dials, buttons, and gizmos that were all probably very important. Garrett chose to sit up front with the pilot, while Iannis, Director

Chen, and I settled next to each other on the long bench seat behind them.

Technically, Iannis should have been up there, since he was the mission leader, but the ship *was* provided by Garrett's department. And besides, I wasn't about to complain— I was happy to have Iannis sitting next to me for the flight. His warmth was comforting, and I squeezed his hand tight as the pilot engaged the engines. The small craft began to vibrate with a barely perceptible hum. I hoped the sound would remain muffled enough to evade the notice of the Lion Guards patrolling between the guest pavilions.

"You all strapped in?" the pilot asked sharply. "We're about to take off!"

I double checked my straps, then gripped Iannis's hand with my left and the overhead strap with my right, as the aircraft began to rise vertically into the air. We ascended slowly at first, then gradually picked up speed, the vibration from the small rotating wings becoming stronger. We lurched, then dropped for a long stomach-clenching moment. The pilot yanked on a lever, and I clenched my jaw at the accompanying loud noise coming from outside the aircraft. I assumed it had something to do with the wings, because in the next second, we caught the wind, and the aircraft began to swoop upward. It wasn't until the aircraft leveled out that I finally let out the breath that I'd been holding.

"And so we're off," Iannis murmured, rubbing the back of my hand with his thumb. I scowled at the amusement in his tone, and then remembered that he'd nearly fallen to his death from a dirigible at four times this height and survived. If he could still manage to get onto experimental aircrafts after *that* experience, then I supposed I could stop being a baby and suck it up too.

~

WE FLEW THROUGH THE NIGHT, then landed in a wooded clearing near a small village, where we spent the day resting in a rickety old inn that had seen better days. Still, the hot spring baths were most welcoming and the food was delicious, so it was easy enough to ignore our less-than-stellar accommodations. I would have liked to go out and explore the village a little, but we'd gotten a lot of strange looks when we'd arrived. Though I couldn't understand the whispered conversations, the tone told me enough—the villagers viewed us as a threat.

"Garaians do not take kindly to outsiders," Chen reminded me over dinner when I brought it up. "It is best to have as little contact with the villagers as possible. It's a good thing that the overlord of this province does not live close, and that we will be gone by the time they tell him about us. We do not want the villagers to notice anything too strange, like our flying craft, or the overlord may feel compelled to report directly to the Imperial Palace."

We paid for another night in the inn, then waited until our landlady retired before slipping back to the forest and taking off in the aircraft again. The second night and day went much the same, and as we boarded the aircraft on the third night, the sky was clear, and our spirits were up.

"Only this last night, and we'll be at Leniang Port," Garrett said, sounding downright cheerful as the aircraft soared through the sky smoothly, as it had been for the past four hours. "Will your sister be surprised at your unannounced arrival with several companions?" he asked Chen.

She gave a delicate shrug. "I suppose so, but life is full of surprises." She did not sound worried. "Once we explain our aims, it is in Asu's own interest, as a Garaian mage, to help us stamp out these traitors as they deserve."

"We'll have to hide the flying machine outside the port city and enter on foot, unobtrusively," Iannis said. "Will that be a problem?"

"Not at all," Chen assured him. "The main part of Leniang is on an island covered by wooded hills, surrounded by smaller islands. Discreet back entrances are a dime a dozen, and hiding such a small machine will not be difficult at all."

"I suppose we will just have to hire a carriage," Garrett said, "and pretend we arrived on a ship."

"That should be easy to arrange in a port city," Iannis said. "Just make sure you keep your belongings close. There may be drivers and merchants aplenty in Leniang Port, but with that also comes plenty of pickpock—"

A strong wind buffeted the right side of the aircraft, slamming the three of us sideways. Director Chen cried out as she took the brunt of the blow beneath all of our weight, and I quickly righted myself, grabbing onto the strap hanging from the wall. Iannis grabbed the one dangling above him, and not a moment too soon, as another gust hit the other side of the aircraft and sent us careening in the opposite direction.

"Blast it!" the pilot cursed as rain began to splatter against the windows. "We've run right into a storm!"

"I can *see* that," Garrett snapped, his fingers digging into the arms of his chair. His face had turned white, and fury flared in his hazel eyes as he glared at the pilot. "How did you allow this to happen? Don't you have weather gauges?" He gestured wildly to the console between them.

"Yes, but they don't seem to be working!" The pilot slapped at the console, fear and frustration oozing off him. "I don't know why—I tested them just yesterday!"

"You should have tested them again before we took off!" Garrett yelled, and Henning flinched.

"*Silence*," Iannis demanded, and the two of them snapped their mouths shut. "Quarreling isn't going to get us out of this mess. Stop yelling at the pilot and let him fly the damned plane."

Garrett's cheeks colored as he clenched his jaw. "Very well. Is there anything we can do to assist, Henning?"

"Can't we do a similar spell to turn the storm away, like we did with the ship?" I asked.

"That spell requires at least ten mages, and is specifically designed for use at sea," Director Chen said. Her ivory face was pinched with worry. "I suppose we could try to improvise—"

Another wind gust slapped against the side of the airship, and we tightened our hold on the straps. Fear leapt into my throat at the sound of metal buckling, and Garrett's eyes nearly popped out of his skull as a tear burst open the craft's thin outer wall. Rain began to sputter in through the opening, and Iannis hastily smacked his hand against the leak and spoke a Word. The metal began sealing itself up, but before it had quite closed, we got hit from the other side and a new tear opened in the opposite wall. Ice crystalized in my veins—it was only a matter of minutes until the entire craft dissolved around us, and we went hurtling into the murky depths below.

"We *can't* hold against this storm," the pilot shouted as I ducked to avoid the spray of water. "I have to land, now! Brace yourselves!"

My stomach lurched as the aircraft took a sharp nosedive. Terror gripped my heart in an icy vise, and I grabbed Iannis and held him tight to me. Fuck the strap—it wasn't going to save me if we crashed. If we died, I wanted to be holding Iannis.

"We're going to be fine," Iannis said, his arms banding tight about me. He pressed my cheek against his chest, and I felt his heart hammering beneath his clothes, just as hard and fast as mine. He could sound as calm as he wanted, but under the surface, he was just as terrified as I was. "We can't stop the landing, but at least we can slow it down."

"Yes, we can," Director Chen agreed firmly. She clasped her hands together, and along with Iannis and Garrett, began to chant the Words to a spell. I managed to string it together with my improved Loranian—it was a spell to temporarily lighten something's weight. Hope rose in my chest as the aircraft began to slow. Maybe we would make it through this after all!

But then I looked out the window, and that hope plummeted as I noticed we seemed to be heading directly for a river.

"Seriously!" I shouted, my turn to be angry at the pilot now. "You couldn't aim us toward land instead?"

"Be grateful we're landing anywhere at all," the pilot shouted back as we crashed into the water. The impact wasn't as hard as it should have been, but it still rattled my brain, and I slammed into the hull. Waves engulfed the craft, obliterating any visibility at all, and we went under for a second before bobbing to the surface. The pilot slapped at a button near his seat, and the hatch popped open.

"Let's go before this thing sinks," he shouted, and he didn't have to say it twice—the leaky airship was already sinking back into the water. With no choice left, I tore the seatbelt off me, then dived out of the hatch and into the cold, wet, roiling darkness of the unknown.

16

"*T*his is fucking awful." I grimaced as we huddled beneath a tree to wait out the storm. There was basically zero visibility out here with these howling winds and torrential rains, which had made swimming to shore very difficult. Iannis had conjured a glowing light over the river to ensure that we stayed together, and we'd eventually crawled onto the banks. Once we'd accounted for everyone, we erected a dome-like magical barrier beneath a tree ten yards from the river to keep out the storm. We'd also dried ourselves and started a little fire to keep warm, but it was still pretty damn miserable.

"You're telling me," Henning agreed gruffly, staring into the fire. His expression was bleak, and my heart sank for him—as the pilot, he had to be taking the loss of the aircraft harder than the rest of us. "We could have been in Leniang Port by morning if not for this damned storm."

"How is it that the aircraft was unable to withstand the storm?" Iannis asked sternly. "Didn't you claim it had been tested several times?"

"Ah, yes, but now that I think back, the tests were always done in dry weather," Henning confessed. He glanced nervously at Garrett, who was scowling. "I guess it'll be back to the drawing board for the next prototype."

"This weather is likely a remnant of a typhoon, like the one we hit on the way in," Director Chen mused. Her arms were folded over her knees, which she'd drawn to her chest, and she stared out at the frothing river. "We're lucky that we weren't badly hurt by the crash landing, or separated. You did a good job, Henning, considering the circumstances."

"I suppose we'll have to find the nearest town tomorrow morning, and secure transport," Garrett said. He sat cross-legged, his hands curled into fists atop his inner thighs, and he looked a bit like a wild man with his hair sticking out every which way. I didn't even want to know what my own hair looked like—we'd dried off, but we hadn't concerned ourselves with grooming, and everyone else around me was dirty and disheveled from our battle with the river. "Any idea how far we are from our destination, Henning?"

"At least three days' ride on horseback," Henning said glumly. "*If* we had horses and found a road southward."

"That's too long." Garrett's features tightened. "The Minister will have our heads if we're not back in time."

"He will do no such thing," Iannis said calmly. Of the five of us, he looked the least ruffled—his pale skin was clear of smudges, his dark red hair tied back from his stern face with a tie he'd procured from that magic sleeve of his. I wondered if he kept any blankets in there, and if so, why he hadn't produced one yet. "Your hysterics are not helping the situation, Director Toring, and are unbecoming of a mage of your stature."

Garrett's eyes narrowed, and I stiffened at the ire rolling off him. "I refuse to be spoken to as a child," he said stiffly.

"Then stop acting like one," Iannis said. "We will do as you say and head to the first town to find proper transport. Director

Chen, are there any trains passing through this area? Surely that will be faster than horseback."

"There might be. I will ask the locals in the morning. One of them will be able to point us in the right direction."

We all settled into an uneasy sleep after that, taking turns at the watch so we could ensure no one snuck up on us. The fire wasn't quite enough to keep out the chill of the storm, so I changed into panther form and cuddled close to Iannis. The sound of his heartbeat, and his hand gently stroking my fur, lulled me into a dreamless slumber that I didn't wake from until Director Chen called my name to wake me for my watch.

Wanting a better vantage point, I climbed up into the tree and perched on one of the branches. The rain had finally let up, and the barest hint of dawn had touched the horizon, giving shadowy shape to a range of mountains that we had been very lucky not to crash into during our landing. The river had begun to calm, and now that it wasn't pitch dark, I was astounded to see that it was at least a mile wide, and seemed to stretch on forever in either direction. I turned my gaze east to see how far along I could follow it with my gaze... and caught sight of a junk sailing our way.

"*Iannis,*" I called in mindspeak, my voice urgent. "*We have company.*"

It was a moment before he answered. "*What are you talking about? I don't see anything.*"

I growled, swishing my tail in agitation as I watched the ship approach, too rapidly for my liking. "*I guess you wouldn't from your position. There's a ship approaching from the east.*"

"*A ship? Not a river boat?*"

"*Looks like a ship to me. It's got sails and everything.*" I watched the ship steer toward the river bank on our side. It sported black sails rather than white, which sent a bad feeling shivering down my spine. "*Are you seriously not seeing this?*"

"*I see them now—cutthroats from the looks of it,*" Iannis confirmed my impression. "*I'm going to alert the others, and extinguish the fire. Perhaps they haven't spotted us. Keep a lookout up there.*"

"*Aye, aye, boss,*" I said, narrowing my eyes on the junk. I forced my tail to stop swishing around—I didn't want the motion to draw any attention. The dawn light grew stronger, and as the ship drew closer to the riverbank, I was able to get a good look at the men on deck. My heart sank a little as I noticed their scruffy appearance and the large, curved swords they wore at their hips and on their backs. Many had shaved heads, and I picked out what looked like tattoos on quite a few. A man in slightly nicer clothes than the rest, wearing a large, oddly shaped hat, came to the deck railing with a spyglass in hand. He trained it in our direction, then grinned and said something to the man next to him, pointing at us.

"*Don't look now,*" I said, dropping to the ground in the middle of the clearing and startling the other mages. "*But I think we're about to be attacked by pirates.*"

"Those certainly look hostile," Chen said, unruffled, as Iannis relayed my warning. The others got to their feet as the ship dropped anchor in the river, and the pirates began descending via a rope ladder. Several had their swords drawn, the tips of their blades gleaming in the early dawn light. One of them jabbed their sword in the air and shouted something in Garaian at Chen.

"We should be able to torch the entire crew between the five of us," Henning said, magic glowing at his fingertips as he raised his hands. "What do you guys say?"

"Hang on," Iannis said, placing a hand on Henning's shoulder, and I was surprised to see a positively devious smile on his face. "Let's not be too hasty."

Annoyed that I couldn't interject myself into the conversation, I changed back into human form. Just as the light was fading from my eyes, I watched Iannis blast the group of approaching pirates—about ten of them—with a burst of ice-blue energy. The pirates froze mid-step as the blast hit them, and two fell over as they had just been raising their feet. Their knives clattered to the packed earth, of no use to the immobile pirates now.

"I thought you said not to be too hasty?" I shouted as the other pirates, who'd been watching from the safety of the ship, let out cries of rage. I swallowed hard as I watched them draw swords and descend from the ship, *en masse*. "Why the hell are you drawing them all out at once?"

"Because," Iannis said, calling more magic to his fingers as he turned back to face the pirates. "I want that ship, and I don't want to accidentally destroy it when we get rid of them all."

17

*K*illing an entire crew of pirates off was pathetically easy. So easy that I felt bad as I burned, stabbed, and sliced them to death. They were an entirely human crew, and stood no chance against four mages and a shifter-mage hybrid. Especially since we were on a mission and determined to get hold of their ship.

Thankfully, Iannis knew how to navigate as a sailing master, and Henning did too, so between the two of them and our unskilled contribution, we got the junk started down the river again. Once the vessel was briskly moving along, Chen and I went below decks to inspect the quarters and supplies. It was no surprise that the place was filthy and infested with rats. She taught me a spell to drive vermin from the ship, and we went from bow to stern and cleaned out the place, while the men stayed above deck and did who knew what.

Typical, I thought, and I was only half-joking.

"If you are feeling bad about killing all those men, don't," Director Chen said quietly as we inspected the meager stores in the pantry. There wasn't much aside from a few bags of rice and dried fish. "They were all thieves, and almost certainly murderers or rapists as well." Her voice, which was normally always so smooth and calm, darkened in disgust. "They deserved their deaths."

"Yeah." I let out a little sigh, hating that Director Chen sensed my tension. "You're right." I decided not to tell her that it wasn't their deaths that weighed down my thoughts, but rather, how easy it had been to kill them. It was truly impossible for anyone to stand against the might of the mages, no matter how clever the Resistance thought they were. What if peaceful protests and negotiations were not enough to get the regime to change? If one day they decided to crush us beneath their magical thumbs, what could shifters and humans really do against such terrible power? It had been five against twenty, and yet we'd massacred those pirates so efficiently, without a single loss of life on our end, or even any major injuries.

"Why didn't that pirate crew have any mages or shifters aboard?" I asked as we left the pantry and went to inspect the weapons stores. I was unsurprised to see gunpowder and pistols, along with sabers—more than a few of the pirates had carried guns, although they were technically outlawed in Garai too. "How is it that they haven't already been wiped out by another mage?"

"This section of Garai is populated by human villages," Director Chen said. "There is a mage warlord who oversees the area, of course, but the villagers themselves hold no magic. They rely on the warlord to protect them, but he cannot be everywhere, and the pirates take advantage of that by passing through and hitting villages they know to be defenseless." Her lips twisted into a grim smile as she picked up a heavy pistol, her fingers dancing across the barrel. "It's a pity we left no survivors, because they would have spread the word far and wide and perhaps deterred other pirates. Unfortunately, the nature of our mission prevents us from eradicating all the pirates along this river." The smile faded, replaced by a look of sadness, and I stared.

"Why are you looking at me that way?" she asked, frowning.

"Sorry." I cleared my throat, dropping my gaze. The truth was that this was the most emotion I'd ever seen from Director Chen, and it was a bit disconcerting. "I guess I'm just a little tired. Why don't we go and get breakfast started?"

"Excellent idea," she said, following me back to the pantry. I hoped we could find some spices if we dug around a little more, because if not, we were in for some seriously boring food.

"I DIDN'T THINK it was possible to burn rice," Garrett said, wrinkling his nose in distaste. He poked at the charred grains in his bowl with his chopsticks, clearly hunting for some white grains amongst the sea of blackness. "At least the fish looks somewhat edible."

"I'm pretty sure it's possible to burn anything," I growled, giving him a death glare that he ignored. He tried to pick up a piece of fish with his chopsticks, and I took savage pleasure in the fact that he failed. "We proved that a little earlier today, didn't we?"

"Sunaya," Iannis warned, laying a hand on my thigh beneath the table. We were all sitting in the bridge on deck, with Henning at the helm and the rest of us seated at a small table inside, eating the miserable meal that I'd attempted to cook in the sad little room that passed for a kitchen down below. I turned and held his gaze, daring him to say more, and a few seconds passed in dead silence.

"Perhaps assigning you and Director Chen cooking duties wasn't the best idea," he finally conceded. "I had hoped you would be able to cook rice, since it's a staple of Garai," he said to Chen.

"We had household servants to do the cooking and cleaning," Chen replied, her voice chilly. "It is not an activity in which I have ever had to take an interest before."

"Sounds to me like we need to stop someplace where there *is* a good cook," Henning said from the helm. He was remarkably cheery, and I suspected it had something to do with the fact that he was once again behind the wheel of a ship, even if it was on water instead of in the air. "There's got to be plenty of villages along this massive river."

With that idea in mind, I shifted into beast form and climbed up the main mast, so I could perch on the crossbeam and survey the surrounding land. The sun had well and truly risen, and the golden light spilled over the verdant mountains and into the breathtaking valleys and plains. From here, I could see terraced fields of rice with modest huts near them. There was one coming up just around the river bend.

"Stop here, after the bend!" I called to Iannis in mindspeak.

Iannis did as I ordered, and we left Henning and Garrett behind to watch the ship as we went in search of food and information. Half a mile inland, we came across a small hut of clay with reed thatch that looked worn and mildewed. Chickens and a skinny rooster pecked for insects in the muddy earth. The few trees and small vegetable patch right by the humble dwelling did not look big enough to support a family. A young, painfully thin-looking girl in rough-looking robes was chasing the chickens in the front yard, but froze at the sight of us, her eyes growing wide. She stared for just a moment, then turned tail, her skinny legs kicking up dust as she rushed into the house.

"Let me take the lead on this," Director Chen said, stepping forward. "These are simple farming people, and they will be more at ease if speaking to a fellow Garaian."

"Very well." We followed Director Chen to the front of the house, and then stood back at a respectful, non-threatening distance as she knocked. The door opened slowly, revealing a haggard-looking Garaian man in his thirties who was wearing a homespun tunic that looked like it had seen better days. A triangular bamboo hat hung down his back, secured by a cord around his neck. As he bowed to us with a fearful expression, I caught a glimpse of the girl and three younger children peeking out at us from behind their father. I smiled, trying to put the children at ease. The girl from before stared at us with those wide eyes, then disappeared inside again, pulling her smaller siblings behind her.

Chen and the farmer began speaking, and from the way she gestured toward us and spoke our names, I gathered she was introducing us. They continued to talk for some time, and as several minutes passed, I wondered exactly what Chen was asking him. The two seemed to be negotiating, though I wasn't sure about what. The price of breakfast, maybe?

"This is Yu Wai," Director Chen finally said, turning back toward us. "He is a poor farmer and does not have very much to offer us in the way of food. However, his eldest daughter Liu is a fine cook, and he is willing to sell her, and two of his chickens, for a bronze coin."

"Wait, his *daughter*? You mean that little girl?" My mouth dropped open in shock. "He can't just sell her like she's some kind of object!"

The farmer said something to me in Garaian, a troubled look on his face. Director Chen instantly began speaking to him in a soothing tone, and he relaxed again, nodding. He bowed to us both, then returned inside the house and closed the door.

"I asked him to give us some privacy while we discussed the offer," Director Chen said coolly once he was gone. "He was most puzzled by the anger in your tone, and I had to explain that you were a foreigner who did not understand our ways." I opened my mouth to protest, but Director Chen bulldozed right over me. "Slavery is a very common practice in Garai, Miss Baine, whether you approve or not. It is not uncommon for poor folk to sell their children to pay a debt."

"I know this sounds horrible to you," Iannis said gently, squeezing my shoulder. "And you are right to feel so. It is barbaric and deplorable. But under circumstances like this, where parents cannot afford to properly feed their children, sometimes the children are better off with their new masters, where at least they will have a job and ample food. I believe this will almost certainly be the case for Liu here."

"You're damn right it will be," I snapped, still recovering from the shock. "We'll take good care of her, and she's not going to be a slave. She'll be a paid employee until we get to Leniang Port, and after that, we'll make sure she gets placed with a good family." I couldn't help but wonder whether or not that was really the right thing to do. Wouldn't it be better to just give the father more money, so he could afford to keep the girl here with her own family?

He'll probably just sell her to the next prospect when he runs out of money, I admitted to myself glumly. And besides, we really did need a cook.

"As you wish," Director Chen said with a small shrug. She turned away and knocked on the door again, and the farmer opened it almost instantly. I both hated and pitied the hopeful, eager look on his face—he was clearly looking forward to selling his daughter.

"Don't allow your own issues with your father to affect your judgment here, Sunaya," Iannis said quietly. He slid his hand down my back so he could rest it against my waist, and the gentle touch soothed me a little despite myself. *"This farmer views this*

as an opportunity to give his daughter a better life, as well as make a little profit."

"*I guess you have a point,*" I admitted, my outrage subsiding a little. The farmer called his daughter, and Liu came forward, her hands clasped behind her, her eyes glued to her dirty, bare feet. I could smell the waves of fear rolling off her, and my heart clenched in pity. Director Chen crouched down in front of the child and placed her hands on Liu's shoulders, speaking quietly. The little girl raised her head, and though her lower lip trembled a little, she shed no tears from her dark, slanted eyes. They spoke for a few moments, and then Liu turned back to her father and threw her arms around him. The farmer closed his eyes and hugged his little daughter. As he squeezed her tighter, I could see her shoulder blades jutting through her thin shirt, as well as the outline of her ribs. By Magorah, she had to be starving.

My mind made up, I said nothing as the farmer took his daughter inside so she could take leave of her younger siblings. If buying this little girl could help her get a better life, then we would do it. Before we left, Iannis slipped the astonished farmer another coin, and the knot in my stomach loosened as I caught the glint of silver. I took comfort in the knowledge that even though we were taking away their eldest sister, the younger children would be taken care of.

---

18

*A*s her father had claimed, Liu was an excellent cook, and she managed to turn the two chickens, our stores of rice and fish, and some herbs she'd brought along from her father's garden, into very satisfactory meals. She didn't speak any Northian, but using Chen as a translator, I discovered that she wanted to open her own restaurant when she was old enough. I promised to support that venture when the time came, and, in the meantime, to get her a job with the Palace cook when we finally got home to Northia.

We traveled the rest of the day along the river, and thanks to the swiftly flowing currents and favorable winds, soon found ourselves approaching the South Garaian Sea—another part of what we Northians called the Western Sea. I spent the night in beast form, draped along the main mast so I could watch for any danger and keep an eye out for our destination. Part of me would rather have been snuggled up inside with Iannis, but there was something both peaceful and breathtaking about being alone so high up in the night sky, with only the salty breeze and the cold blaze of the stars for company. The wind whispered sweet nothings into my furry ears and gently caressed my flanks, lulling me into a catnap.

It was only as dawn crested the horizon once more that the muddy yellow river merged with the salty seawater. The latter was a deep blue-green that lightened where the ground was sandy. Henning turned the boat south, following the shoreline at a distance. Soon after that, I caught sight of sailing masts sheltering in a blue bay with an inviting beach.

I frowned as I noticed there were far fewer ships than I would have expected from a big port like Leniang. Had we missed our destination? The port nestled in a sheltered area at the back of a large island facing a peninsula jutting off the mainland. Steep hills covered with dense vegetation rose right behind the shore, and only a few houses dotted the landscape—a sign that there were not many permanent residents. Most of the houses were wooden, except for one further up the hill that was much bigger and made of stone.

"Iannis," I called via mindspeak. I felt his consciousness stir, and waited a moment before continuing. *"I can see Leniang Port from here, I think, but it's much smaller than I thought. We're only an hour or so out."*

I climbed down from the mast and changed back to human form. Leaning against the port beam, I waited for the others to come up from below decks. When Director Chen came up, her face tightened as she spotted the port.

"This is not Leniang Port," she said, gripping the railing. "I forget the name, but this is a much smaller port that serves as a backdoor to Leniang City on the other side of the island. It's where smugglers unload their goods to avoid the scrutiny of port officials."

"Smuggling?" Garrett asked, crossing his arms over his chest. "Are you telling me we're about to sail into a pirate's cove?"

"I'm afraid that's exactly what she means," Iannis said. "We'd best be on our guard when we arrive."

By the time we arrived in the smuggling port, the atmosphere on deck was tense. I wasn't sure if I should be excited or alarmed that we were about to walk into a pirate's den. After all, these pirates were no match for our magic, and something about the place beckoned to my sense of adventure. But on the other hand, I really hoped that we wouldn't have to kill them to get out of here. I was getting a little sick of all the bloodshed.

We glided up alongside one of the two piers, where a gangly youth in a white linen shirt and trousers waited with a clipboard in hand, ready to collect our names and docking fee. Apparently, Director Chen's information was out of date, and the port officials were now in business on this side, too. We dropped anchor, and his eyes grew round as he watched us disembark, no doubt surprised at the fact that foreigners were sailing on a Garaian junk.

"Your name and business?" the youth asked in heavily accented Northian, addressing Iannis.

"Trade," Iannis said, pressing a coin into the young man's hand. "Is that good enough for a name?"

Greed entered the youth's eyes as he stared down at the money, then looked back up at Iannis. "A name is worth two coins."

"Why you—" Garrett hissed, but Iannis held up a hand.

"Pleasure doing business with you," he said, and gave the youth another coin.

The boy grinned, then pocketed the money and took his clipboard elsewhere. "It is not worth haggling over what amounts to small change for us," Iannis said quietly to Garrett as we made our way up the pier.

"We're going to need every coin we have," Garrett argued

under his breath. "We lost all our supplies when the aircraft sank, and, on top of that, we have no transportation."

"We have the ship," I pointed out, glancing back at the junk over my shoulder.

"With no crew to guard it, I wouldn't be surprised if it was stolen by nightfall," Garrett snapped. "This place is crawling with thieves and pirates."

"I should think Henning can hold his own against mere pirates," Iannis said mildly. We'd left the pilot and Liu aboard the ship, as they weren't really needed for the rest of the journey, and we did need someone to look after the junk anyway.

"Speaking of thieves and pirates," Chen said tightly. "I believe we are about to meet up with some."

I glanced up ahead, and my stomach tightened at the sight of five muscular Garaians headed our way. While they were all at least a head shorter than Iannis or Garrett, their swagger and confidence showed they considered themselves masters of all they surveyed. All but one were shaved bald, and they wore broad leather sashes over showy silk clothes. Gold rings and chains clanked from their necks and ear—a gaudy display of wealth. They were a lot better dressed than the pirates we'd killed, but the wickedly sharp swords and cutlasses swinging from their sides, and the dangerous gleam in their eyes, told me that they were probably going to be more trouble.

The man in the middle, whose head was shaved though he sported a long, thin mustache, stepped forward and addressed us in Garaian. The smug tone in his voice got my back up, and my fingers drifted toward my chakram pouch. Who the hell did these bastards think they were?

"These men work for Bao-Sung, the local pirate overlord. He says that Bao-Sung would like to meet with us," Chen translated. "Immediately."

"That sounds more like an order than an invitation," I said, my hands on my hips. And not one that I liked the sound of.

"We could kill them," Garrett mused, his eyes narrowed thoughtfully. "But that would cause a scene, and we do not want to draw the attention to the local authorities so quickly after our arrival."

"Indeed," Iannis agreed. He showed absolutely no emotion on his face as he regarded the pirates. "Director Chen, tell these fine men that we are happy to meet with their boss."

Director Chen relayed the message, and the head thug grinned, nodding. The five immediately closed ranks around us, and my spine stiffened as several of the pirates raked me with lecherous stares. Not that I feared them, but it was pissing me off that I couldn't just punch them in their pockmarked faces. Instead, I had to stay quiet and let these bastards herd us up the docks and into the big stone house that squatted a little higher up the hill, dominating the cove.

Turning my head back at the picturesque beach and the colorful sails of the boats, I wondered why such a pretty place was so infested with criminals. We had to step over the lower rim of the door—a custom that was followed all over Garai, I had learned, to keep out evil spirits—and were conducted to a small open-air inner courtyard, where a middle-aged man was smoking a water pipe. He did not rise from his divan as he surveyed us with his dark eyes. The place was crawling with more servants and guards, who all regarded us with derision. Not a single woman was in sight, but my sharp ears picked out the sounds of childish laughter and soft female voices from deeper inside the building.

"Play along," Iannis told me as the thugs motioned for us to bow. *"We're not in any real danger. We can get out of this at any time."*

I swallowed my retort as I shallowly bowed to the pirate lord, along with the others. From his scent, he was displeased that we were not prostrating ourselves at his feet, but then again, we were still dressed very plainly, and the pirates didn't know what we were capable of. It made sense not to reveal our true nature until the last possible moment.

The pirate boss himself wore a Garaian silk tunic and pants, and unlike many of his henchmen, had long hair braided down his back. He would have looked respectable if not for the gold hoops in his left ear and the tattoos showing on his neck and his left forearm. His dark eyes gleamed with greed and curiosity as he looked us over, lingering on me much longer than the others. My nose twitched as I smelled his lust, and I forced myself not to react. He spoke to Director Chen briefly, and then turned to the rest of us and began speaking again.

"He says to tell you that he is confiscating our ship, and that he is going to sell us as slaves," Chen translated, "as punishment for coming to the port without his official leave."

"That's preposterous!" Garrett said, taking a step toward the pirate leader. "This is a public port! You don't own it, and you can't control who comes and goes!"

One of the pirates jabbed Garrett hard in the back with the butt of his spear. Garrett let out a startled yelp, and I grabbed the spear out of the pirate's hand and pressed the blade against his throat before he could so much as blink. I kept my eyes trained on his, cold and hard, even as I heard the click of pistols being cocked from around the room.

Bao-Sung let out a hearty laugh, and I saw him wave his hand out of the corner of my eye, ordering the others to stand down. "Feisty," he said to me, speaking in Northian. "My captives are not usually so fearless."

"Yeah, well, that's probably because you don't usually capture mages," I snarled, throwing a fireball at him. The pirate overlord's eyes widened, and he jumped to his feet as he drew his sword. To my surprise, the steel blade glowed bright blue, and Bao-Sung batted the fireball back in my direction.

Damn, I thought as I twisted away from the fiery missile. *His weapon must be spelled to repel magical attacks!*

"I've had enough of this!" Garrett shouted, swinging toward the pirate nearest him. He sliced his hand through the air, and the pirate fell back, a huge gash opening up in his throat. Blood poured down the front of his shirt as he went down, and pandemonium broke out as the rest of the pirates charged us with swords and pistols. Iannis flung out a hand and turned three of them into ice, and Director Chen conjured a shield to stop the bullets as gunfire exploded through the air. The pirates cried out in surprise as she grabbed one of the brutes by his throat and lit his entire body on fire. Screams and burning flesh laced the air, and I jumped out of the way as two pirates rushed me, conjuring a shield to deflect their bullets as well. Spinning around, I kicked one in the back and sent him crashing into the other one.

"*Enough!*" Bao-Sung roared in Northian, and the entire room froze. Dead pirates littered the floor, several struck by their own bullets. But plenty were still alive—the door to my right had swung open and more were pouring in, drawn by the shouts. Bao-Sung yelled at them in Garaian, and the surviving pirates grudgingly backed off, grumbling and shooting glares at us as they retreated to the edges of the room. Garrett looked like he wanted to pursue them, but Iannis shot him a warning look.

"My apologies, honored lords," Bao-Sung said, reverting to Northian. The devious gleam was gone from his eyes now, and his expression was grave. "I did not realize that I was dealing with mages. You do not dress like people of importance," he added, his tone accusing now. "How was I to guess?"

"We are trying not to draw attention," Iannis said calmly, though his eyes glittered with cold fury as he held the pirate overlord's stare. "And we would have succeeded, if your thugs had not intercepted us at the docks."

"May I ask what your business is?" Bao-Sung drawled, twirling the ends of his long beard around his forefinger. He was remarkably cool, considering that his reception room was littered with the dead bodies of his henchmen. "There must be great need of secrecy, if you would risk arriving here dressed little better than peasants. Your Garaian woman must know that anyone who comes to my port looking like prey... becomes prey." His eyes flicked back toward me, and he grinned, revealing a gold tooth where one of his incisors should have been. "Though that one does rather look like a predator."

"That's none of your business, pirate," Iannis said. "And since we have the upper hand, I don't see any reason to tell you." He raised his left hand and the same ice-blue energy from earlier crackled around his fingers. The hairs on the back of my neck stood up, and I tensed, wondering if he was going to smite Bao-Sung in his own home.

"That might be true, but you could hardly keep a low profile if you wiped out my entire household," Bao-Sung said, not the slightest bit ruffled. "You are strangers, presumably in need of local help. We might yet do business."

"Perhaps we might," Iannis agreed to my surprise as he reached into his sleeve. He pulled out a fat brown leather purse, then tossed it from hand to hand. Bao-Sung's eyes lit as it made a clinking sound with each toss. "Do you happen to have an airship and pilot on hand that we could hire for a long-distance journey in two or three days' time?"

Bao-Sung's eyes were glued to the purse. "That might be arranged. Your ship is part of the deal?"

"Indeed, and don't pretend we are not overpaying. We require discretion, mind you." He handed the purse to the pirate.

"Hmm." The pirate hefted the bag, then pulled out one of the gold coins and bit down on it. Satisfied, he nodded, then tied the pouch to his belt. "Yes, I do believe this is a fair exchange. But there is something else I want from you."

"Which is?"

"Your shifter female." The pirate nodded toward me, and I stiffened beneath his lecherous grin. "I am even willing to trade one of my own concubines for her. I love taming the feisty ones."

"You slimy *bastard*," I spat, stalking forward before Iannis could reply. "I'm done with you treating me like a piece of meat. If you think you're so much better than me, why don't you get down here and fight me like a real man?"

"Sunaya!" Iannis snapped, and, if looks could kill, I'd be dead. But I refused to look at him, instead holding the pirate lord's glittering gaze. My blood was boiling now, and I really wanted to spill his.

Bao-Sung arched his brows. "Are you challenging me to a duel?" he asked, sounding incredulous.

"You bet your ass I am. No magic, just hands and weapons. Now get down here." I stepped back a little, toeing one of the dead bodies away so that we could make enough space for a small arena. "If you win, you can have me for a night."

"Like hell!" Iannis snarled, surging forward, but he stopped as I pinned him with a glare of my own.

"Do you seriously have such little faith in me that you think I'm going to lose to a human?"

"No, but the fact that you would even make such an offer—"

"Is tempting," Bao-Sung finished for him, rising slowly from his seat. "Prepare yourself, then, Miss...."

"None of your business." I knew better than to give this sleaze ball my name, and I couldn't be bothered to come up with a fake one. Instead, I drew my crescent knives and assumed a fighting stance. "Are you going to talk me to death, or are you going to fight?"

Bao-Sung laughed again, and then the next thing I knew, he was in my face, his sword swinging straight down at me. I raised my right hand just in time to block him with my crescent knife and continued the arc, pushing his sword away and slashing out with my other knife. He dropped to the ground, avoiding my blade, then kicked out with his leg and swept my legs out from under me.

"Oof!" I grunted as I crashed to the ground. I rapidly rolled out of the way as he stabbed at me, then bounced back up onto the balls of my feet. Our blades clashed again as he closed the distance, and I went on the offensive, slashing furiously. He parried each of my strikes with astonishing skill and force, and, for a moment, I regretted my promise not to use magic.

But only for a moment.

I slashed with my blades again, then pretended a moment of weakness, slowing my movements and allowing my eyelids to droop a little. Bao-Sung took immediate advantage of the opportunity, charging in with amazing speed for a human. But I was faster, and I stepped out of the way, then kicked him as hard as I could in the back. Bone splintered beneath the heel of my boot as at least one rib gave way, and he cried out, stumbling forward.

"You witch!" he hissed, whirling about, and I was impressed that he managed to keep the grip on his sword steady. His face was white now, beads of sweat trickling down into his mustache, and I knew he must be in incredible pain. He charged me again, but this time when I caught his sword with my crescent knife, I swung it around and used my curved blade to catch his sword and pull it from his weakening grip. The sword clattered to the ground, and the room fell dead silent as Bao-Sung looked down at it.

"You stayed true to your promise, and yet you still beat me."

Bao-Sung bowed, and his body buckled beneath the pain. Two of his pirates rushed forward, each catching him by the underarm before his knees hit the ground. "A shame, as I was greatly looking forward to having you in my bed."

"Yeah, yeah." But I couldn't help the grin that tugged at the corner of my lips at his determination, and at the playful note in his voice despite his broken ribs. "Now why don't you have your men show us that dirigible?"

19

*A*s it turned out, we didn't leave right away. Iannis took pity on Bao-Sung, and not only healed his broken ribs, but also an old ankle injury that had been paining him for some time. The pirate offered to host a banquet in our honor as a show of gratitude, but we declined, claiming that we had to be on our way. We did take him up on his offer to care for Liu, though, leaving her with his own seven children until we could return for her. His principal concubine, a stunning Sandian woman with long, dark hair and coffee-colored skin, promised me that Liu would be well taken care of, and instantly took to fussing over her and dressing her like a doll in much prettier clothes. All but one of Bao-Sung's children were boys, so I imagined she was thrilled to have another little girl to care for.

Once the child was settled in, the pirates showed us the hidden footpath to Leniang City. It wound upward across the hill under dense tropical foliage, allowing the pirates to come and go undetected. Smuggling goods were carried by donkey, our guide told us, or moved on small "fishing vessels" under cover of darkness.

At the top of the hill, we paused at our first sight of the large city and the huge, busting port. Half of the city was perched on the pirate island, at the foot of the steep hills we had just climbed, while the other half stretched out across the harbor on the mainland side. In between, hundreds of ships in various sizes, with colorful sails, were plying the green water.

"Amazing," I said as we surveyed it, "I can't believe this place was completely hidden from the back of the island!" Leniang Port was not quite as huge as Maral, but the hilly island was a much prettier setting. Large falcons were circling overhead, looking for fish or game, and up here, among the lush trees, colorful butterflies flitted around. I took in a deep breath of the humid air, which was fragrant with exotic plants.

"Yes, it's impressive." Iannis took my hand. "Now why don't we go down there and see it for ourselves?"

We quickly made our way down the hillside. In less than an hour, we found ourselves at a busy market with stalls selling every imaginable, and unimaginable, kind of goods. There were colorful masks, live toads and frogs, and even snakes—which I guessed were for food—as well as fake coins and other objects that were meant to be burned as funeral goods, raw meat buzzing with flies, and fish still flopping around, gasping for air —the current day's catch.

"We need to buy better garments before we go exploring further," Director Chen reminded us. "We cannot possibly arrive anywhere in these rags."

I looked down at my own clothes, then at the others. Chen was exaggerating, but only a little—though we'd magically cleaned our outfits and mended them as best we could, our swim in the muddy river and other adventures had resulted in significant wear and tear.

"We don't have time to waste on such trivialities," Garrett argued. "We can simply transform our clothes before we arrive."

Chen stopped dead, then turned sharply toward him. "My

sister and her husband are mages, and they would immediately notice the deceit. It is considered terribly gauche to supply your clothing with magic. Did you not see how our lack of fine clothes confused that pirate?"

Garrett looked like he wanted to argue the point, but he stopped short at the cold anger on Chen's face. Iannis proclaimed that Chen was right, settling the matter, and she led us toward the market's textile section. The rows of stalls selling clothing were truly a sight to behold. I'd never seen so many different colors and styles of fabric in my life! Annia would have been in paradise, I reflected wistfully. But despite the sea of shimmering silks and colorful jewels that surrounded us, Director Chen looked unhappy.

"I don't see a lot of finished clothes," I remarked, wondering if that was why she was upset. Most of the stalls were offering rolls of silks, velvets, and other fabrics.

"That's just it," she said. "Everyone who is anyone has their garments made to measure from these fabrics; they can be finished in a single day or two. But we don't have enough time."

"Oh." I pursed my lips as I surveyed the stalls again. "Surely there has to be someone around here who sells finished clothing."

"Yes, but they won't be nearly as fine as I would like." She shook her head, then let out a resigned sigh. "Oh well, we'll just have to make do."

Director Chen steered us to a stall that had a sort of wooden shop attached in the back, and to her relief, found a variety of finished clothing there. We purchased robes for all of us that seemed flashy enough to me, and as I stood in the small dressing room, I decided I rather liked the dark red silk of my new outfit. Even so, Director Chen's lips pressed together as she surveyed us all, disapproval clear in her eyes. But there was nothing better to be had, so she said nothing as we paid for our clothes and left.

Once we finished procuring some additional supplies, we hired a carriage to take us to the home of Asu, Chen's sister, who lived with her husband Loku only half an hour from the port. As we bumped along the winding road, I allowed my mind to wander back across the Western Ocean, to Solantha. How were Cirin and Fenris faring, running the city in Iannis's absence? Was the ether parrot harassing Rylan in my absence? Had Comenius returned from Pernia with his daughter? And, if so, how was she acclimating to the new country? I hoped the little girl would get along with Elania, though it was unlikely they would have a smooth start. Would she have strong magic, since both her parents were hedgewitches?

Thinking of Com's daughter reminded me of Tinari, who was also without a mother now that hers had cruelly rejected her. How was she doing? Had the Guild found her a suitable home yet? I wished we were close enough to send an ether pigeon, so I could inquire after her welfare. I knew Fenris and Rylan would keep their promise to check on the children, and Janta as well. But it would still be nice to know for sure.

And what about Annia? She had to be down in Southia by now, probably in some seedy bar playing cards and drinking with the locals, or getting into trouble. She'd taken the job so that she could put Noria out of her mind, and for Annia, that meant she'd be partying as hard as she was working. I wished that she was here with me now, taking in the exotic sights of Garai. She would have gotten a kick out of the pirates. Knowing Annia, she probably would have had them wrapped around her finger in ten seconds flat, and gotten them to hand over their dirigible without throwing a single punch.

"We're here." Iannis gently squeezed my thigh, pulling me away from my wistful thoughts. I peered out the window to see that we'd arrived outside a large home that was the equivalent of a Northian mansion. It sat a little higher on the slope of the hill, and I imagined it had a magnificent view of the entire harbor, including the opposite side that connected to the Garaian mainland. Blue-green water reflected the blue sky. Flowering trees and plants everywhere, and at least two hundred different ships moving around or at rest, made for a fascinating backdrop to Asu's home.

The house boasted a forbidding outer wall with a gate of carved wood painted red, to protect the privacy of the occupants and discourage trespassers. Once an elderly servant in a long, dark robe had admitted us, and Director Chen explained we wanted to visit with her sister Asu, we crossed a garden with a tiny pool in which colorful carp languidly sunned themselves. These fish were supposed to bring good luck and wealth to the household, Director Chen explained to us.

"Lalia!" the lady of the house cried, surprise on her pretty face as she met us in the hall. She greeted Director Chen with a deep bow and more respect than I would have expected among sisters. The two of them talked fast in Garaian for a few minutes, and I used the time to study Asu. She was a few inches shorter, and a little curvier, than Chen. She wore her long hair mostly unbound, with only some of the strands near her face pulled back and secured with a gold chain. Since Asu hadn't been expecting us, I gathered that her beautifully embroidered and perfectly tailored dark blue silk dress was everyday wear for her. It was certainly fancier than anything I'd wear around the house, and I suddenly understood why Director Chen had been so unhappy with the ready-made garments we'd purchased. Chen's fuchsia robes with blue silk embroidered flowers were beautiful, but they were not even equivalent to what Asu wore now. And we hadn't brought anything suitable for a grander occasion.

Finally, Chen and Asu turned back toward us, and Asu bowed again, addressing us in Northian. "Good afternoon, honored guests. My name is Asu Bai, Lalia's younger sister. I am very pleased to welcome you to my home."

"Good afternoon," Iannis said, bowing in return. "We have been looking forward to meeting you, Mrs. Bai. I am Iannis ar'Sannin, Chief Mage of Solantha, and these are Sunaya Baine, my fiancée, Garrett Toring, who works for the Northian Federal government, and Henning Mogg, our pilot." He gestured to each of us as he introduced us, and we bowed as well. "We are here unofficially, so please do not tell outsiders of our visit to your city."

I hid a frown at that. Would it not have been better to use pseudonyms, if we didn't want Asu telling others about us? But then again, it was important that we gain her as an ally and she already knew Director Chen, so lying to her probably wasn't the best way to go.

"You are all most welcome to stay for as long as you like." Asu bowed again, and as she did, I caught a whiff of unease coming off her. She wasn't being entirely truthful, but I wasn't going to call her out on it. I couldn't blame her for her unease— we probably looked like trouble. "My husband is not home right now, but I will introduce you as soon as he comes back. In the meantime, why don't we have lunch?"

I can get behind that, I thought as Asu led us down the hall and into her dining room. It was a simple but elegant space, with beautiful scrolls depicting Garaian artwork and characters on the walls. In the center of the room, a long, narrow table of dark wood sat low to the ground. It was already laden with various spicy-smelling dishes, and my stomach grumbled a little in anticipation. Standing off to the side in a single line, with their hands clasped in front of them and their posture perfect, were five children in tailored silk robes who all resembled Asu to varying degrees. They bowed in unison as we entered, and I could scent their nervousness despite the expressionless set of their features.

"These are my children," Asu said proudly, and then began to introduce them one by one. The oldest, who looked about fourteen, was Arai, a stunning young woman who, according to her mother, was highly skilled at flower arrangements and also showed signs of strong magic. Next was Busou, twelve, a stocky young boy with intense eyes. He and his younger brother, Kori, were both learning the art of the sword from their father. The two youngest, Shirai and Yusai, were twin girls, and they were adorable with their shy smiles and matching outfits, though Shirai wore green and Yusai wore pink. All of them knew basic Northian. Asu introduced Director Chen as their aunt, and the rest of us as her foreign friends, then we sat down on the legless, but comfortable cushioned chairs to eat our meal.

"My nieces and nephews are very well behaved," Director Chen remarked with a smile as we served ourselves. I was thankful for the ivory serving spoons that supplemented the chopsticks—it would have been embarrassing to spill food all over the glossy wood or onto the silk carpet beneath our feet. "You must be very proud."

"I am," Asu agreed, and the children ducked their heads to hide their smiles. "I am pleased that you are finally getting the chance to meet them. You have been gone for several decades. I would have expected you to have a husband and children of your own by now, actually." Asu gave her a puzzled frown. "Why do you not yet have a family of your own?"

I bit back a grin as Director Chen's scent changed, indicating irritation, though her expression remained placid. But before she could answer, a stocky Garaian dressed in bright red robes walked into the room. He wore his long hair in a queue at the nape of his neck, and the pointed tips of his mustache nearly reached his sternum. His black eyes were cold as he measured us, only warming slightly as he looked at his two boys, and Asu stiffened almost imperceptibly as his gaze landed on her. He barked something in Garaian, and Asu and her children immediately rose from their seats. I shifted in my chair, not sure if we should rise as well, but Iannis laid a hand on my thigh, so I stayed seated.

"This is Loku, my sister's husband," Chen murmured as the two exchanged heated words in Garaian. "He did not know that we were coming, and the sight of us in his dining room gave him an unpleasant shock."

"Indeed." Loku turned toward us, hiding his displeasure behind a smug smile. "Do forgive my rudeness, sister-in-law," he said to Chen in fluent Northian. "I have been out on business since the early hours of the morning, and was expecting to come home to a quiet household."

"Of course," Director Chen said smoothly. "Please allow me to introduce you to my boss, Lord Iannis ar'Sannin, Chief Mage of Canalo." She gestured to Iannis, who inclined his head, then introduced the rest of us as well.

"What an unexpected treat—so many guests arriving all at once," Loku said, a sour note lurking behind his words. "Why don't we sit and enjoy the rest of this delightful meal?"

We settled back down to eat, and Loku engaged Iannis and Garrett in small talk, mostly about the principal trade goods shipped from Solantha. He included his eldest son now and then, but ignored Chen and me completely. I forced myself to focus on my food and not betray my anger at Loku's utter dismissal. I had a feeling, based on the way Asu had reacted when he walked in, and the way he'd smiled so condescendingly at Chen, that he didn't think very much of women.

"So, Mr. Bai," I said loudly when I'd finally had enough, interrupting their conversation and forcing his attention to me. "What sort of business do you run?"

Annoyance flashed in Loku's eyes for just a moment before he turned that patronizing smile my way. "I am most invested in the fireworks business," he said. "They are very popular not only in Garai, but also around the world. I own a factory down here by the wharf, and several others around the country."

"Fireworks, huh?" I smiled back, just as patronizingly. "I'm guessing that means you do a lot of shipping, since you said you sell to other countries. Does that mean you own ships?"

"Not exactly," Loku said, his eyes narrowing a little even though his smile did not waver. "My business is vast and complicated. It would take too long to explain to someone like you."

"Oh, do you mean because I'm a woman?" I said sweetly, then stabbed a piece of meat with my chopsticks, which I knew was very rude.

"Why don't we discuss business over tea later?" Asu said swiftly, glancing at her children. The children had been glancing back and forth between Asu and me like they were watching a tennis match, their eyes wide.

"That is a good idea," Iannis said firmly. *"He may be an ass, but you should still pick your battles,"* he said to me in mindspeak, though he didn't so much as glance at me. I stifled the urge to stick my tongue out at him, focusing my efforts on clearing my plate instead.

We finished the rest of the meal in peace, then adjourned to a sitting room furnished in pink silk wallpaper and black lacquer accessories, where we were served hot tea. Deciding it was best not to ask for coffee, which they probably didn't have anyway, I gingerly cradled the hot cup of tea in my hands and blew on it as the others sipped. The fragrance, I had to admit, was growing on me—the trace of dried flowers amongst the tea leaves was pleasant to my sensitive nose.

"So, Mr. Bai," Garrett said, setting his cup down on the low table with an audible chink of ceramic against wood. "Have you heard anything about a factory in these parts supplying guns to rebels in the Northian Federation?"

"I may have heard something," Loku conceded, arching his brows. "May I ask what your interest is? I did not think mages from your country would be interested in illegal firearms."

"We are when they are being used to terrorize our own citizens," Garrett said. "The Northian government, for which all of us work in some capacity, takes a dim view of smuggling proscribed arms, Mr. Bai. It can only harm relations between our countries. Surely you would see fit to help us with this."

"I care not for relations between countries," Loku said with an airy wave of his hand. "What I do care about is money, and, unfortunately for you, it is not in my best interests to help you with this matter."

"Why, because you're secretly smuggling in the guns yourself?" I accused. My hand itched to slap the smug bastard, and it was all I could do bury it in my lap.

Loku gave Iannis an unpleasant smile. "Does your fiancée always talk this much? Such forwardness is a very unattractive quality in a woman."

"Why you—" My leg muscles bunched as I prepared to jump to my feet, but Director Chen grabbed my wrist. Surprised, I glanced in her direction—she'd never laid a hand on me before. Her face was expressionless, but the tension in her grip gave me pause, and I reluctantly settled back down.

"Northian women are very different from Garaians," Iannis said, sipping from his cup of tea and looking very relaxed. "But Sunaya does raise an interesting question. Are you directly involved in the gun-smuggling trade, Mr. Bai?"

"Of course not," Loku said, smiling. "I am a law-abiding citizen."

"He's lying," I said dryly. "I don't even need my shifter nose to confirm that."

Loku's smile dropped. "I do not appreciate such baseless accusations."

"We mean no offense," Iannis said. "However, it is obvious that you know *something*. The use of firearms is meant to undermine mages' control of the population, though the main victims are helpless humans and shifters. They will be angry with Garai when it becomes generally known where those illegal arms come from. If you know anything useful, it is in your own interest as a mage to help us put a stop to this gun-running."

"I have a human partner," Loku said slowly, "named Ma-San, who may be involved, though this is only a suspicion and has nothing to do with me. I lease one of my warehouses to him, so he can conduct business safely without being harassed. What he keeps there is his own affair."

"So you are involved, then." Garrett's green eyes darkened. "The Federation will not stand for such treachery, Mr. Bai. You and your partner must cease providing guns to the rebels, immediately!"

Loku laughed. "You have no authority to forbid anything here, and I doubt you'll want to bring it to the attention of the Imperial Palace," he said. "Then you would have to admit to conducting a clandestine operation without the approval of the Garaian government."

"We may not be able to do that now, but we *will* take action," Director Chen said firmly. "Please, brother-in-law, look past your greed. Have you no honor?"

"Do not bring honor into this," Loku growled. "We may be family, but I do not owe allegiance to your boss here." His eyes flashed, and he held Director Chen's gaze for a long moment. But when she did not back down, he reluctantly relaxed against the cushions again. "Why should we lose out on all this profit? If Ma-San does not sell these guns, there are a dozen other arms dealers who will trade with anyone willing to pay the price. If it happens that the customers are Northian, well, that is your problem, not mine. It is up to your authorities to prevent their entrance and use in your Federation. Even if you did appeal directly to our new Mage-Emperor, it is unlikely he will be able to do anything about it. His plate will be very full as he assumes his new role."

"This is all true," Iannis said mildly, "but you are mistaken if you think this problem only affects the Federation."

"And how is that, exactly?"

"The firearms are the least of the problem. Our sources tell us that the person manufacturing the guns is not simply selling arms. He is also producing and distributing dangerous diseases that the Resistance has developed as weapons specifically to kill mages. Mages like you and your family."

"That's preposterous!" Loku protested, his eyes going wide. "Ma-San holds no grudge against mages. Why would he do such a thing?"

"For the same reason that you are willing to sell arms to Federation rebels, I suppose," Iannis said with a shrug. "You don't care for anything that does not directly affect you, and he likely takes the same shortsighted position when it comes to these diseases. Or perhaps your partner secretly hates mages and plans to use these diseases to kill you and take over your fireworks business."

"That is ridiculous," Loku said stiffly, but the fear and anger in his scent belied his words. "Ma-San may be greedy, but he is not a fool. He needs me."

"Are you willing to risk your life on it?" I asked.

Loku scowled at me. "Of course not." He stroked his moustache, thinking deeply. Eventually, he let out a sigh, his scowl falling away. "I cannot simply brush aside what you are saying —that would make me just as foolish as you are accusing Ma-San of being. I will investigate these claims of yours, and if it turns out that they are true, I will help you get rid of the threat."

"Excellent," Iannis said, smiling grimly. "Remember, time is short. Once you find out that our information is accurate—and you will—we must discuss the best way to locate and destroy the local lab producing these substances. We do not want to endanger civilians if we can avoid it, or draw too much attention to either of us."

"Of course," Loku said smoothly, though I had a feeling he wouldn't give a damn if innocent bystanders did come to harm.

"While we're on the topic of investigation..." Henning said, speaking up for the first time. "Have you heard about a group of three Northian mages visiting this area about six weeks ago? We have not heard anything back from them."

"This is a big port, there are always some foreigners visiting town," Loku said carelessly. "All kinds of misadventures tend to befall foreign tourists. I don't know anything of those men."

"He's telling the truth," I told Iannis, who nodded almost imperceptibly.

"If you like, I can inquire with Ma-San's wife about your missing friends when I visit her this evening," Asu offered. She smiled at Henning, ignoring her husband's disapproving frown. "I can see that you are very worried about them."

"I am," Henning said. "I would appreciate the help, ma'am."

"My wife is very gracious," Loku said, patting Asu's hand and giving her a patronizing smile that she did not react to. "However, I do not think she will learn much, as the women in Ma-San's house know nothing about his business. A man does not tell his secrets to his womenfolk, after all."

Asu and Chen exchanged a look, and I restrained myself from rolling my eyes. I had no doubt that Asu would have a lot to say about her husband's own business practices in private, though of course she wouldn't speak out against him while he was right there. I was glad Iannis wasn't such a sexist tyrant—we might have a vast power disparity between us, but at least he treated me with respect, and he valued my intelligence, ability, and opinions. If this was Loku when he was well behaved, and with guests, how did he treat Asu behind closed doors? She didn't look like the type to talk about private affairs readily, but maybe we could persuade her to give up something we could leverage against Loku.

I hope she does tell us something useful, I thought. Because the way that Loku regarded us, as if we were fresh meat, told me that we were engaged in a game of cat-and-mouse that was far from over.

20

Though we wanted to get started right away, Loku insisted he would not be able to begin his inquiries until later in the day, when his partner would be playing a local board game in his favorite club. He also argued it would be easier to scope out the suspected warehouse under cover of darkness, which Iannis agreed with, so we found ourselves with some free time on our hands.

Loku took the men out onto the back porch to play chess, while Chen and I sat in the front garden with Asu and enjoyed the warm summer breeze and the beautiful fish swimming in the koi pond.

Now that we were away from the men, Asu spoke more freely. I asked her why she had agreed to marry such a chauvinistic man, and Asu explained that the match had been arranged between their families. I gathered that even though her husband was a womanizer, he was also a powerful and widely respected businessman with his fingers in many pies. Being his wife gave Asu higher status than she would have had on her own, and much more freedom of movement than she would have enjoyed had she married a less wealthy man or remained single. And despite his flaws, she added, he was a good father to their sons, with whom he practiced sword fighting and other martial arts daily.

After a delicious early dinner of spicy fish stew and a variety of other elaborate dishes, Asu and Loku bid us a good evening, suggesting we rest up until full dark. Chen decided to go along with Asu for some sisterly confidences, leaving me alone with Garrett, Iannis, and Henning. A servant showed us to a well-appointed guest suite, with a lavish common area that was connected to several guest bedrooms.

"I am really tired," Garrett said, rocking a little as we entered the suite. "I suppose the travel took more out of me than I thought."

"Yeah, me too," Henning slurred. "Think I'm gonna hit the hay." He took a step forward, then stumbled sideways.

"Hey!" I grabbed him by the elbow before he fell to the ground, then jerked him around to look into his eyes. They were extremely heavy-lidded, the pupils dilated. "What's with you?"

"I do believe these two have been drugged," Iannis said, his arm around Garrett. The Director of Federal Security was listing against Iannis, his own eyelids nearly closed. "There must have been something in the soup they gave us."

"Bastards," I hissed, hefting Henning up into my arms. I carried the now-snoring agent into one of the bedrooms and deposited him onto the mattress, while Iannis floated Garrett into the other one using a levitation spell. A quick check of Henning's pulse, and a hand against his forehead, told me that he was perfectly fine aside from being unconscious.

Pissed at this subterfuge, I stormed back out into the common room, where Iannis was waiting. "How can you be so calm about this?" I raged. "Loku is probably planning to kill us in our sleep when he comes back!"

"Yes," Iannis agreed, settling onto one of the couches. To my surprise, he was completely relaxed, and there was even a hint of amusement in his voice. "It would seem that our host has underestimated us greatly. He is going to be quite surprised when he returns."

"He can't have gotten far. I'm going to give him a piece of my mind." I stalked over to the front door and twisted the doorknob, then snarled when the ornate handle wouldn't budge. A faint glow hummed to life around the handle and doorway, indicating a ward had activated. "That bastard!"

Iannis scoffed. "Loku is a fool indeed if he thinks such a simple ward can keep us locked within these walls." I turned to stare at him, and he patted the cushion beside him. "Stop worrying, Sunaya, and come sit down with me. We may as well make ourselves comfortable as we wait for his return."

Sighing, I let go of my anger and joined Iannis on the couch. His arm came around me, and I snuggled into his powerful chest, comforting myself with the sound of his steady heartbeat. "You're really not worried?" I asked, inhaling his familiar scent of sandalwood and magic.

"Not at all," Iannis said, stroking my hair. Tiny, delicious shivers skipped down my spine at his touch, and my skin began to warm beneath my new robes. "Loku is a reasonably strong mage, but he is much more attuned to business than to war. No mage in Solantha or Manuc would be as obsessed with profit as he seems to be," he added, his lip curling in distaste. "He will be easy enough to overpower even if he brings friends, especially once Garrett and Henning wake up."

"Can't you just wake them up with a spell?" I asked, turning my face so I could peer into Iannis's eyes. "I figured you'd want them to be awake and ready."

"I do," Iannis murmured, sliding his hand beneath my chin as his violet eyes darkened with desire. "But this is the first chance I've had to be alone with you for some time, and we might as well take advantage of it."

He kissed me, and the spark of desire in my lower belly bloomed into a full-on flame. My arms twined around his neck as he coaxed my mouth open, and I savored the taste of him as his tongue stroked hungrily against mine. His scent was like a drug, and I took it in greedily, clinging to him as we lost ourselves in the kiss, in each other.

"We should really take this to the bedroom," I mumbled against his mouth as he dragged me into his lap.

"Why?" He began trailing kisses down the edge of my jaw, shooting sparks of desire through my veins. "It's not like they're going to wake up at the noise."

I opened my mouth to protest, then let out a little whimper as he bit down on the sensitive spot near my collarbone. His skilled fingers quickly undid the ties of my robe, and the soft silk spilled down my shoulders, baring me to the waist. Iannis growled hungrily at the sight of my bare breasts and drew me closer. I gasped as he flicked my nipple with his hot tongue, my fingers digging into his broad shoulders. The hand on my back dipped lower, pushing my robe further down as he sucked and licked my nipples, teasing me until I was moaning his name, my core molten with need.

"Enough," I growled, pushing him away so I could tug at the ties of his robe. His velvet skin was warm beneath my hands as I glided them down his torso, enjoying the ridges of muscle there that were honed by discipline and effort, during early morning hours when he thought I didn't notice him slipping away to exercise. I licked my lips as his length sprang straight into my waiting hand.

"Yes," he groaned as I squeezed, and a wicked grin came to my lips. Before he could think to stop me, I slid to my knees on the carpet, then took him into my mouth. His hips came off the couch as he stifled a shout, and then his fingers were tangled in my curly hair, urging me on with low moans of encouragement as I pleasured him. I'd become very familiar with his tells and knew just how much to push. I waited until his whole body was tense and trembling, then pulled back. His snarl of frustration would have cowed a lesser woman, but I only grinned at him as I stood up, shucking off my robe completely. It puddled on the floor as I straddled Iannis, and the slightest breeze from an open window across the room kissed my already damp skin as I impaled myself on him.

"Oh," I moaned as Iannis's magic twined around us, heightening the pleasure we both experienced. I braced my palms against his broad chest as we began to move together, savoring the blaze in his violet eyes as he looked up at me. His beautiful face was savage with lust, but there was tenderness in his gaze as it drank me in, and his touch was soft as he lifted his palm to my cheek.

"You're so beautiful," he breathed, sliding a thumb across my lip. I bit down on it, and he grinned. "Beautiful and mine."

He cupped the back of my head, bringing me down for another kiss. And we finished that way, entwined both in body and soul as we finally tumbled into bliss.

AFTER WE'D MADE ourselves presentable again, Iannis used a variation of a healing spell to wake up Henning and Garrett. Henning was disoriented, while Garrett was absolutely livid.

"How *dare* that slimy, two-faced snake drug us," he spat, his cheeks turning bright red. Magic crackled in his fist as he clenched it, bright yellow, and I backed up a little as a stray spark popped off his fist.

"Garrett!" Iannis said sharply. "Calm yourself."

Garrett's nostrils flared as he took in a deep breath, and it occurred to me that he was one of the most temperamental mages I'd ever met. But his ire cooled as he let out the breath, and that calm mask that all mages wore slid over his features once more.

"Very well," he finally said, "But we cannot allow this to stand. Loku must be punished."

"And so he shall be," Iannis agreed. "Do any of you have suggestions?"

"I think we should beat him into a pulp," I said, placing my hands on my hips. "But before that, we need to find out just what the hell he was planning on doing to us."

"I agree," Garrett said immediately. "Did he really want to kill us in our sleep? Or is he secretly working with the Resistance, and perhaps planning to extract information from us?"

"Given that he is a Garaian mage, that does not really make sense," Iannis pointed out. "He did not even know of our existence until we showed up."

"Could be that he does know what happened to my fellow agents," Henning growled, his brows drawing together. "And that he was going to deliver us the same fate."

"Nah," I said, twirling a curl of hair around my forefinger. "He wasn't lying when he said he didn't know where those agents went, and his reaction when we told him about the diseases seemed genuine."

"You don't think maybe we should just make a break for it right now?" Henning asked. "We could probably disable that ward, or bust a hole in the wall and leave if we really have to. I don't see why we should stay with this treacherous snake if we have to worry about him killing us in our sleep."

"I am not going to run from Loku," Iannis said, sounding affronted at the very idea. "Between the four of us, we should have no problem subduing him, should he try to attack us."

In the end, we disabled the ward, then went out to the sitting room off the main hall to wait for Loku to return. The servants seemed both surprised and nervous to see us out of our rooms, but they served us tea and almond cookies. Iannis pulled his poison-detecting ring from his right ring finger, where he'd taken to wearing it, and carefully passed it over our food and drink. The square-cut, milky-white stone did not change color, and I let out a sigh of relief. It was good to know that the servants, at least, were not trying to poison us.

It was past nine o'clock before the front door finally opened, and I stood as I caught Loku's scent. The others rose as well, and Iannis held up a hand in warning as I made for the hallway. Reading the look in his eyes, I stepped back and allowed him to walk out first, the rest of us following to make a barricade so that Loku could not enter further.

"Lord Iannis." Surprise flickered in Loku's eyes, and he stopped dead. "I expected you to be resting in your rooms."

"Indeed," Iannis said flatly. "Or rather, you expected us to be lying in our beds in a deep sleep, judging by the drugs you slipped into our—"

The rest of Iannis's sentence was cut off as Loku shouted a spell in Garaian, calling that same strange green magic that the assassin-mage had used on me. Iannis and Henning conjured shields to defend against it, bouncing the magical energy back in Loku's direction. Loku managed to avoid the blast, but Iannis hit him with an identical one. Our treacherous host froze in the middle of the foyer, one foot suspended off the ground mid-step, his mouth open in a snarl of rage.

"Oh, shit," I said aloud as it finally hit me. "That's the same spell Chartis used to immobilize me back in Thorgana's mansion, isn't it?" No wonder I'd gotten the chills when the assassin mage had tried to use it on me, and again here!

"The very same," Iannis confirmed, stepping forward so that

he was toe to toe with Loku. He regarded him thoughtfully, then tapped Loku on his long nose. "Now what exactly are we going to do with you?"

21

"I apologize about the misunderstanding," Loku said with a thin smile as a servant poured more tea for all of us. I was getting sick of drinking the stuff, but figured it would be impolite to bitch about it, so I took my hot cup and sipped gently. At least I was acclimating to the temperature. "Your demeanor and plain clothing confused me into thinking that you were of a lower stature than I realized."

"We introduced ourselves by name and title," Garrett said stiffly. "How could you possibly misunderstand our status? We are high officials in our own country."

"I do not know much about ranks or titles outside of Garai," Loku said, and I wrinkled my nose as I smelled the lie.

"You mean you don't *recognize* any ranks or titles outside of Garai," I sneered.

"What I do recognize is power, and you have demonstrated that you have it in abundance," Loku said coldly. He turned back to Iannis with a smile. "I'm going to assume that the reason you unfroze me is because you want the information I gathered for you tonight?"

"Did you?" Iannis asked, arching a dark red brow. "Or did you go out and conspire against us with your human partner?"

"Of course not," Loku said dismissively. "I took your accusation seriously and did some investigating, just as I promised. And even now, though I doubt it will help, my wife and her sister are visiting with Ma-San's wife. It would seem that you are correct—Ma-San's lab is not actually in my warehouse, but it is right next door in another building I own that he said he's been using for storage." A muscle in his jaw twitched. "I am most displeased to find out that my partner is manufacturing diseases meant to kill mages, and on my own property, no less. I passed by that place just the other day with my older son. He could have been harmed if any of those diseases had gotten out." His eyes flashed at that.

"He clearly underestimates you," Iannis said, then took a sip of his tea. *"Much like Loku underestimates us, not that he would recognize the irony,"* he said privately to me in mindspeak, amusement in his voice. I nearly choked on my tea, and lifted the cup a little higher to cover my grin.

"That is the last mistake he will ever make," Loku said. "I will have him killed for endangering my children."

"If that's how you feel, then why the hell did you drug us?" I demanded.

"Because if it turned out that you were lying, and secretly trying to destroy my business, then I was going to kill *you*." Loku smiled, then lifted his tea cup as if to toast us. "It is just as well for all of us that this was not the case."

The four of us exchanged looks of incredulity. "How do you suggest we go about destroying the lab?" Iannis asked Loku. "We need to ensure that no human or animal escapes, that could spread diseases into the general population."

"I suppose we could do the Suffocation spell," Garrett suggested before Loku could answer.

"Suffocation spell?" I asked.

"It is a powerful spell that blankets an area with a deadly fog that will choke and kill every living thing, from tiny insects to humans," Iannis explained.

"I would be fine with that," Loku said. "From what I understand, the victims die slowly and painfully." His lips curved in a reptilian smile, and a chill ran down my spine. Were we really going to do this? I hated the Resistance as much as anybody, but this was tantamount to torture.

"That spell requires a special herb called *loqualis,* which I do not believe is native to Garai," Iannis said. "You do not have any on hand, do you?"

"Unfortunately not," Loku said with a sigh. "What about this —we have a magical bell in Leniang City that, if struck with a special rod, produces a sound so horrible that it will scramble the minds of anyone listening for a good hour. That will immobilize the lab staff very effectively."

"No way," I snapped. "My ears are way too sensitive for that."

"We would use a spell to protect ourselves, Miss Baine," Garrett said, a thoughtful look in his hazel eyes. "And wax in our ears, for added safety. I rather think this is a good idea. There is minimal chance of innocent bystanders losing their lives."

"What are the chances of obtaining this bell?" Iannis asked.

"Not very good," Loku admitted. "The owner owes me a favor, but she is a collector and very possessive of her artifacts. It would take time to persuade her to give it up." His expression twisted, as if in disgust over the idea that he would have to bargain with a woman. But then his eyes lit up, and his face cleared. "I have it! There is a special gas my master used to make long ago that causes extreme nausea and will make enemies too sick to fight back. It causes no actual illness and wears off in a few hours."

"Is there an antidote?" Garrett demanded. "One that we can

ingest beforehand, that will actually work? We will not be tricked by the likes of you again."

"Of course," Loku said smoothly. "I will head to town and gather the necessary materials tomorrow morning. You all will be well protected. Tomorrow night, we will go to the lab and destroy these vile weapons."

With that settled, Loku bid us goodnight and retired to his rooms. Since Asu and Chen had not returned, the rest of us decided to remain in the sitting room and wait for them. Henning in particular was anxious to know if they had any news about his missing comrades.

"Did you sense Loku was telling the truth, about giving us the antidote?" Iannis asked.

"I'm not sure," I admitted. "I didn't smell a lie when he said those words… but there was still something malicious about his intent. I can feel it."

"We can't trust him," Garrett said, glaring at the opening into the hallway as if expecting Loku to come charging back through to attack us once more. "We should just go to the lab tonight without him and destroy it, Lord Iannis. We have little time left, and we don't need 'help' from this treacherous snake."

The front door opened, and I sighed in relief as I scented Asu and Chen. Their footsteps clattered on the wooden floorboards as they rushed down the hall, and I hurried to the entryway so that they wouldn't miss us.

"Miss Baine!" Chen's eyes widened in surprise, and then she let out the most brilliant smile I'd ever seen from her. "I am so glad you are all awake. We bring good news!"

"What good news?" Henning cried, practically elbowing me out of the way as he made his way into the hallway. "Have you found out what's happened to my colleagues?"

"Yes," Asu said, though her expression was not nearly as

happy as Chen's. "The agents are still alive, and we know where to find them."

_____

su and Chen settled down in the sitting room, then told us their findings. They had discovered that the three Federation agents had been captured and sold, the female to a brothel, and the others to a slaver who had not yet put them up for auction as they were still being trained. The men and I were astounded to learn this, and Henning demanded to know who could reduce three powerful, highly trained mages to such a helpless state.

"They will have used the confusion spell, I expect," Asu said.

"What's that?" Henning asked, frowning. I leaned forward a little, curious as well—Iannis had never mentioned such a spell to me, and judging by the expressions of the others, they'd never heard of it either.

"It is not known outside the region, and it is only passed down within some local families," Asu explained. "The spell was invented a century ago by a mage called Ghom. It can erase a mage's magic and training from his memory, effectively turning him into a human. Ghom used it on the young sons of a rival mage, and then forced the father to hand over his whole fortune before he consented to apply the counterspell."

"A very risky gamble," Iannis commented.

"So it proved," Asu agreed with a slight grimace. "His rival called on his wife's clan for help. They invaded Ghom's mansion at night, and, in revenge for his blackmail, slaughtered him with his entire household. However, one of the servants managed to escape. She had memorized the spell and sold it to a local warlord. Loku's great-grandfather, as it happens."

"By Magorah," I murmured, shaking my head at such a terrible, and senseless, conflict. "What's the difference between the confusion spell and a magic wipe?"

"A mind wipe permanently erases the ability to do magic, whereas it sounds like the confusion spell simply makes a mage forget his powers," Garrett said absently. "If this confusion spell is reversible, it must work on a different principle. What I find strange is that it has not become known outside Garai by this point."

"Mainly because it's in the local dialect, not Loranian," Asu said. "If you heard me use it, you would not be able to memorize it correctly—every single syllable must have exactly the right intonation. And you are right, it is different from a magic wipe since, in reality, the mage still has his magic, but is unaware of it. Any time a victim begins to think of magic, a terrible headache descends upon them, and they quickly stop trying. For all intents and purposes, they simply become a very long-lived human. Slavers love capturing mages because of this, though they don't do it very often to Garaians because it would draw too much notice. The penalty is death by drawing and quartering."

"But, of course, a foreigner would not be missed by anyone important," Henning seethed.

"No," Asu agreed. "And now that they have been effectively turned human, I don't see that they would be much use to you. It might be better to leave them to their fate, as punishment for their incompetence."

"Northians are not that ruthless," Iannis said sternly. "We would not abandon our own to such a terrible fate."

"It is hardly their fault that they were victimized by such a nasty spell," Garrett added. "Especially since they did not know of its existence."

"I've heard of it before," Iannis admitted with a sigh. "During my previous travels in Garai, I heard rumors that it was a closely guarded secret in certain mage families. Apparently, it is not amenable to normal healing spells."

A gloomy silence descended upon us, and I breathed in against the heavy weight on my chest. What would happen to these operatives if we couldn't cure them?

"I do know the spell, and also how to reverse it," Asu said, drawing surprised glances from the rest of us. "I can teach it to you, Lalia, in return for a favor in the future."

"Very well," Chen agreed readily. "As Lord Iannis says, we cannot leave loyal Federation agents to suffer and die out here. I assume we can just buy them back?"

"That would be the easiest way." Asu turned her flat gaze toward Iannis. "How much are you willing to pay for them?"

It turned out that Iannis had ample gold and jewels hidden in his magic sleeve, more than enough to buy back the agents. Life was cheap in Leniang Port, and Asu and Chen were confident that the matter would be easily settled without putting a significant dent in Iannis's purse.

"Even after I apply the counterspell, your friends will be confused and helpless for several days, sometimes as much as several weeks," Asu warned. "It takes time for the brain to properly realign itself. Are you certain you want to bother with such a burden?"

"We'll manage," Iannis assured her. "And we are grateful for your help."

Asu took Chen aside to her private quarters to teach her the spell and its counter, and the rest of us retired for the night. We rose very early the next morning, before Loku or the children had woken, and under Asu's direction, hired a carriage to Leniang Port. Once there, we found a Northian vessel that was leaving the next morning, and then arranged transport with the captain for the three agents as well as Henning. We decided it would be best that he accompany them, since they would still be recovering from the confusion spell. Besides, now that we were hiring an airship and pilot from Bao-Sung, we didn't really need Henning anymore.

"We'll stop at the brothel first," Asu said as we climbed back into the carriage, ready to go and retrieve the operatives. "It is closest to here. I happen to know the owner, who is quite a local character and one of the richest women in town."

"Oh good," I said. "If you two are acquainted, that should make this rescue easier."

"Not necessarily," Asu said as the carriage bumped and rolled along the rough streets. "She hates Western men with a passion. While she has never explained her reasons, I suspect it has to do with her early history about how she became a courtesan in the first place."

"That is very unfortunate," Iannis said, "considering that most of us in this carriage are Western men."

"Yes." The carriage came to a stop. "She would never do a favor for one of you, so I suggest that you men stay in the carriage while we retrieve your friend."

I put a hand on Iannis's arm; he looked reluctant. *"If she's right, then we'll never get Narana out if you come along,"* I said to him in mindspeak. *"Just go with it—I'll call for backup if we get in trouble."* Not that I thought we'd need it— Asu and Chen were powerful mages, and I could kick magical ass too.

"Very well," Iannis agreed aloud. "I suppose you three shouldn't need our help to handle a brothel owner."

"I don't like this," Henning growled, "but so long as you bring Narana back safe and sound, I'll deal with it."

"I promise we will, if she's in there," I told him.

Asu, Chen, and I climbed out of the carriage and went inside the brothel. From the outside, the house looked like any other, the broad door painted a discreet green instead of the more popular red. We were admitted by a muscular fellow who eyed us with suspicion, but relented when Asu proffered a silver coin. He said something to her with a coarse laugh, but Director Chen spoke to him sharply and he deflated. A mage, whether male or female, was clearly far above him in the local hierarchy.

"He was asking if we wanted the big room, for a group orgy, and if he should send some handsome lads," Chen explained in a low voice as the man led us across the garishly decorated entrance hall. "I reprimanded him," she hastened to add, "but he probably does not see many female groups like us."

My nose clogged up instantly at the overpowering scent of incense, which was meant to hide the smells of sex but did not quite succeed against my shifter senses. Swiping at my watering eyes, I muttered an air-filtering spell that Iannis had taught me after the assassination attempt back in Bilai, and the air around me instantly cleared.

The place was furnished entirely in shades of red and rose, with a bit of gold trimming here and there. A gilt statue of a robed old mage with an oversize erection stood opposite another of two naked women intertwined, groping each other with silly looks on their faces. Two Garaian women, beautiful and petite, crossed the corridor in front of us, and we ignored them—they were clearly not our target. Both were dressed in loose, skimpy silk dresses covered by some kind of dressing gown, meant for easy access to their lithe bodies. As we passed, they lowered their eyes and scurried out of the way.

We were shown into a large sitting room on the first floor,

mercifully free of suggestive statuary or prostitutes. While I waited for my nose to finish unclogging, Director Chen and Asu spoke to the brothel owner, an older woman who must have been very attractive at one time, though the expression on her powdered face was cold and crafty. She narrowed her eyes and shook her head, and Asu's voice grew lower and more insistent. They argued back and forth for several minutes. More than once we rose, pretending to leave. Finally, the owner gave a satisfied nod and led us into a room a little way down the hall.

"She has agreed to sell Narana back to us," Director Chen told me as the woman slid the door behind us. "We are to wait here while she gets ready."

"That's great," I said, then relayed the news to Iannis via mindspeak.

The smell of sex was stronger here, and I decided to refrain from sitting on the low couch or the futon, or touching any of the furniture at all. It all looked clean, but not clean enough for someone with my senses, and my skin crawled as I watched Asu and Chen make themselves comfortable on the couch.

A few minutes later, the door slid open, and the owner ushered in a beautiful woman with long, red hair and pale skin. She wore the same loose, colorful robes as the other prostitutes, and her face was heavily made up.

"Are you to be my new owners?" she asked, her dark blue eyes wide with confusion as she glanced between us. She had probably not expected us to be female.

"No," I said gently, my heart clenching with pity for her. Rage followed quickly on its heels, and I stepped forward, curling my hand into a fist as I confronted the owner. "How could you *do* this to her?"

"Miss Baine!" Director Chen grabbed me by the arm and pulled me back, then placed herself between me and the brothel owner. The woman's eyes narrowed at me in annoyance, and she snapped something at Chen. Chen said something back, her voice apologetic.

"Foolish girl," Asu hissed at me under her breath. "Do you want to rescue your friend, or not? This woman does not understand your ways, and does not believe she has done anything wrong. This is her world, her place—there is no point in arguing with her."

"Someone should teach her, then," I growled back at Asu. But instead of confronting the brothel owner again, I turned my attention to Narana, who was standing nearby and watching the exchange with a horribly vacant expression in her pretty eyes. She looked every inch the vapid whore she'd been made into, and not at all like a mage, never mind a cunning government agent. Horror coated my throat at the idea that magic could be used to change someone's personality so drastically, and I swallowed it down. I didn't have time to dwell on such things.

"Do you have any belongings?" I asked, touching her arm gently. Her long hair fanned out behind her as she whipped her head around to look at me. "Anything you need to gather before we go?"

"Everything I own is here." She hefted a small cloth bag she held in her hand that I hadn't noticed before. "What is it that you plan to do with me? Are you taking me to another brothel?"

"That's enough," Director Chen said firmly before I could answer. She dropped a clinking purse into the owner's hand, and the owner inclined her head, then hefted the purse. Satisfied, she left the room, though not before shooting me a glare.

"Narana, come here, please," Chen said in a soft voice, once the brothel owner's footsteps had faded away.

The woman did as Director Chen bade, her face expressionless. I could smell the anxiety coming off her, though, and I wondered what this woman had endured. She'd been sold into prostitution, forced to open her legs for countless men. It was rape, essentially, and my blood boiled with the need for retribution. I could hear soft laughter and grunts coming from the room next door, where another man was taking his pleasure, and more further down the hall. It would be so easy for me to rip through the wall and grab the man by the throat. I could kill him, or crush his balls. After all, he was probably cheating on his wife. He deserved it, didn't he?

But I didn't do any of these things, because deep down inside, I knew Asu was right. What good would it do? The men behind these walls were simply paying for a service, and most of the women here were just trying to make a living in whatever way they could. It was impossible to know which ones were slaves, and which ones were here of their own free will. And yes, I could kill or threaten the owner, and free all these women, but what would that do? The willing ones would simply find another brothel, and the slaves would be lost without someone to take responsibility for them. If I involved the local authorities, I would jeopardize our mission.

I couldn't save everyone. Much as I would like to, I couldn't help these women. Like Iannis said, I had to pick and choose my battles.

But at least we were going to save this one.

Director Chen placed her fingers on the woman's temples, then began to chant in Garaian. After a few seconds, her fingers began to glow white, and Narana cried out, squeezing her eyes shut in pain. Her body started to shake, but Chen remained steadfast, pushing whatever magic Asu had taught her into Narana's mind, forcing her to remember.

A shockwave of magical energy rippled outward, ruffling my hair and sending tingles up and down my skin. The burnt-sugar scent of magic filled the air, and a vase sitting on a small table crashed to the floor, shattering into small pieces.

"Wha..." Narana breathed as Chen finally removed her

hands. Her face was white with shock, and her knees buckled. Chen and I each grabbed her by an arm, then helped her to a chair. "What is going on? What am I doing here?"

"You've had a very bad dream," I told her gravely. "One might even say a nightmare. But it's okay now. You're going home."

∼

WE VISITED the slaver's pen next, where Iannis and Garrett successfully bargained for possession of the other two mages. Henning was overjoyed to see his fellow agents alive and mostly unharmed. Although they were all very disoriented when Asu and Chen brought them around with the spell, they did recognize Henning and were happy to see him.

We set them up at a hotel room near the docks, where Henning would stay the night with them before boarding the ship the next morning. Asu returned home with the carriage, and the rest of us got a late breakfast from one of the street vendors, then headed across to the manufacturing district so we could check out the lab for ourselves. The ferry ride across the harbor only took about twenty minutes, and Asu had given us directions to her husband's warehouse, so the journey was pretty easy.

As we approached the other side of the harbor, it became apparent that it was as busy as Leniang Island, if not more so. It was like one gigantic market close to the piers and ferry, with small street stalls and vendors of all kinds. Since we had a little time, we paused to sample freshly pressed mango juice and admire the view of the island beyond the narrow harbor, beautifully framed by the hills over which we had entered the city. Despite the difficulties of our mission, I knew I would remember Garai fondly for these gorgeous vistas alone. It was really too bad that we weren't on vacation—there was so much to explore!

After fifteen minutes of winding our way through the thronged narrow streets, we reached the manufacturing district, where goods were produced in a series of warehouses. The long, flat-roofed buildings were separated from each other by narrow lanes, and some of the owners thought nothing of clogging up traffic with heaps of industrial garbage. I covered my face with my sleeve—the stench was as overpowering as the brothel had been, and even worse in some places. I wished I could use the air-freshening smell again, but I needed all my senses about me now, and the spell interfered with my nose.

"This is a good place to hide an illicit operation," Garrett said as we walked along the main road, parallel to the wharf about half a mile away. There were rows and rows of warehouses, each on their own pier, and plenty of dockworkers moving crates in and out of the buildings. Loku's warehouse had a firework logo painted on the side of the building and above the entrance, next to a series of Garaian characters that probably spelled his company name.

"Lots of gunpowder in there," I confirmed, sniffing as we walked by it. "It really is a great place to hide illegal arms. I can't tell what belongs to the guns, and what belongs to the fireworks." I sniffed again. "On the other hand, there are thousands of rats in the adjacent building, way more than what's normal. I bet they're lab rats, and that this is the building we're looking for."

We walked on, so as not to alert any guards that we were taking an undue interest in the place. "I find it puzzling that it's not bigger," Iannis said, frowning as he looked at the long, narrow wooden structure. "Compared to the bunker in Osero, this structure is tiny and terribly ramshackle. I can't imagine they have an underground facility here. If this is supposed to be a lab, it is operating on the cheap."

"No kidding," I muttered darkly. The Resistance scientists in

Osero would probably have been horrified if they'd been given such a rickety and unsecurable place to conduct their science experiments. Sure, they'd intended to kill off mages and shifters, but at least they'd been concerned with basic safety when they'd set up their facility.

"Definitely no cellars," Director Chen said. "The ground here would not permit it, and the neighbors would be far too nosy to hide any large excavations. As for operating on the cheap, that's the local practice, to squeeze every last drop of profit out of any enterprise. Public safety is not a priority here."

"By Magorah." I crossed my arms and scowled at the building. "This is a catastrophe waiting to happen. Those crowds we passed through are only a few minutes away. What would happen if even one of these rats escaped, carrying an infection?"

Garrett scowled. "Perhaps it has already happened, and that rat is even now traveling on some outbound ship."

Anger sizzled in my veins at the thought of such carelessness. Were human lives really so meaningless to these people? Weren't they humans themselves? I forced my features into a neutral expression—there were still people walking by, and we were drawing attention as it was. Some of the Garaians we passed sent us curious looks, but nobody challenged us. We were close enough to the harbor that foreigners would not look too out of place. After all, we could have been Northian merchants looking for a lucrative cargo.

"It's a pity we can't just destroy the place now," Garrett said as we walked back to the main part of the city so we could hire a carriage to take us back to Asu's. "I don't trust that Loku fellow to keep his end of the bargain."

"I agree," Iannis said, "but we are not prepared, and it is broad daylight, with too many bystanders around. Best to wait until nightfall, and if it turns out Loku really is going to help us, so much the better. But one way or another, this place will be destroyed by tomorrow."

After riding on the steam ferry again, we caught a cab to Asu's home. As we sat in silence on the bumpy ride back, I couldn't help but worry about the lab. This small warehouse, with its thin wooden walls, was hardly like the airtight, secure bunker we'd destroyed in Osero. While that would make our task much easier, it was very likely that the rat cages were equally flimsy. What if the rats managed to escape through holes in the walls, and infect passersby? If this problem wasn't handled soon, Garai could very well end up with an epidemic of their own....

WE ARRIVED BACK JUST in time for lunch, and had another delicious meal with Loku, Asu, and the children. There was a bit of tension at the beginning of the meal when Iannis insisted on checking the dishes with his ring, but once he determined that the meal was safe, everyone relaxed.

"I have started mixing the materials for the gas and the antidote," Loku said after a nanny had taken the children away. "I spent the entire morning gathering all the supplies, which were quite expensive."

"I am more than happy to reimburse you for your expenses, Mr. Bai," Iannis replied. "We appreciate your assistance and expertise."

"It is nothing," Loku assured us with a wave of his hand. "I have just as much of a stake in this as you do, at this point. This gas does take time to mix, though, so please excuse me while I get back to work."

"Do you need any help?" Garrett asked as Loku rose from his chair. "I have been told I'm fairly handy with potions."

"Oh no, please don't trouble yourself," Loku insisted, bowing. "You are honored guests, and I would not have you do work while you are here. Please enjoy your afternoon, and rest. We will be up very late tonight, after all."

"Is he telling the truth?" Iannis asked me as we watched Loku leave the room.

"He is, but I still don't like this," I said. *"Something isn't right."*

As we rose to leave the room, Asu leaned in and whispered something in Chen's ear. She spoke in Garaian, so I couldn't hear what she said, but her voice was full of warning, and my stomach sank as Chen nodded. We walked in silence back to our suite, and I waited until the footsteps outside in the hall had faded, and I couldn't scent anyone else nearby.

"Okay, what did she tell you?" I demanded as we sat down on the couches. "Your sister was obviously warning you about something."

"Asu told me that, under no circumstances, are we to fall asleep tonight," Chen said, her dark eyes diamond hard. "The confusion spell that the slavers used on the agents we just rescued is best applied when the subject is asleep, and Asu strongly suspects her husband is planning to use it on us."

"I knew it!" Garrett said, his green eyes blazing with fury. "That bastard was planning on double-crossing us this entire time!"

"But why?" Iannis said, frowning. "As Loku said earlier, our goals happen to be the same. Why does he feel the need to eliminate us still?"

"Loku is a member of a powerful secret society that despises all foreigners," Chen said, deep disapproval in her voice. "They do not consider foreign mages worthy of the same rights as Garaian citizens. Therefore, in Loku's eyes, any promise made to you is not binding and does not need to be honored."

"This is crazy," I said, letting out a disgusted huff. "The

sooner we get back to Solantha, the better. I'm tired of all this backstabbing bullshit."

"That makes two of us," Garrett agreed heartily. "So what do you suggest we do about Loku? Do we ambush him again, as we did last time while you were out with your sister?"

"I think that it's time to give my brother-in-law a taste of his own medicine," Chen said with a feline smile. "Asu cannot use the confusion spell on her husband without breaking her marriage vows. My sister believes that without this binding oath, Loku would use magic to control her whenever they have a dispute. But *we* are not bound by any vow, so we shall use it on him when he comes to us tonight."

"Damn." I let out a low whistle. "Are you gonna undo it before we leave?"

"Perhaps," Chen said lightly. "Or perhaps I will leave the timing of his release to my sister. She has had enough of her husband's bullying and womanizing ways, and I have a feeling she will enjoy holding the reins for once."

23

---

*S*ince the initial plan was to leave for the docks at midnight, we decided to pretend to sleep while we waited for Loku to make his move. Garrett, Iannis, and I retired to our rooms in the guest suite after dinner and several games of Garaian chess, while Chen went to sleep closer to her sister in the family quarters.

"Do you think my father has tried to visit me while we've been gone?" I asked Iannis as we spooned on the bed. My head was tucked under his chin, his arm around my waist, and the heat from his body was so soothing that I had to fight sleep.

"It's possible," Iannis said carefully. *"Did you want him to?"*

I sighed. *"I don't really know."* The Minister and the rest of our delegation would have turned him away, claiming that I was too ill to see visitors. *"Part of me wishes I could just tell him and get it over with. I know he can't publicly acknowledge me, but it would be nice if he could at least accept me privately."*

"I understand how you feel," Iannis replied, pressing a kiss to the top of my head, then nuzzling it. The affectionate gesture made me feel warm and fuzzy inside, and I snuggled my back a little closer against his chest. *"Perhaps we will get to speak to him*

when we return. After all, we need to find out whether he was behind those assassins. Your keen nose will be able to discern the truth when we question him."

"*That's true.*" My heart sank at that. In all this excitement, I'd forgotten all about the assassins back at the capital. What would I do if it turned out that my own father was behind the attempt to kill me? He'd seemed so genuinely friendly when we'd met. I had a hard time believing he was secretly hiding murderous intent behind those green eyes I'd inherited from him. Would my mother have fallen for him, if he were that evil?

But then again, mages excelled at hiding their emotions when they wanted to. My father was as easily capable of subterfuge as the next mage. He was a politician, after all. They were good at that sort of thing. And the mage who'd attacked me had been hiding his scent. Why would he do that, unless he was afraid that we would cross paths later or already had done so earlier?

The sound of the hallway floorboards creaking drew my attention away from my worries. I tensed in Iannis's arms as Loku's footsteps, so silent that I barely heard them myself, pattered down the hall, then came to a stop outside the suite door.

"*Are you ready?*" Iannis asked. "*You remember the words of the spell?*"

"*Like the back of my hand. Do you remember the confusion spell?*" Chen had taught it to Iannis earlier, and I'd been impressed that he was able to learn such a complicated phrase in a foreign language as quickly as he had.

"*Of course. I have memorized much harder ones before.*"

We ceased our conversation, lying silent as the grave as Loku opened the door and walked into the room. His footfalls were muffled by the carpet, and I was sure the bastard thought he was doing a great job of being stealthy. Guess he didn't have much experience with sneaking up on shifters. Dumbass.

Garrett was awake and ready too, or at least he'd agreed to be, in case Loku went to his room first. But as predicted, our doorknob was the one to turn. The moment the door opened, Iannis and I sat up and shouted the Words to the very same immobilization spell Loku had tried to use against us, and that Chartis had successfully used on me in the past. Loku let out a very un-manly shriek as he ducked Iannis's green blast, but mine hit him square in the chest before he could activate a shield, and he froze right there, his eyes bulging in fury and fear. His mouth was twisted into a rigid snarl, his hand extended in the midst of preparing to shield and counter attack.

"We've got him!" I crowed as Iannis and I leapt from the bed. I grabbed Loku and hauled him out to the common room, then carelessly let him drop to the carpet. Garrett rushed out of the room as Iannis knelt down beside our treacherous host.

"Good riddance," Garrett gloated as Iannis pressed his fingers to Loku's temple, much like Chen had done to Narana when she'd cured her of the confusion spell. But this time, an ugly, reddish-yellow magic began to glow at his fingertips. An unpleasant feeling crawled down my spine as Iannis pushed the magic inside Loku's head, and I couldn't help but think that if he hadn't been frozen, Loku would be thrashing about and screaming in pain. It had to be extremely violating, to be held down while someone basically took your magic and memories from you.

Not that I was feeling sorry for Loku, mind you. The slimy bastard deserved it, and more.

More footsteps came rushing down the hall behind me, and I turned to see Chen and Asu burst through the door. "Oh good," Chen said when she saw Loku on the ground. She clapped her hands twice, activating the magical lanterns on the walls, and I blinked hard at the sudden light. "You got him."

"Indeed." Iannis got to his feet and regarded Loku for a long moment, his face stony. "I think I will leave him with the immobilization spell for now, so that he does not get in the way. Unless you would rather have me undo it, Asu?" he asked Chen's sister.

"Oh no, you may leave him there," Asu said, a sly smile on her face. "I find that I quite like looking at him this way. I will unfreeze him when I see fit."

"Do you plan to leave him in a confused state?" I asked, grinning at the gloating look in her eyes. I couldn't help but be happy for Asu—she was finally getting her revenge. "I mean, I guess you have to let him out at some point to take care of the warehouses and stuff, but still. I'd milk this for as long as I could."

"I'll leave him like this for a few days," she said airily. "That will give me time to get rid of the mistress he keeps in the back house and to take certain measures to ensure that he can no longer bully the girls or me." Her expression turned hard. "He may be my husband, but I have had enough of his antics. He is not much more powerful than I am as a mage, and I can make gold if I need. His business activities are more for flaunting his power than for any real need of money."

"Still, the authorities will eventually come looking if Loku is missing for too long," Chen said worriedly. "And he seems the vindictive type. I would not want you to put yourself in such a dangerous position, sister, by keeping him in this state too long."

"That is true," Asu said, biting her lip. "Hopefully we can come to some kind of agreement once he is back to normal." She had no choice, after all—mages married for life, so Asu was bound to Loku until he died.

"If worst comes to worst, I will arrange asylum for you and

your children in the Federation," Chen said firmly. "You have been a great help to us, and I will not abandon you in your time of need." She gathered Asu in a hug.

"Thank you, Lalia." Asu hugged her back, then gently pushed her away. "Now go, and carry out your mission. You do not have all night."

24

*A*s it turned out, the concoction for the sickening gas was not ready, so we found ourselves standing outside the warehouse building without a plan. The clouds were thick in the night sky, obscuring the light from the half-moon, leaving us cloaked in shadow as we studied the outside of the wooden building. We needed to figure out the best way to go about destroying the lab within, while avoiding collateral damage.

"It looks like it'll go down with a good, stiff wind," I muttered, shoving my hands into my pockets. I'd changed back into my leathers for this, and Iannis, Garrett, and Chen wore the same black robes that they'd donned while sneaking out of the Imperial Palace. "I'm amazed the Resistance, or at least their Garaian partners, chose such a cheap place."

"Clearly, they did not think it would be discovered," Garrett said, somewhat snidely. "They've obviously been relying on bribery to keep the local officials out of their business. I hope the new Mage-Emperor does something about all this blatant disregard for law and order. It's inexcusable."

"We can debate that later," Iannis said. His eyes were trained on the building, and he tapped his chin thoughtfully. "I think we can do a boosted sleeping spell if we do it together; that should render every human in range unconscious, as well as the rats. That way there is no danger of any infected animal escaping accidentally."

"Okay, well, let's hurry," I said as I caught sight of a stealthy movement on the rooftop. "We're sitting ducks right now, standing out here in the open like this."

We quickly joined hands, with Iannis standing in the middle, and I willed my power to flow from my body into Iannis's. Iannis chanted the Words of the spell aloud, and I bit back a gasp as power rushed through me. Not just my own power, but Chen and Garrett's as well. Iannis's hands blazed like twin suns for a split second, and then the energy in his hands rippled outward, heading up and over the warehouse.

A knife hissed through the air, and I hauled Iannis back right before it would have sliced his neck. The blade hit the ground with a thunk, burying itself to the hilt, and I caught a whiff of poison in the air. Grabbing a chakram from my pouch, I glanced up at the roof just in time to see the figure I'd noticed earlier slump sideways.

"Looks like it worked," Iannis said as I let out a sigh of relief. "Thank you for that." He squeezed my hand. "Now let's go and check inside."

Before we did that, I climbed up onto the roof, using my claws to gain purchase, so I could see how many guards we were dealing with. Only two, thankfully, one on each end of the roof, and they both snored peacefully. I confiscated their poisoned weapons, then used the immobilization spell on them, happy to get to practice it again so soon. I didn't know how long Iannis's sleep spell would last, and there was no point in taking chances.

"All clear," I told the others after I'd hopped back down to the ground.

"Good," Garrett said, stepping around me. He held up his

hands, calling magic, and used a spell to lift the heavy oaken wood bars from the large doors. They swung open, and we entered carefully, splitting up to search the rooms.

The rats I'd smelled and heard from outside were kept in bamboo cages, some of which showed signs of gnawing and had been mended with rusty wire. They were all asleep, and there was something creepy about the way their whiskers trembled and their tiny bellies rose and fell. I wished we could save them, but when I leaned closer and sniffed at their cages, I caught a sour, decaying scent that sent a chill down my back. Whatever that sickness was couldn't be allowed to survive with them.

"By the Lady," Director Chen said, eying the bent wire on one of the damaged cages, "these people are playing with fire, keeping dangerous diseases in such conditions. Such careless-ness is almost worse than the Resistance."

"As long as these diseases don't affect humans, then they probably did not care much," Garrett observed critically.

Luckily, the rats seemed to be the only prisoners in this place. We found five human lab technicians in white coats sleeping at their desks, lots of lab equipment and chemicals, and refrigerated boxes filled with tubes that were labeled mostly in Garaian characters.

Chen and Iannis inspected the tubes and went through the paperwork, while Garrett and I kept watch to make sure no addi-tional enemies snuck up on us. But the night was dead silent aside from Iannis and Chen moving about the rooms. I almost wished someone would charge through the door—I was getting antsy, and all those sleeping rats, full of death and decay, were creeping me out. I wished I could read Garaian characters, but since Garrett and I couldn't, we had to stand back and wait.

Eventually, Iannis and Chen finished, and we reconvened. "From what we've determined from these documents, as well as the equipment and products here, this place has not been conducting any original research," Chen said. "It would seem that Ma-San has been involved in the wholesale production and export of the diseases that the Osero lab had already developed. He simply injected the rats with the serums he got from the Resistance, then harvested and processed their blood. They were going to start using dogs as well, but had not yet arranged for the extra space."

Thank Magorah for that, at least, I thought as my gut roiled with disgust. I was *so* glad we were about to destroy this place.

"Was there any indication how many shipments they dispatched, and where?" Garrett asked, his face tense. "If this stuff is contagious, we may have arrived too late to prevent the worst."

"The place has not been in operation for longer than five months, and it took them a few weeks to collect sufficient rats, streamline their process, and get production up to speed," Chen replied. "From what we could tell, they were just gearing up, and no major shipments have gone out yet. However, there are large stores ready for shipment. It looks like we arrived in the nick of time."

"Several of the crates prepared for shipping had Northian labels," Iannis said. "Inside, we found sealed vials of the diseases packaged and ready to go out, very likely to remaining Resistance camps. At least now we know exactly what diseases they were. Some of the vials were labeled specifically for use on shifters."

"Magorah curse them!" I swore as a wave of fury swept through me. Now that word of the Resistance's plans to betray their shifter members was spreading, they must have decided to decimate the shifter population before we could be mobilized against them. My claws bit into my palms, and I forced my hands to uncurl before I started gouging myself.

"By the Lady." Garrett scrubbed a hand over his face. "We must destroy this entire place immediately."

"What about the technicians?" I asked, glancing toward the nearest one snoring away on his desk. "Do we just blow them up along with the lab?"

"They certainly deserve that fate," Iannis said. "But we are not in our home country and need to strive for discretion, so perhaps we should avoid leaving a trail of dead bodies behind," he added reluctantly.

"Perhaps we cannot kill them," Director Chen said slowly. "But we can do something to them that is tantamount to the death penalty here in Garai, and that will ensure they never lift a hand to aid the Resistance again."

"As much as I'd love to punish these humans, I think the rats should be killed now, while they're still sleeping peacefully," I said. "They don't deserve to suffer—it's not their fault they got caught up in this."

Director Chen gave me an odd look at that, which didn't surprise me. Most mages and humans wouldn't feel empathy toward rats, but as part-animal myself, I knew very well that animals had thoughts and feelings. Even the ones I would normally view as prey.

"Of course," Iannis said, his face solemn. He swept his right arm out, murmuring a spell too low for me to catch, but I still felt the magic ripple outward from him, an invisible wave rolling through the room. A stillness settled in the air in its wake, and it took me a moment to realize that all the rats had stopped breathing.

"I stopped their hearts," he explained. "They did not suffer."

"Thank you," I said, my chest lightening even as my heart twisted with sadness. It was too bad the rats had to die, but at least no one else would have to suffer from these awful diseases.

We rounded up the sleeping technicians and the guards on

the roof, and Iannis and Chen performed the confusion spell on each of them while they were still out. The strange, reddish yellow energy once again made my stomach knot, and I was glad that these humans were not awake.

"W-where am I?" the first one said after I woke her, using a spell Iannis had recently taught me. "Wh-who are you?"

"We are no one," Iannis said, his voice layered with suggestion magic, and the technician's wheeling eyes went glassy. "You will leave this place and forget that you were ever here."

A strange sadness filled me as the technicians and guards stumbled out of the warehouse under Iannis's suggestion, babbling and muttering all the way. It was horrible to see anyone reduced to such a state. "Why is it that they're acting this way, but that the agents we rescued seemed pretty normal?"

"Humans are affected much more strongly by the confusion spell than mages," Director Chen said. "Their minds do not cope as well beneath the strain."

"No kidding. I wouldn't be surprised if they get themselves killed tonight, stumbling around as they are."

"If they do, it is no less than they deserve," Garrett said coldly, and I glared at him. "Now, how shall we destroy this place? Should we simply set it aflame?"

"We could do that," Iannis said. "But I think there's a better way, where we can kill two birds with one stone."

We did one last check of the lab to make sure there was nothing we'd overlooked, then snuck over to the fireworks warehouse next door. There were only a few guards, and Iannis used his sleep spell to incapacitate them while Garrett magically unbolted the heavy doors. Chen used a levitation spell to float the guards out of the warehouse and deposit them on the next street corner. They were scum, but we didn't need their deaths on our conscience if we could help it.

"Oh, man," I said, fighting not to sneeze at the gunpowder

scent as we opened up boxes of crates filled with fireworks. Some of the crates contained guns and ammunition too, proving that Loku was lying about his "hands-off" approach to the gunrunning. I grabbed armfuls of the explosives and began piling them in the center of the warehouse, along with Director Chen, Garrett, and Iannis. "This is gonna draw a lot of attention."

"Yes, but at least it will look like an attack on the fireworks warehouse, rather than the secret lab behind it," Iannis said. He hefted a rocket that was nearly as tall as himself onto the pile, then grinned at me. "Would you care to do the honors, Miss Baine?" He held up the large wick of the rocket in my direction.

I couldn't help it—I grinned back. "I thought you'd never ask."

"Uh, I think we'll get clear first," Garrett said, hastily retreating from the massive pile of fireworks on which I was standing. For once, he actually looked nervous.

"I agree," Director Chen said as he took her by the elbow. "We'll be waiting outside."

"Scaredy cats," I teased, sticking out my tongue, but I couldn't blame them for wanting to get clear. I waited until they were well past the doors, then conjured a flame and lit the wick.

"Race you to the door," I challenged Iannis as the wick began to spark and spit. I made a mad dash for the front door, and Iannis laughed as he blew past me in a gust of wind, outpacing me easily with his Tua super speed. I was halfway to the door when he zoomed back toward me, and then the next thing I knew, I was in his arms.

"Show off!" I shouted as he burst out the door with me. The first explosion went off as his feet hit the pavement, propelling us forward, and my heart leapt into my throat. Thankfully, Iannis didn't fall, and we made it across to the other side of the street just in time to watch the fireworks show.

"That was uncharacteristically foolish of you, Lord Iannis," Director Chen observed as the warehouse went up in a spectacular burst of light and flame.

"Indeed, but it was worth it." Iannis flashed a brief grin, then turned serious. "Now let's stop standing around. We have work to do."

The four of us joined hands again to lend Iannis power, and he conjured winds to blow the fire onto the adjacent building that housed the secret lab. It didn't take long for the roof to catch fire, and once a good blaze was going, Iannis let up, allowing nature to take its course. While the fire raged, he taught me a spell to put anti-flame protection on the adjacent buildings, to ensure that the fire did not get out of control and harm innocent bystanders and neighbors. We applied the spell to all the nearby warehouses together, and to my very pleasant surprise, I got it right on the second try. Guess all those magic lessons were paying off!

"Are we going to go home now?" I asked as we walked away from the conflagration. My ears were still ringing from the explosion, and I was exhausted and hungry from using all that magic. "I'm ready for a serious—" I stopped as the wind shifted.

"What is it?" Iannis asked as I sniffed the air.

"A couple dozen humans." Now that I'd smelled them, I could hear their hurried footfalls from just a block away. "Sounds like a mob of them."

"Blast it," Director Chen cursed. "That must be Ma-San and his thugs! He should not see us. We must leave, now."

But it was too late. The group of men charged around the corner, carrying swords and guns. Their boss was taller than the average Garaian, with a balding head gleaming above his olive-colored velvet jacket. He might have been handsome if he hadn't been practically foaming at the mouth with rage, I noted dispassionately. His henchmen were bare chested and muscular, all sporting similar blue-colored tattoos of striking cobras on their upper arms, and brandishing their weapons in businesslike fashion. These were men used to bathing in the blood of their enemies, and they no doubt intended to kill us with great relish.

"Are you fucking serious?" I shouted, grabbing a chakram from my pouch and flinging it straight at Ma-San's head. He ducked, and the blade beheaded the man behind him instead. The rest of the thugs howled with rage, probably pissed as hell that a woman had struck the first blow, and those who had guns fired straight at us.

"Oh, I have just been looking for a fight," I snarled, jumping high out of the range of the bullets even as Iannis conjured a shield to deflect them. Several of the men cried out as the bullets ricocheted and hit them instead. Served the bastards right. I drew my crescent knives mid-air and came down slashing, cutting throats and ripping into stomachs as I did so. A sword cut into my upper arm, but it was a glancing blow, and I kicked the offending man so hard that he went flying straight into the wall of the closest warehouse. The rest of my comrades had jumped into the fray, using magic to slice, stab, burn, and disintegrate the enemies.

"Die!" a male voice cried in Northian, and I let out a cry of my own as a sword stabbed through the back of my left shoulder. Agony exploded through my upper back, but, thankfully, the man pulled the blade out for a second strike—the last mistake he would ever make.

"Maybe you should take your own advice," I growled, spinning around and catching his next blow with my crescent knife. The man's eyes widened, and I grinned viciously as I realized it was Ma-San himself who'd engaged me. I swept the knife in my left hand into a curve, knocking his sword arm wide so that he was off balance, then came in and sliced his throat open as he stumbled backward. The evil bastard went down sputtering and choking in a pool of his own blood, and I spat on him. Not just for me, but for those all the innocent people the Resistance had experimented on, alive or dead, to make the diseases that he was making profit on.

Not to mention the dead rats burning inside, I thought darkly. I wished I could have made his death more painful, but there wasn't time.

"Let's go, Sunaya," Iannis said quietly as the remaining thugs ran off. I turned to see flecks of blood on his alabaster skin and weariness in his eyes. "We're done here now."

Yes, we are, I thought, giving Ma-San's dead body and the burning buildings one last look over my shoulder as Iannis led me away. We were leaving a trail of dead bodies in our wake after all, and needed to get clear of them before the authorities arrived.

25

*W*ith our mission concluded, we stayed at Asu's only long enough to catch a few hours' sleep. I was surprised to realize that despite our unpleasant mission and treacherous host, I was going to miss staying here. The place was beautiful, and it would have been nice to relax for a few days and get to know Asu and the children better, without her bastard of a husband breathing down our necks. I would have had a lot of fun exploring Leniang City, too. I resolved to come back as a tourist someday, so I could take in the sights without the pressure of an urgent mission on my shoulders.

"It was truly a pleasure having you all," Asu said to us as she saw us off in a carriage, and I could tell by her scent and her smile that she genuinely meant it. The children had gathered around to see us off as well. "I do hope that you will come to visit again, Lalia. I have not experienced this much excitement since before I married Loku."

"Duties permitting, I will visit more often," Chen promised, hugging her sister.

"Do you have to leave now?" one of the twins asked, her eyes round and sad as she looked up at me. "You have not stayed long, and now that Father is sleeping all the time, he cannot scold us for playing with you."

I smiled at her, then crouched down to meet her at eye level. "I would stay and play with you, but our friends are waiting for us, and we have to get back. But I can show you a cool trick before we leave."

"Really?" Her face lit up, and the other children began bouncing on the balls of their feet, even the older ones. "Show us, show us!"

I got down on all fours, then reached for my inner beast and changed. The children gasped as white light engulfed my body, hiding it from sight as the magic stretched and changed me. Muscles and bones rearranged, fangs, claws, and fur grew where there were none, and my senses sharpened, scents becoming stronger, visual details becoming clearer.

"A *cat*," the little girl crowed as the light faded away. The other children gasped and shouted, some in fear, others in delight. "A really big cat!"

"A panther," the oldest sister corrected. "Be careful!" she said as the younger ones rushed up to me, gliding their hands along my sleek, black fur and playing with my ears. I allowed it for a few minutes, rolling onto my back so they could stroke my belly even though, as a general rule, we cats didn't enjoy that. Eventually, even the older ones joined in, and I found myself purring as Busou, the oldest boy, scratched a really good spot beneath my chin with his strong fingers.

"All right," Asu said, her voice both stern and affectionate. "That's enough, children. Let Miss Baine up. She has to leave."

The children whined and pouted a little, but they obediently returned to their mother's side. I got to my feet and quickly licked Shirai's face—the twin who had asked me to play. She shrieked in delight, then ran back to her mother and clutched at her skirts.

I had half a mind to climb into the carriage as a panther, but there wasn't enough room for me to stretch out, and I doubted Garrett or Chen would appreciate it if I lay on their laps. So I changed back to human form, then joined the others in the carriage.

It took about two hours via a steep, winding road for us to reach Bao-Sung's stone house overlooking the small port he unofficially commanded. We met him in the same room as before. This time, his principal concubine was there as well, her dark, manicured hands resting on Liu's shoulders. My heart lightened to see the little girl so at ease despite being surrounded by pirates—she was wearing a sunny yellow dress with white flowers, and looked like she'd put on a little weight in the past few days.

"Thank you for caring for Liu while we were gone," Iannis said. "We can see that she has been very well taken care of."

"Tulai has a way with children," Bao-Sung said easily, smiling at the woman. "I believe she would keep your little slave if she could."

"Liu is very clever," Tulai said in a voice like raw honey. She patted Liu on the shoulder, then gently pushed her forward. "But a pirate cove is no place for a young girl. She will be better off with you."

Liu gave Tulai a grateful smile, and, though she seemed reluctant, returned to us. She came to stand between Director Chen and me, and I squeezed her hand briefly to reassure her.

The pilot Bao-Sung was sending with us was a short, stocky Garaian with several missing teeth, a shaved head, and a gold hoop in his left ear. But despite his rough looks, he was courteous and professional. He spoke only Garaian, so Director

Chen dealt with him, sitting up front with him in the gondola of the airship while the rest of us occupied the passenger seats. The airship was a little rickety, and nowhere near as luxurious as any of the ones Iannis owned, or even my own second-hand dirigible, but it did the job. Soon, Leniang Port was but a speck on the ground as we headed north for Bilai.

Since we were running behind schedule, Iannis and Garrett used magic to strengthen the favorable winds and push us toward the capital, forcing the craft to make the journey in one day rather than the three we had taken to get to Leniang Port. While they powered the spell, I helped Liu practice her Northian. Tulai had already begun teaching her words and phrases, and I was astounded at how much she had picked up in the last couple of days.

"Are you sure you want to be a chef when you grow up?" I asked her. "I could see you being a doctor or a scientist very easily."

Liu bit her bottom lip. "I no know much about doctor or science," she said. "I know food."

"Everyone likes good food," I said with an encouraging smile. "I'm sure you'll be a fantastic chef, and people will come from all over to eat at your restaurant."

Liu smiled back, but the happy expression quickly faded as she turned to look out the window. The sun had completely set by now, but the Imperial Palace was easy to spot, the lights blazing like a beacon in the center of the capital city.

"What's wrong?" I asked when she began to tremble. "Are you nervous?"

"They... kill me," she whispered softly. "I no be... allow... to enter."

"You'll be fine," I assured her. "You'll simply be counted as one of our five servants, now that we've sent another one of them home. Lord Iannis and I will not let anything bad happen to you. You have my word."

Liu nodded, but she still looked worried, and I had a feeling she didn't believe us. After all, we were foreigners, so what could we do if the new Mage-Emperor did take offense to her presence?

"Should we not have brought her back with us?" I asked Iannis worriedly, using mindspeak so that Liu would not overhear and grow even more agitated.

"It will be all right," Iannis said. *"She'll be inside the pavilion for the remainder of our stay. We'll bribe the staff to look the other way. Besides, no one else notices servants. Since Northia is racially diverse, it wouldn't be strange for us to have another Garaian with us, even if she is a bit young for the role."*

The winds began to pick up in strength as we approached the Imperial Palace walls, so Iannis and I broke off our discussion so he could focus on controlling the weather. Visibility worsened as the dirigible dove lower, as thick clouds were moving in from the west, hanging close to the ground.

"These clouds have one advantage," Chen said as I scowled out the window. "We could land close to the guest pavilions, right inside the walls."

"Not with this craft," Garrett pointed out. "There is no landing space big enough. And how would we see it anyway, through this fog?" He pressed his lips together as he studied the view of the ground below. "How close can the pilot get us?" he asked Chen.

"Lord Iannis," Director Chen said after a brief, but tense conversation with the pilot. "The pilot is not going to be able to land here. And the moment the guards see this big airship, the jig would be up. It would mean a death sentence for the pilot to be caught in there without authorization. We will have to levitate down the rest of the way."

"Very well," Iannis said, his eyes still focused outside as he wrangled the winds. "But tell the pilot not to hover too high up."

After a quick discussion with Chen, the pilot agreed to get us as close above the guest pavilions as possible. Since Iannis was the main one controlling the winds, he would leave the airship last, so he could send the pilot on his way with a nice gust at his back.

"We can't hover for long," he shouted over the roaring wind as Garrett opened the door. I grabbed Liu, fearing that the strong currents would whip her away, and held her trembling body close to mine. "Someone from the Imperial Palace might notice this aircraft, and send guards out to investigate!"

"Guess we better hurry then." I scooped Liu up in my arms, then walked over to the open door. But instead of jumping, I leaned up on tiptoe and kissed Iannis, quick and hard. His mouth opened in surprise, and I nipped on his lower lip, satisfying myself with a small taste. After all, there was always a chance I could fuck this up and die.

"See you down below," I said, and then jumped out into the roiling fog.

I LANDED on top of the nearest pavilion, my shoes smacking against the rain-slicked tiles harder than I would have liked. Liu whimpered as I tottered a little, and I quickly regained my balance, then pressed myself against the roof. The incline was steep, but the edges were curved upward, so that we could not easily slide off.

"Are you all right?" Iannis whispered as he landed next to me. Chen and Garrett were still floating down, doing their best to control their descent despite the buffeting winds.

"Yes, I'm fine." We watched as Chen landed gracefully.

Garrett had less luck, banging his shin against the glazed tiles as he alighted.

"Shh!" I admonished as he let out a sharp curse.

"Who is that?" a male voice, laced with sleep and suspicion, demanded from below, and we all froze.

I glared at Garrett, who quickly scurried to the edge of the roof and looked down. "Very sorry to wake you, sir!" he called down as quietly as he could. "I couldn't sleep, so I decided to come up to the roof to enjoy the night sky."

"In this weather?" the man asked incredulously. "You can't see a thing with these clouds!"

"I like the rain," Garrett said simply as the rest of us listened, rooted to the spot. If that guy came up here to investigate.... "I didn't think sitting on the roof was a crime."

"It is if you wake others up in the middle of the night," the man grumped. "Be more considerate of others."

His footsteps crunched against some stray pebbles on the path as he walked away, and my shoulders slumped in relief. We stayed up there for a good five minutes more, and then I crept to the edge of the roof and scoped out our surroundings with my night vision to make sure that no one else was around.

"All clear," I told the others, and we levitated down to the front porch silently. It was somewhere around four in the morning, still an hour before dawn, so I doubted anyone could see our descent. Even so, it made me nervous that we were so exposed.

Once we reached the Northian pavilion, Iannis did not knock on the front door, but used the unlocking spell to let us in. Solar came rushing out of one of the rooms as we shut the door behind us, a lantern held aloft and a scowl on his face.

"Oh, Lord Iannis!" Solar lowered the lantern, looking relieved. "You've made it back!" His expression turned wary as he looked us all over. "Where is Henning? And who is that girl?"

he added, staring at Liu, who was peeking out from behind Chen's robes. Her eyes were wide as she glanced about the common room, taking in the splendor of the guest pavilion.

"Why don't you wake the Minister?" Iannis suggested. "We have much to report."

26

*T*he Minister was relieved that we'd managed to return on time. The presumptive new Mage-Emperor, Kazu, was scheduled to undergo his ritual testing bright and early this morning, and it would look very bad if half our delegation were missing. He was even happier to learn that we'd not only destroyed the lab and some of the firearms, but also recovered the missing agents, and praised us for a job well done. We introduced him to Liu, explaining where we'd gotten her from and that we planned to take her back home with us. For a moment, I worried the Minister would refuse to let her join the delegation since she was only a human. But to my surprise, he accepted her without protest, and immediately assigned one of our actual servants to look after her.

After a few hours of very much deserved sleep, we all rose early and dressed in our finest to attend the testing ritual. It was being held in a huge open-air amphitheater normally used for sporting events. Unlike the funeral, it was open to the public. Half of the capital's population must have been crowding the venue, filling the air with palpable excitement as they chattered amongst themselves.

It's a good thing Garaians aren't overweight, I thought to myself, eyeing the wooden benches. Those seats might have broken down under the masses otherwise. As it was, I heard some ominous creaks beneath the buzz of conversation as red-clad ushers led our group to the reserved section of prime seats. These seats for official guests were covered in red velvet, unlike the bare wooden benches for the common people.

The sky was still overcast and cloudy, and many spectators had brought umbrellas. I wondered if the velvet covers and our elegant robes would be soaked during the event. It was a good thing we were mages and could conjure a rain barrier above our heads if we had to.

"There seems to be a lot of betting going on," I muttered to Iannis as we settled into our pre-assigned seats. We were in the top row of the cordoned-off area, which was awesome, because it gave us a good view of the arena while keeping us far away from harm. On our way up, I had watched money exchange quite a few hands, though discreetly.

"Naturally," Iannis said with a hint of a smile. His expression was stern, but there was a glint in his violet eyes that told me he was looking forward to the event, and that he might have even placed a bet himself. "Such events always encourage gambling, even if there is no official bookie."

I'd heard that Garaians were very fond of gambling, and imagined that on a historic occasion like this, fortunes were changing hands. It was a bit surprising the government allowed it, but then again, there was no Emperor at this moment; the ceremony we were about to witness would decide if the heir would be crowned, or if one of his brothers would be allowed to take the test. It made sense to allow gambling, so that people would be encouraged to attend and witness his success.

The center of the amphitheater was bare except for a loosely built wall some thirty-feet high and twenty-feet wide, made of heavy stones stacked together without cement. Only three feet beside it, a white spot was marked in the carefully raked sand surface.

"So how exactly does this testing stuff work?" I asked. "Is it like the kind of testing you do at the end of your apprenticeship?"

"Oh no," Iannis said. "Kazu has already done that long ago. These trials are more of a local tradition, but a very important one. Today is the day that he must prove to his people that he has the strength to lead them."

"And how does he do that?"

"There are three trials," Director Chen explained. "Prince Kazu must overcome two maddened bulls, stop that stone wall from crushing him, and defend himself against ten well-armed enemies without carrying any arms himself. Only if he proves he can withstand such challenges will he be allowed to wear the mantle of Mage-Emperor and appoint the officials he trusts as his government."

"Really?" I wrinkled my nose at that. "I'd think any competent mage could do those things."

"As I said, these tests are more about tradition," Iannis said, and from the tone of his voice, it sounded like he agreed with me. "I think it would be good to have a test for wisdom and justice as well, though such a test might be more difficult to devise."

We debated that for a little while, but as Chen and Iannis began to delve into more complicated ideas, I grew bored. Tuning them out, I scanned the crowds as I waited for the testing to begin. My heart skipped a beat as I caught sight of Haman coming up the aisle, with Isana and his son Malik in tow. Haman's eyes met mine, and I raised my hand in greeting, figuring it would be insulting to pretend as if I hadn't noticed. He smiled back, and Isana gave me a half-hearted wave as they headed to their seats a few rows down from us. Malik, on the other hand, only raised his chin and stared straight ahead. I frowned at the snub. Had I done something to offend him? Or was he just prejudiced against me because I was a half-shifter?

I don't know why you're acting surprised, a snide voice said in my head. *He's acting just the way you expected your family to.*

A loud gong echoed throughout the arena, jarring me from my thoughts, and the crowd instantly went silent. I looked up just in time to see Prince Kazu, the eldest son of the former Mage-Emperor, stride onto the sanded arena. He hadn't attended any receptions before we'd left for Leniang, so this was my first sight of him. He looked about forty, tall, strong, and warrior-like. He had dressed in leathers and half-armor, likely to remind the people of his long career as a successful general. If he was at all worried about the high stakes he was facing, it could not be seen from his tranquil expression. A murmur of admiration and speculation blew through the crowd as he strode to the spot marked in white.

I glanced sideways at the dais of the widowed Empress, accompanied by her adult children, who looked effeminate compared to their half-brother. My hackles rose at the gloating half-smile on the face of the Empress. She looked not a day older than thirty, younger than the Emperor-designate.

"*She's planning something,*" I said to Iannis in mindspeak. "*Some kind of sabotage?*"

"*Without doubt. I imagine her stepson will be on his guard.*"

An opening in the amphitheater's walls was raised, and two huge black bulls burst into the arena. I blinked at their behavior, surprised they would rush to attack so quickly. They would usually have done some stomping and sniffing before deciding to attack the lone mage by the wall. But then I noticed their bloody red eyes and the white foam coating their nostrils. I was too far to sniff at them, but it was obvious they'd been drugged, and my stomach turned at the sight of such disgusting treatment.

To his credit, Prince Kazu stood calmly on the white spot that had been marked for him to make his stand, unfazed by the mad rush. He held up a hand and shouted a spell, and the stampede stopped in an instant as the bulls were immobilized. The beasts stood there in their strange poses for a moment, until the heavier one slowly toppled onto its side. Attendants rushed from the sides and pulled their heavy bodies across the sand with ropes.

"Even I could have done that," I remarked in a low voice.

"Don't sell yourself short," Director Chen murmured to my surprise. "You may be an apprentice, but you are more powerful than most, or will be when fully trained. Not every mage can handle two bulls at once."

I frowned, unconvinced. Then again, maybe being trained by one of the most powerful mages in the northern hemisphere had left me with unrealistic expectations of other mages' abilities. I would have to think about that more later, after the test was over.

The next test involved the wall. Another mage struck it with a spell, and the stones all came clattering down atop Kazu's head at once. I expected him to react with a spell, so my heart leapt in my throat when he was instead buried beneath the avalanche of rocks.

"He could have put up a barrier," the Minister said critically, and I privately agreed. Why the hell had he just stood there?

"I believe he did," Iannis said mildly. Before our eyes, the stones flew backward and neatly stacked themselves into an orderly heap. From underneath, Kazu emerged, looking completely unruffled. Not one hair out of place, or a single smudge on his clothing. He had to have been shielded.

The Empress looked disappointed, though she quickly smoothed out her features.

"He used the body shield technique, as I thought," Iannis concluded. "A small but impenetrable shield about two inches from the skin," he added to me. "We must practice it soon. It's quick and efficient, appropriate for a soldier, but requires steady nerves."

"Good idea," I said, doing my best to hide my disappointment at how fast the trials were going by. Indeed, the first two tests had ended so quickly, it hardly seemed worth coming all this way to witness the ceremonial testing. It was all over bar the shouting, I decided, since fighting off armed opponents, the last test, would be child's play for a seasoned mage general.

The ten fighters came into the arena from the same door where the bulls had entered, but instead of rushing the prince all at once, they separated and tried to encircle Kazu. Then three of them made a dash straight at him from the front, while the others approached more slowly from behind, brandishing their spears and swords.

"Why doesn't he immobilize them, like he did with the bulls?" I asked.

"They were too far away at the entrance, and you can only immobilize enemies you see," Iannis explained. "He can do it to the ones in front, but not simultaneously to all ten."

Huh. Perhaps it wasn't that easy after all. I'd have to try it myself sometime, if I could arrange to have ten attackers practice with me at once.

The general made a gesture and shouted a spell, but the attackers, all ten of them, kept coming, their movements only growing swifter as they tried to rush him.

"They must be using *alarain*!" Director Chen exclaimed. Her scandalized words were drowned out by the crowd as they suddenly began shouting and yelling from the stands. Many of their faces were red, and they shook their fists in outrage. Others remained carefully blank but for the smug gleam in their eyes, and I noticed that Chari, the widowed Empress, was one of these. Was there some sort of foul play occurring?

I opened my mouth to ask Director Chen what was going on, but pandemonium broke out in the arena, and I whipped my gaze toward it. Kazu had somehow managed to take away the sword from one of his attackers, and he'd erupted into a whirl-wind, disarming and killing the men who now crowded and attacked him from all sides. I frowned, unable to discern whether or not he was using any magic. Why didn't he just blast them with magical fire, as I had done to that rhino shifter so long ago on that fateful day?

But Kazu didn't incinerate his enemies, or attack them with anything but his fists and sword. He spun through his attackers like a tornado of death. As he cut down his enemies one by one, an awed silence descended onto the amphitheater. The smug glint in the Empress's eyes faded, and every other face showed either shock, admiration, or horror at the display of unre-strained violence.

The last man fell to the ground with a hoarse cry, and the crowd seemed to flinch collectively as Kazu stabbed him straight through the throat with his sword. His death scream echoed throughout the amphitheater, and everyone watched in utter silence as Kazu spun away from the dead man and stalked toward the dais. He'd defeated all the attackers with an incred-ible display of strength and skill, despite the wound in his arm that one of the more fervent attackers had dealt him.

Blood stained the linen sleeve beneath his cuirass as he stood before the Empress and her courtiers, dripping to the ground from his fingertips as he silently stared them all down. His face was expressionless, but I had no doubt he was in a towering rage. I would have been calling for blood if they'd tried to sabotage *me* like that! I hoped he gave the Empress a taste of her own damned medicine, once this was all over.

As Kazu met each of their gazes, the courtiers prostrated themselves before him, one by one. The eldest of them stood, then waved a hand to Kazu and shouted something to the audience. The crowd rippled as the spectators all lowered their heads in a respectful bow, and there was no need for Chen to translate when the meaning had been so clear.

The Gods had spoken, and Kazu was Garai's new Emperor.

"JUST WHAT THE HELL HAPPENED?" I demanded as we were carried back to our quarters. "What is *alarain*, and why didn't Prince Kazu use his magic?"

"A very rare and extremely expensive potion that protects humans against all kinds of magic," Iannis explained. "It only exists in Garai, and is strictly controlled. Whoever gave it to the team of attackers was trying to ensure that Kazu would be unable to stop them with magic and that he would be killed. The chief suspect is obvious. A political problem for the new Emperor to solve."

Would he order the execution of his stepmother, or merely exile her? It must be horrible to have such deadly enemies in your own family.

But then again, it seemed I was in a similar position. My heart sank into the pit of my stomach, and I suddenly wasn't sure if I wanted to run into my father again.

27

"Minister Graning," a cool voice said. "The Mage-Emperor would like to see you in his chambers."

I turned to see a Garaian man dressed in ornate robes standing at the Minister's elbow. I'd seen him at the Mage-Emperor's side before—Director Chen had told me that he was the late Mage-Emperor's most trusted aide. We were in the Hall of Dragons once again, suffering through one of many interminable receptions after yesterday's very opulent coronation ceremony. There were several going on in different halls, being hosted by different political leaders, and I had a feeling that my father was in one of those other ones. I'd been craning my neck since we'd walked in here, hoping and dreading to catch a glimpse of him, but so far, I'd been sorely disappointed.

"Certainly," the Minister said. "May I ask what this is about?"

"His Majesty will explain," the aide said. He paused, then added, "Bring the rest of your delegation as well."

Iannis and I exchanged looks, then fell into step behind the Minister as the aide began to lead us to the Emperor. *Do you think he's suspicious of us?* I asked Iannis in mindspeak as we walked through the halls. Our surroundings became increasingly ornate as we approached the imperial family's chambers. I couldn't help but stare as we passed priceless artifacts, statues, and a collection of historic armor and weapons. I wished we had time to stop so I could admire them properly.

"It's possible," Iannis replied. My stomach tightened at the implications, and my toes and fingers tingled with worry. *"We were rather exposed in that airship. Someone could have noticed it hovering over the Imperial Palace grounds."*

"And assume that it had something to do with us?" I resisted the urge to bite my bottom lip and kept my expression calm—the guards we passed were watching. *"Wouldn't the Minister have mentioned if the Mage-Emperor or his family inquired after us?"*

"He should have," Iannis agreed, sounding annoyed. *"But it is possible that someone else brought our absence to his attention. He has many eyes and ears, and we did ask the Imperial Guard to investigate the attempt on your life."*

"Oh, right." I narrowed my gaze on the Minister's back. Had the guards come to interview me after the funeral, to check if I had any enemies among the other guests? If I were them, I would have done so. What did our fellow delegates say to them? I wished I'd thought to discuss this beforehand, but it was too late now.

The private audience chamber to which we were led was relatively small, and decorated in imperial gold. A pair of Lion Guards in human form stood at each of the four doors. Another one of them, in beast form, lounged on the floor next to his master, watching us out of unblinking amber eyes.

The Mage-Emperor regarded us lazily from the raised dais on which he sat on his throne. If he were a jaguar, his tail would be swishing back and forth. His expression was relaxed, but my senses told me he was waiting for an opportunity to strike. After his display in the arena, I had no doubt any strike this man made would be swift and deadly.

After we had bowed respectfully—the Minister merely inclining his head, as one head of state to another—Kazu moved over to a set of gold-colored sofas and motioned for us to sit, facing him, while his guards and various courtiers hovered in the background. I tensed, and I guessed Iannis was not fooled by the show of hospitality either. Enemies tended to be most dangerous when pretending to be affable.

The Emperor spoke to us in Garaian. "His Majesty wishes to know how you are enjoying your stay in Garai, Minister Graning," the translator standing to the Emperor's left said.

"Very well. Please thank His Majesty for his lavish hospitality," the Minister replied. "Our every need has been seen to, and we have appreciated this rare opportunity to visit the Imperial Palace."

"The Emperor is glad to hear that," the translator said as Kazu spoke again. "But he is concerned that all may not be well with some of your delegates. He has heard about the attempt on Miss Baine's life, and her resulting sickness as well. The Imperial Guard heard that she was indisposed, and were denied the opportunity to speak with her, as well as Director Toring, when they tried to interview them last week. Yet the offer to send one of our healers was also declined."

I forced myself to meet the Mage-Emperor's gaze steadily, even as trepidation sent warning tingles down my spine. Those black eyes took my measure, and in them, I saw the truth. He knew where we'd been, and maybe even what we'd done.

"We were grateful for the offer of a healer, but it was not needed," the Minister said blithely, as if he were not aware of the growing tension in the room. "Thankfully, Miss Baine is fully recovered now, and she was able to attend the trials and coronation with the rest of us. We were most impressed by your performance in the testing, Your Majesty, especially the last part. You are more than worthy of your ancestors' crown."

"His Imperial Majesty thanks you," the translator said. I kept my eyes on the Emperor. His expression was reserved, but I could scent the anger coming off him, and I knew we were in deep shit. "He would like to know what sort of illness Miss Baine had, that could not be cured for an entire week by one of the most talented healers in all of Recca." The Mage-Emperor gestured to Iannis, who inclined his head, acknowledging the compliment.

"Your Majesty is most gracious to say so," Iannis said. "But I am not all powerful, and Miss Baine did indeed need several days of rest to recuperate."

"Oh, stop it," I snapped before the Mage-Emperor could speak again. Iannis and Chen shot me warning looks, and the Minister's eyes snapped fire, but I ignored them all. "The Mage-Emperor knows I was not that sick. We're just making ourselves look like idiots by engaging in this stupid charade. We should just tell him what happened." I met that black gaze head-on. "You deserve to know what is going on in your own country."

Director Chen gasped in shock and jumped up to step in front of me. I caught the look of fury in her eyes right before she bowed very low and began speaking very quickly to the Mage-Emperor in Garaian, her tone conciliatory. She was probably telling him I was a crazy half-shifter, and not to believe a word I said.

"No," Kazu said in Northian, surprising us all. He held up a hand, stopping Chen mid-speech. "There is no need to apologize, though I appreciate your bravery in trying to protect your fellow delegate. Please, Miss Baine, tell me what it is going on in my own country—that you feel I do not know about. Perhaps you can start with telling me where you, Lord Iannis, Director Chen, and Director Toring all returned from via airship, when

you should have been within the Imperial City this entire time."
His tone turned dangerous, though his placid expression did not
change.

"It's a long story," I said, refusing to show fear even though
the Mage-Emperor looked like he could strike me down at any
moment, and though I could feel daggers slicing through my
back from the Minister and Director Chen's stares. Straightening
my spine, I told Kazu everything, except for the existence of the
three missing agents, that we had received help from Chen's
sister, and of her husband's involvement. A bead of sweat
trickled down my back, and I hoped that my gamble would pay
off. If not, the Minister would skin me alive. If we made it out of
here in one piece.

"That is quite a tale," the Mage-Emperor said slowly, after I
finished. He looked at the closest Lion Guard, the one in animal
form, who gave a tiny nod, and I knew Kazu had used his guard's
shifter senses to confirm my story. "I shall have to look into the
matter personally. I cannot allow mere humans to put our mages
at risk."

"I would appreciate that very much, Your Highness," the
Minister said. "And yes, what Miss Baine has revealed is true.
We felt we had to act quickly, and regret, in hindsight, not
involving the Garaian authorities from the outset." I hid my
smirk at the half-assed apology, which I could tell did not come
easily. I doubted the Minister was accustomed to groveling in
front of anyone.

"Since your mission has not harmed me or my realm, I am
willing to overlook that you conducted a clandestine operation
in my country, *this one time*," Kazu said calmly. "But do not think
to do so again, Minister. I have a much lower tolerance for such
things than my father before me."

"I understand," the Minister said, though I noticed that he
hadn't agreed. Then again, the guards would be able to detect

the lie, so it was probably best for him to be as ambiguous with his words as he could.

"How is the situation with the Federation rebels evolving?" the Mage-Emperor asked. "I heard that the Resistance attempted to take Solantha while you were missing, Lord Iannis."

"Yes, but we were able to beat them back," Iannis said. "Miss Baine has been instrumental in helping to locate these dangerous Resistance camps and shutting them down. And Director Chen has been invaluable as well by holding down the fort while I was gone."

"I'm sure she has been," the Mage-Emperor said, and I arched a brow at the way he looked Chen up and down. The gleam of interest in his eyes was unmistakable—he definitely wanted a piece of her.

"Your Majesty," Chen said, putting on a gracious smile for him. "It would be extremely helpful in our fight against those unscrupulous rebels if you could put a stop to the gun-running as well. We managed to destroy some guns and ammunition, but illegal firearms dealers are rampant in Garaian ports, and I fear the Resistance will simply find a new supplier."

"Hmm." The Mage-Emperor tapped his chin, appearing to give the matter some thought. But the gleam in his eyes had not gone away, and I got a bad feeling as he looked Director Chen up and down again. "You would not need to bother your pretty head about such matters if you had remained here in Garai, Miss Chen. Why don't you come back home? I am looking to enlarge the Imperial court, and there are never enough lady mages in one's household." He added something in Garaian, in a low, intimate voice, and the hairs on my arms rose. Had he just asked her to become one of his concubines?

"Oh!" Director Chen's cheeks colored as she lowered her gaze. "What a very flattering offer, Your Imperial Majesty." Her voice sounded slightly giddy, but I knew it was just an act—I could smell the panic coming off her in waves.

"It is," the Mage-Emperor agreed. "Do you accept?"

"I'm afraid that you've stunned Director Chen speechless," I said with a laugh, drawing Kazu's attention back to me. Patting Chen on the arm, I added, "Of course she could not refuse such an offer, as it would be a great honor. But I'm afraid it would break her fiancé's heart, and he is waiting for her back in Solantha."

"I see," the Mage-Emperor agreed. To my relief, he did not glance at his Lion Guard for confirmation about the truth of my claim. The gleam in his eyes faded away, replaced by disappointment. "I would not want to come between two hearts already entwined. Please, go and enjoy the rest of the festivities. You have told me all I need to know, and I would not keep you here any longer."

We thanked the Mage-Emperor, then left the room and headed back to the Hall of Dragons. Chen walked at a sedate pace, her face expressionless, but the fear continued to come off her in waves. It did not abate until we were nearly back at the hall.

"Thank you for doing that," she said quietly to me.

"You're welcome," I said. "I figured that refusing him yourself would have put you in an awkward position."

"Very much so," she said with feeling. "The Garaian government considers anyone born in Garai to be a citizen for life, even those like me who have renounced their nationality and made a career in a different country. To refuse his offer directly would have been an unforgivable insult. Such a slight would have severe repercussions against the family I have still living here, never mind international relations."

"Indeed," the Minister said, frowning. "We are very lucky that he took the rejection so well—amongst other things." He gave me a pointed look. "That was a very risky gamble you took."

"Yes, and it paid off quite nicely, didn't it?" I said, smiling sweetly. "I could tell that he wasn't buying our excuses, and that he was growing angrier by the minute. Magorah only knows what would have happened if we'd kept lying to his face."

"But that is the essence of international relations," Garrett said with a quirk of his lips. "You lie, and they know you lie, and yet have to pretend to accept it. Most of the time."

I could only shake my head at *that*. If politics were conducted by shifters, matters would be a lot more straightforward. There would be much less lying and subterfuge, and disputes would be settled quickly, by tooth and claw if necessary. My lips twitched as I imagined the Minister's reaction to such a suggestion—he'd probably find it barbaric.

"I'm sure it helped that he was in a mellow mood, no doubt from securing the throne at long last," Iannis said, placing his hand on my waist and steering me toward the crowds and chatter. "Now let's do as the Mage-Emperor bid us and get back to the festivities, before we find ourselves in any more trouble."

28

I tried to do as Iannis asked and keep out of trouble, but I found myself bored within minutes. The rest of our delegation easily fit into the international crowd, practiced at conversing with other politicians, but I wasn't quite so polished. Besides, Iannis had warned me against allowing members of the other delegations to lure me into spilling secrets, so I was hesitant to talk too much to the other guests for fear that I might accidentally reveal something I shouldn't. Quite a few tried to engage me in conversation, but when it was clear that I would only make small talk, they quickly gave up and moved onto better, more inebriated targets.

Just as I was considering the idea of slipping out early, I saw Isana on the other side of the room. She wore midnight blue today, and her black tresses were pulled back from her head and styled artfully, revealing the gemstones that dangled from her ears. She was in deep conversation with a Sandian delegate, and I approached from the side, waiting until the man had disappeared before making my move.

"Hello, Miss ar'Rhea," I said, and she jerked as I appeared

before her. I grabbed a glass of wine from a passing servant and offered it to her. "Care for a drink?"

"Thank you." She took the glass gingerly, a hesitant smile on her lips. "Usually it's the men who ply me with these," she joked, taking a small sip.

"Big surprise." I settled onto the low couch she was perched on, draping one arm over the back. "How have you found your stay in Garai?"

"Very pleasant," Isana said. "This is my first time visiting, and I find the culture fascinating in its strangeness. What about you?"

"Oh, I think it's lovely," I agreed. "But I've been having trouble sleeping ever since that assassination attempt."

Isana's eyes widened. "Oh yes, I remember hearing about that. Someone mentioned you were wounded. Did the attacker do any lasting damage?"

"No," I said, keeping my expression carefully blank. Isana sounded sincere, but her scent told a different story—she was nervous. "I'm a shifter, and I heal easily from most wounds."

"I am happy to hear that," she said. This time, I could smell the lie.

"I'm not sure you are." I allowed my eyes to narrow, watching with satisfaction as Isana's sun-kissed skin paled. "Did you know that shifters can smell lies, Isana?"

"N-no," she stuttered, her face blank even as her scent grew sour with fear. "We have no shifters in Castalis."

"Ah, yes, that's right," I said, as though I'd forgotten. "I've heard that Castalians are rather prejudiced against them. Makes me wonder whether *your* family was the one who targeted me."

"I resent that implication," Isana said stiffly, her green eyes flashing. "I am sorry that you were attacked, Miss Baine, but I do not know who assaulted you, and I don't appreciate you fingering my family for the blame. Your poor manners and unreasonable paranoia no doubt make you lots of enemies, wherever you go."

Her cheeks grew pink with genuine fury, but underneath that, she was still nervous. What was she hiding?

"Isana?" Haman called before I could probe further. I tore my gaze away from my half-sibling to see him approaching our little corner. Malik was at his side, and while Haman's face was drawn with concern, Malik's green eyes glittered with anger, echoing his sister's.

Haman came to a stop before us, his gaze shifting back and forth between Isana and me. Those green eyes, identical in color to mine, lingered on mine for a long moment, and I held my breath. Did he suspect the truth?

"Is everything all right?" he finally asked, turning back to Isana.

"Of course." Isana let out a breath, then smiled at her father. "Miss Baine and I were having a spirited conversation is all."

I arched a brow at that. Why would Isana lie to her father about what we'd been discussing? Wouldn't it behoove her to tell her father about my accusation?

"Very well," Haman said, though he didn't look like he believed her. "Miss Baine, would you mind letting me borrow you for a few minutes? I'd like to speak privately, just the two of us."

"Borrow me?" I repeated, excitement and fear bubbling up inside me all at once. Was he going to acknowledge our relationship? But if so, why would he not invite his son and daughter?

"Yes." He held out his arm to me. "I need to speak to you privately."

What if he's planning to kill you?

I scanned the crowd quickly, looking for Iannis, but he was

nowhere to be found. For a split second, I considered calling out to him via mindspeak and asking him what I should do.

No, I scolded myself. In the end, this was my demon to face and mine alone. I couldn't rely on Iannis to tell me how to handle every situation—that would only encourage his overprotective instincts. If I asked, he would insist that I not to go anywhere alone with Haman. But my own instincts told me to accept Haman's offer, and they rarely failed me. Looking into my father's eyes, that bottle-green color so familiar, I could detect no malice or fear. And though his scent betrayed his nerves, I did not sense that he feared or distrusted me, as Isana did.

"Very well," I said, taking his offered his arm. "Please lead the way."

"I KNOW that you are my daughter," Haman said as we sat down on a stone bench next to a koi pond in the Palace Gardens. A gingko tree extended its branches over us, hiding us from the waning moon and anyone who might look this way from a distance. "The moment I laid eyes on you, I knew in my heart. But I had to investigate, had to make absolutely certain, before approaching you about it."

"I guess that must have been an unpleasant surprise, given the way your country feels about shifters." I kept my voice even, as though my heart wasn't hammering against my chest, as though my palms weren't sweaty against the cool stone of the bench beneath me. As though the words I spoke didn't coat my tongue with bitterness.

"By the Lady, no." Haman sighed. "I feel guilty, mostly, but also amazed. If I ever shared that stupid prejudice against shifters, meeting your mother, Saranella, would have cured me of it. I adored her."

"Is that so?" I couldn't keep the scathing note out of my voice. "Is that why you left her without a backward glance? Without even telling her who you were?"

"I had no choice." His voice was pained now. "I could not stay with her, much as I wanted to. I was bound by duty and obligation. I still am."

I wanted to snort in derision, but decided to hear him out first. "That doesn't make me feel a whole lot better." I paused, then added, "I used to hate you, you know. Even though I didn't know who you were for most of my life."

"I'm not surprised..." He trailed off, then turned to face me. There was sadness in the lines of his face, but curiosity gleamed in his eyes as he regarded me. "How did you find out about me? Did Saranella tell you before she passed away?"

"No," I said quietly, a pang of sadness hitting me as my mother's face swam into my mind's eye. "I tracked down your old master, Ballos, after finding out that my mother had gone to him for information about you all those years ago."

"Ah." His face softened with something like nostalgia. "How is the old fellow?"

"He's a cantankerous bastard," I said, and, to my surprise, Haman's lips twitched. "But I guess you already knew that."

"Master Ballos is... eccentric," Haman allowed. "But very knowledgeable nonetheless. I learned much from him during my stay in Solantha."

"When you weren't gallivanting about with my mother." Haman grew silent, and I shifted as the tension grew between us. "How did it happen?" I finally asked the question I'd been dying to know the answer to. "How did the two of you meet?"

Haman let out a heavy sigh. "I guess I owe you an explanation, no matter how painful and unflattering it might be to me." He ran a hand over his face. "When I met your mother, I was at loose ends. Ballos was a good teacher, but I swiftly grew bored of

his pedantry, and I was missing my family. To relieve my frustration, I decided to explore the city in human guise, practicing my
skills. I ended up at a small concert in Rowanville, and that was
how I met Saranella."

His eyes lit up, and my throat tightened at the transformed
look on his face. "She was unlike anyone I'd ever met before.
Gorgeous, passionate, with a fine sense of humor.... She lived
her life to the fullest, and her infectious energy never failed to
rub off on me. Being around her was like an addiction. Perhaps
all shifters are the way she was—I had never spent time with
one before. But I could never get enough."

"We shifters are a passionate race," I said, smiling despite the
strangeness of this conversation. "But there was no one quite
like my mother."

"No, I imagine not." Haman was silent for a moment. "I
adored her, and she was fond of me too, but I could never show
her my true face. I regretted that most, after it was all over. That
she would never know who I truly was."

"So the two of you clicked, and you had a hot affair," I
summed up, trying to pretend as if it wasn't a big deal. "And then
you left when you realized there could be nothing more between
you."

"Yes," Haman said simply. "We should not have 'clicked' as
you say. I was already promised to someone else, and we were
from two different races. But I could not help myself, and I
found myself thinking of her at all hours, even when I was
supposed to be focusing on my studies. I spent my nights staring
up at my bedroom ceiling in Ballos's house, forming mad
schemes to leave my country and heritage behind... but none of
them would have worked."

"No, I guess not." I swallowed against a sudden lump in my
throat. Hearing Haman's story made me realize just how

precious my relationship with Iannis was. Most people in my situation didn't end up with the love of their life. Too often they had to abandon their dreams and deal with reality, as my father had done. "Still, I'm not sure why you didn't reveal the truth to her before you left."

Haman shifted uncomfortably on the bench. "One night, not long before I broke things off with her, Saranella and I had a discussion about magic. I found out that she hated it with a passion, and harbored unbridled resentment toward the mage community for what she called the oppression of her kind. I knew then that things would never work out between us, which was why I left without saying anything. She would have never forgiven my deception."

"We'll never know that for sure," I couldn't help but point out, even though I knew it was digging salt in the wound. "You never gave her a chance."

"No. But even had I stayed there, I would have always felt guilty for abandoning my heritage, my betrothed. The shadow of my betrayal would have forever darkened our door and ruined our happiness. So I moved on with my life, and she moved on with hers."

I said nothing to that. What could I possibly add? In the end, Haman had made the right choice. He had gone back to his home, his family, and had married the woman who had been lined up for him. He had a beautiful family, a beautiful wife, and an entire kingdom.

He hadn't known that he had me, too.

"Even so," Haman went on. "When Ballos wrote years later that Saranella had died, all those old feelings came rushing back as though it had been yesterday. The pain of her loss was inde-scribable, and to make matters worse, I could not tell anybody about it." His eyes gleamed with grief for a few moments, and then his brows drew together in a scowl. "I don't understand why Ballos didn't tell me about you in the letter."

"He felt you were better off not knowing," I explained, feeling a little sorry for him now. His absence in my life had truly not been his fault. "He made my mother promise not to contact you. In exchange, he bound my magic so I could attempt to live as a shifter." *Not that* that *had worked out*, I added silently.

"I can see the logic, but even so, Ballos had no right to keep your existence from me." Haman's eyes burned—he was clearly incensed at the old mage's deception. But then his broad shoulders sagged, and he dropped his gaze back to the shimmering pond. "I suppose I only have myself to blame, though. You have every right to hate me."

"I don't hate you." My throat was tight as I said the words, and I meant every single one. It was clear that he'd loved my mother, whatever his faults, and that he hadn't meant to abandon me. "Maybe I did when I was younger, but I don't now."

"It means very much for me to hear you say that." Haman met my gaze again, gratitude in his eyes. "You look so much like Saranella," he said wonderingly, lifting his hand. His fingers brushed against my cheekbone for just a moment, then fell away. "Your faces are nearly identical, though you have my coloring. It's like a miracle."

"I've got your mouth, I think," I said, smiling. By Magorah, but was this really happening? Was I really having a conversation with my father, as his daughter and not a stranger?

"And my eyes," he said. "Although, it *is* strange to see them as shifter eyes instead of human."

I tore my gaze from him at that, staring hard at the pond. The moonlight glowed against the still water, making it hard to see the fish that swam beneath, but every so often, I caught a flash of color from a fin.

"I did not mean offense," Haman said quietly after a long moment of silence. "I brought you out here to tell you that I am sorry I never knew of you, and that I wasn't able to have any role in your upbringing."

"Would it matter if you had known?" I asked. "Given your country's laws and customs, wouldn't you have been forced to hide my existence anyway?"

Haman hesitated. "It would have been difficult, under the circumstances, for me to care for you properly," he conceded. "But somehow, I would have found a way."

He spoke with such sincerity that for a moment, I almost believed him. But those were just feelings talking, I reminded myself. He might believe that he could have found a way, but whether he could have actually done so was another matter. Maybe it was just as well that he'd never had to try—the heartbreak would have been unbearable.

"So, what now?" I asked. "Now that the facts are established, and we've both said our piece, do we just part ways here and pretend this meeting never happened?" My stomach dropped at the thought. It felt wrong to end things like that with my father, even if Iannis might advise it.

"That might be the logical thing to do, but I don't want that," Haman said, sounding a little offended. "I did not approach you so that I could tell you to forget me. I shall write to you, like a friend, now that I know of your existence, and it is up to you whether you want to reply, or visit, once you are married. I wish I could offer more, but it would be folly for either of us to publicly claim our relationship, at least not until I have stepped down from office as High Mage, and Malik takes over."

"That's probably gonna be a couple of hundred years, huh?" I said, and a weight slipped off my shoulders. There was zero chance that he would try to call off my wedding, not if he wanted to keep his position.

"Perhaps not," Haman said ruefully. "Being a High Mage is not as much fun as some people think, and I don't plan to cling to the office forever. It could be as soon as a few decades, depending on whether Malik is ready. He has much growing up to do. In any case, you have nothing to fear from me regarding your engagement to Lord Iannis. I will not interfere in any way, and neither will my family. None of them know about you."

"I wouldn't be so sure of that," I said. "Just a few days before I left for Garai, I received a letter from Isana suggesting that we might be related. She wrote that she'd seen my picture in a magazine and noted the resemblance. And then she went on to say that she really admired what I'd accomplished as a hybrid, and that she wanted to meet me."

"Really?" Haman looked taken aback. "That sounds most unlike Isana. She does not warm easily to people, especially not over something like a mere photograph. Besides, I saw that picture in the papers myself, and I did not make the connection at the time. I find it hard to believe that she would."

"Well, *someone* did," I insisted. "And maybe they put the idea into Isana's head. Whoever it was, though, wants me dead."

"Dead?" Haman scowled. "What are you talking about?"

"I was attacked the morning of the funeral, not far from my own pavilion," I told him. "There were three humans and a mage, all dressed in black with their faces covered. One of them cut me with a magical knife, spelled to inflict wounds that don't heal."

"By the Lady," Haman muttered, running a hand through his curly hair in a way that reminded me of myself. It was a little disconcerting, actually. "I can't believe he would do this."

"Who?" I demanded, alarmed at the sudden anguish in his voice. "Are you telling me you know who's behind the attack?"

"I can't be sure," Haman said firmly. "I must find out more before I say for certain." He rose, his robes fluttering behind him in the gentle night wind. "Rest well, Sunaya. I will come and find you again in the morning, as soon as I know more."

He left me there on the bench, and it was some time before my mind and heart settled enough for me to go back inside again.

"*I* do wish you had notified me about your meeting with Haman before you went off alone with him," Iannis said as we walked back from the breakfast buffet. I'd told him over a large and very satisfying meal what had happened last night—by the time we'd returned to bed, I'd been too tired to go over it with him then. "But I am glad he shows some fatherly concern, and that he has agreed not to interfere with our union."

"I am too," I said, squeezing Iannis's forearm gently. "I wasn't trying to shut you out, you know. I just felt like it was something I needed to handle alone."

Iannis sighed. "You are a grown woman," he said eventually. "I cannot dictate your every move; I can only advise you as to what I think is best. At least you asked me to come along for this next meeting."

Haman had sent a servant to our pavilion this morning with a message for me, asking me to meet him at the same koi pond at nine o'clock. I could have gone without Iannis, but I felt like doing that twice would have been a betrayal of sorts. I was gradually getting accustomed to thinking of myself as part of a couple, a team. I imagined it was even harder for Iannis to get used to the idea, since he'd been single even longer than I had. Hopefully one day, we'd both learn to include each other in all our schemes and problems. It wasn't a matter of trust, but more of habit—we were both used to relying on ourselves.

Haman was waiting beneath the tree, dressed in cream robes with a gold-and-black pattern. His thick, curly dark hair hung free, brushing his shoulders, and there was a hint of stubble around his strong jaw. I tensed a little at the troubled look in his green eyes—he had bags beneath them, as if he'd been up all night.

"Good morning, Lord Iannis, Sunaya," Haman said to us, offering a strained smile. "Thank you for coming so promptly."

"Good morning, Lord Haman," Iannis said, sliding an arm around my waist and pulling me a little closer. "We are more than happy to meet with you, although I am not sure you should be addressing my fiancée with such familiarity."

"I would never do so in public," Haman said stiffly. "However, she *is* my daughter. Unless *you* would rather I not?" he asked, his eyes softening ever so slightly as he looked at me.

"No, it's all right," I said, sighing a little. It was strange—all these years I had hated my unknown father, expected to hate him even worse if I ever met him face to face, but I could not help rather liking Haman ar'Rhea. Perhaps because he had so much of me in him. "Just don't expect me to start calling you dad." I wasn't ready for that. Not by a long shot.

"Why did you call us here?" Iannis demanded. "Sunaya says that you have an idea of who might have attacked her. Do I guess correctly that it is someone close to you?"

"Yes." Haman's expression grew chagrined. "The knife Sunaya described sounded much like a knife that belongs to my son Malik. I questioned him about it last night. In the end, I had to use magic to get the truth out of him. He is a stubborn young man." I could sense Haman's exasperation. He was still very upset, and no wonder. "Malik finally confessed that he was indeed trying to kill you. He was acting on behalf of Lord Ragir, his grandfather and the former High Mage. Not that I'm trying to minimize Malik's guilt. He is old enough not to have gone along with such a murderous scheme behind my back." Haman's voice was heavy.

"Your son and your father-in-law?" I gaped. "But why—what have I done to them?" Iannis, beside me, did not seem particularly surprised. I remembered that he had warned me of the man's ruthlessness when we'd talked about the ar'Rhea family back home in Solantha.

"You don't know Ragir; he is ice-cold, an absolute terror," Haman said. "It was Ragir who dictated that letter Isana wrote to you. He hoped to place an assassin in her entourage if she was invited to meet you, but when he guessed you might be coming to Garai, he roped my son into helping him instead." His expression darkened. "That he subverted my own children like that is unforgivable. I shall forbid him all further contact with them when I return to Castalis."

"Why does he want me dead so badly?" I asked, trying not to sound too hurt about it. After all, I had expected something like this, but still, to actually hear it.... *At least Ragir is not related to me by blood,* I consoled myself. But that excuse did not apply to Malik and Isana. I was glad of Iannis' warm, steady presence beside me as I contemplated how my half-siblings wished me dead.

"Ragir considers you a threat to the family honor, for all the reasons that you would imagine," Haman said gravely. "I would be stripped of my office should the truth come out, and my family's reputation would be in ruins. I suppose in his twisted way, he saw it as a necessity to protect his daughter and grandchildren."

"I assume that you are going to punish your son for his

crime?" Iannis asked, fury simmering just beneath his cool tone. Anger radiated off him in waves, and I squeezed his arm a little tighter. The last thing I needed was for him to attack Haman, though I knew Iannis probably wouldn't do that. He very rarely lost his head over anything. "I would hate to have to take matters into my own hands," he added in a tone that made it very clear that he absolutely *would* do so if he felt he had to.

"Of course," Haman said tightly. "I cannot allow such insubordination, never mind the fact that Sunaya is my flesh and blood." His expression softened as he looked my way. Iannis tensed slightly when Haman reached into his sleeve, but relaxed when he only withdrew a small velvet box.

"Please accept this, as a token of my regret," he said, handing it to me. "It will not make up for my absence as a father, or for my son's deplorable behavior, but I believe you'll find it quite useful."

"T-thanks," I said, opening the box. Inside rested a gold ring with a square-cut emerald in the center. The gemstone flashed in the morning sunlight as I held it up, and the scent of magic tickled my nose. "What does it do?"

"Aside from looking pretty?" The corner of Haman's lip briefly curved. "It will help you tell friend from foe. When an enemy is near, it will grow warm, and when one approaches with killing intent, it will grow hot."

"So it'll scald me in an attempt to save me?" I asked dubiously. With the kind of life I led, I might have burn marks on my finger in no time at all.

"No, it won't get quite that hot," Haman said. "This ring is a family heirloom, said to have belonged to the First Mage's daughter, our ancestress. As it is clearly designed for a woman, it has not been used in my family for some time. I intended to give it to Isana, but in light of recent events, I think you could use it more. And you *are* my first-born child."

"Oh. Well, thank you." Touched, I slipped the jewel onto the ring finger on my right hand. It fit perfectly, as though made for me. "I will wear it always."

"Good." Haman smiled briefly, then grew stern as he looked at Iannis. "Take good care of my daughter, Lord Iannis. I may not be able to claim her publicly, but I won't allow harm to come to her if I can help it."

"I will," Iannis said, something like respect entering his voice for the first time. "She is mine, after all." He pulled me a little tighter against him.

"I can take care of myself perfectly well, you know," I said, a little cross now. I didn't like the way the men were talking about me, as if I were a possession.

"Of that I have no doubt," Haman assured me. He bowed to us both. "Good day, my dear."

As Iannis and I watched Haman walk away, I leaned against him and smiled a little. His possessiveness might be a little much at times, but Iannis wrapped me in his love and was unafraid to stand by me openly in the eyes of the world.

30

*D*espite the happy note on which my meeting with my father ended, I still found myself restless. While Iannis and the others discussed the various treaties they had negotiated over the past weeks, I went outdoors, wandering between the guest pavilions as I tried to sort my thoughts. Yes, my father had acknowledged me, but I couldn't quite ignore the sting of rejection from my half-siblings. Anger simmered in my heart as I remembered the way Malik had snubbed me at the testing ceremony. That the little snot had tried to kill me *really* rubbed me the wrong way. And Isana's subterfuge was hardly any better.

I'm so glad we're going home soon, I thought, my hands clenching into fists at my sides. The extravagant coronation ceremony had come and gone, and there were only a few days of celebration left before we could depart. The sooner I could put some distance between myself and my half-siblings, the better.

My feet ended up carrying me to a shell fountain that emptied out into yet another koi pond. The sound of water trickling, and the scents of blossoming flowers from the trees, teased me out of my angry mood. I sat down at the edge of the pond, then rolled up the legs of my pants and slipped off my shoes so I could dip my toes in the cool water. A golden-red fish popped its head out of the water, and I giggled a little as it nibbled at my toe with its rubbery lips.

I shouldn't let Malik and Isana get me down, I told myself. What happened, happened, and I would just have to trust that Haman would deal with them and their vicious grandfather. I would be back in the Federation in a matter of weeks, safe from Lord Ragir's machinations and hateful ways, and far too busy with my apprenticeship and other duties to spare the ar'Rhea family another thought. Until such a time that my father felt it safe to reach out to me again, I would put the whole bunch of them out of my mind. I'd coped without them well enough for almost a quarter of a century, and I would continue to do so.

My right hand began to grow very warm, and it took me a moment to remember the ring that Haman had given me. I glanced down to see that the emerald was glowing, and the hairs on the back of my neck stood straight on end. Acting on instinct, I jumped high in the air, just in time to avoid a blast of magic from Malik as he sprang out from behind a large statue.

"Filthy half-breed!" he shouted, his tanned cheeks pink with rage. He said something else, but the sound of the fountain shattering beneath the force of his blast drowned out his words. I threw up a shield to avoid the debris, curling my lip as Malik hastily dodged a piece of flying shrapnel.

"What the fuck is your problem?" I shouted, hurling a fireball at him. He deflected it easily, sending it careening back at me, and I was forced to absorb the magic before it hit one of the trees around us and caused a fire. I winced—Malik was very strong for his age. "Didn't your father tell you to leave me alone?" Fury rose in me, quick and deadly, at Malik's unreasonable and unceasing enmity. What the hell had I done to deserve this? Wasn't *he* the one with the name, the pedigree, the wealth and inheritance? How dare he act as if he was the one who'd been wronged!

"As if I could!" Malik swept out his hand, shouting an incantation, and sent a wave of red magic rushing toward me. I threw up another shield, but I couldn't deflect the attack completely, and the wave slammed me into one of the trees. I let out a strangled cry as one of my ribs cracked, and I dug my claws into the bark to keep myself upright. The rib would heal in short order—I was far from down and out.

"Father is not in his right mind, giving such a priceless heirloom to a dirty shifter like you," Malik spat, stalking toward me. Magic glowed at his fingertips, and a chill went down my spine at the cold hatred in his green eyes. "It is my duty to protect the ar'Rhea name."

"By murdering me? How very honorable," I sneered. "It's a wonder I'm not impressed by your noble rank."

"If I must kill you in order to get that ring back," he hissed, his eyes gleaming with relish, "then I shall do so gladly. A byblow like you has no right to it!" The color in his cheeks and the fervor in his gaze told me that he was in no mood to listen—nothing I could say would make an impression while he was high on anger and self-righteousness.

"You can try," I challenged, flinging a chakram at his neck. He deflected the blade easily, but the distraction cost him, and before he knew it, I was high up in the air above him. His eyes widened as I blasted him with ice magic from above, where his shield did not protect him, and he barely managed to get out of the way. Ice crackled across the earth, sending chills through my body as my bare feet touched the ground again, and I had to be careful not to slip as I rushed him again. To my surprise, he flung a small throwing knife at me, and the blade sliced through my left sleeve and upper arm before I could dodge. Blood trickled down my arm, and I hissed at the faint scent of magic mingling with my blood. Was this another blade he'd spelled, so that my wound wouldn't close?

"*Enough*," I roared, grabbing him by the throat. His eyes bulged, both in fear and surprise—he'd obviously expected his knife wound to slow me more than it had. I trembled with rage as I hefted him above me—clearly, this bastard had underestimated me as a *filthy half-breed*. Fury eroded my control, and I slammed him into the dirt. His head knocked against the ground, and had it been hard-packed rather than muddy, that would have been the end of him. But no—he deserved to suffer first.

"You miserable excuse for a mage!" I reared back, then kicked him in the balls for good measure. He shrieked in pain, and I only felt a twinge of guilt beneath my vicious delight. "You can take your ignorant opinion of me and shove it up your ass!" I kicked him again, this time in the ribs, as I grabbed another chakram to put an end to his useless existence. He'd made it clear that this world wasn't big enough for the two of us, and I would make damn sure that I wasn't the one to go.

Stay your hand, a cool voice echoed in my head, and I froze before I could deliver the killing blow. *Do not let hatred guide you.*

I hesitated, reluctant to let go of my anger. Was this the moment, the decision, that Resinah had warned me about when I'd last visited her temple? Some of the red haze cleared from my vision, and I blinked down at my half-brother. He was bloodied up now, his long-lashed eyes closed. Had I knocked him unconscious? His elegant clothes were splattered with mud and drops of blood that seeped from the wound on my arm.

Much as I hated to acknowledge it, Malik was also a descendant of Resinah. As full of bigotry as he was, he was still young. He might still amount to something in his miserable, haughty existence, if I spared him. Or if not Malik himself, then his children or grandchildren. And Haman would be devastated if I massacred his son, regardless of the provocation. Shaking, I sucked in a deep breath, then dispelled my anger with it as best I could.

"I could beat you into a bloody pulp," I said to him, "but that won't make me any better than a scumbag like you."

His eyes snapped open at that—or at least, the right one did. The left one was swelling shut. "You are no kin of mine," he growled.

"Why the hell would I claim kinship to a spoiled brat like you?" I scoffed. "The last thing I want is to be related to the likes of you. I would have killed you with no regrets had Resinah not prevented me just now. You owe the Lady your worthless life, Malik ar'Rhea, and I suggest you grovel on your hands and knees right now and thank her. I have no idea why she'd take pity on you when you only bring shame to her line, but it's not my place to question her."

He gaped up at me, struggling onto his elbows. "A shifter like you would know nothing about the Lady." It was obvious from the incredulity in his voice that the idea that I might have communed with Resinah was inconceivable. "Or of family honor, for that matter. You are just animals that pretend to be human every now and then. I can't understand why Father—"

The rest of his words were cut off with a burble as I pressed my boot against his throat. "Enough, asshole," I growled. "Don't you know when to quit? I swear it's like you *want* me to gut you."

Keeping just enough pressure on his throat to silence him without killing him, I reached out to Iannis via mindspeak. *"You around? I've found my would-be assassin, and I could use a hand."*

"What?" His voice was sharp with alarm. *"Where? Are you all right?"*

"I'm fine. Mostly," I amended as the scent of my own blood grew thicker. *"I've already subdued him, out here in one of the*

gardens. Come find us, quickly." I didn't need to give him directions
—he'd find us with the serapha charm.

Iannis arrived in no time, and from his windblown hair and
the slight flush to his cheeks, I gathered he'd used his Tua super
speed. His violet eyes sparked with rage as he caught sight of my
bloody arm. I'd ripped the sleeve and fashioned a tourniquet
out of it, but the fabric was already soaked with blood.

"This murderous little punk had another one of those magic
knives," I explained, feeling a little unsteady now. The cut wasn't
very big, but since it wasn't healing, I was losing more blood
than I should.

Iannis let out a curse in his native tongue, and, if looks could
kill, Malik would be dead on the spot. Indeed, the kid looked
like he was about to crap his pants, his face going bone white at
the look in Iannis's eyes. I tried not to sulk at that—Malik hadn't
reacted half as strongly when I'd been about to kill him. Guess I
had to work on my intimidation tactics.

"I'll deal with you later," Iannis snapped at him. He jabbed a
finger at Malik and growled the Words to the immobilization
spell. Malik went rigid, his eyes burning with rage though he
could no longer move. Even so, I didn't take my eyes off him
while Iannis gently unwrapped the tourniquet from around
my arm.

"You should have done some healing on this yourself," he
admonished me as he pressed a hand against the wound.

"I couldn't afford to take my attention off Malik," I admitted
as Iannis closed his eyes. Pain zinged through my arm as his
magic accelerated the healing, but it passed quickly. In seconds,
the wound was healed. "And besides, I knew you'd come," I
added with a crooked smile.

"Always," he said, his voice softening for just an instant
before he pulled away. His fury came back in full force as he
turned back to Malik "Your half-brother has a penchant for

poisoned knives, unusual for a mage. I'm surprised you let him live, *a ghrá.*"

"I nearly didn't," I confessed.

Iannis paused. "Why not?"

I considered telling him about Resinah, then shrugged. "Just didn't seem right." I wasn't sure whether Resinah had plans for Malik, or if she'd just been trying to prevent me from doing something I'd regret later, so I decided it was better not to say anything.

Iannis's mouth quirked. "Your control is improving then." He gestured brusquely toward Malik, undoing the spell. "On your feet, boyo."

Malik stumbled to his feet, an arm wrapped around his abdomen. Hatred gleamed in his good eye, stronger than the pain that was obviously radiating from his ribs. With the way I'd kicked them, they must be badly bruised, if not broken.

"I do not understand," he rasped, "why a powerful, noble-born mage such as yourself would ally yourself to a filthy shifter, Lord Iannis. Why would you seek to make her your wife? It is madness to mix the races like that!"

"Be silent," Iannis growled. The air around him began to spark and sizzle, as it did during those rare occasions when his temper boiled over. "That grandfather of yours has filled your brain with his bigotry, but in the wider world, such notions are petty and futile. Be grateful that your life was spared. After what you just said, I am beginning to doubt you will hold onto it for long."

"My grandfather will hear of this—" Malik blustered, but Iannis cut him off with a slice of his hand.

"I don't care about the sob story you tell your grandfather, so long as you also tell him that if he ever goes after Sunaya again, I will have his head. Now swear on the Lady Resinah, who must be writhing in embarrassment at how far her family has sunk, that you will not harm my fiancée again. Or I will send your head back to Castalis myself."

"I s-swear on the Lady Resinah that I will n-not harm Sunaya Baine again," Malik ground out, with obvious reluctance.

"Go on."

"May the Lady strike me dead if I fail in this."

I looked curiously at Iannis. It sounded like an established formula, but I'd never heard that particular oath before.

"Good. Now get out of my sight."

"Would you really have sent Malik's head to Lord Ragir? I asked, leaning against Iannis's shoulder as Malik slunk away with his proverbial tail between his legs. "Wouldn't that cause an international incident?" *It would grieve my father too*, I thought to myself. And though I'd only just met Haman, I didn't want that.

"I don't care what it would cause," Iannis said, turning me to face him. He wrapped his arms around my waist and drew me close. "You're mine, Sunaya, to cherish and protect. I would sooner the world burn than allow anyone to take you from me."

He kissed me fiercely then, his fingers digging into my hips as he held me tight against him. And as I kissed him back, I clung tight to that promise, which was as secure as the strong arms wrapped around me. The world might not always be a safe place, but I could trust in Iannis, and that was enough for me.

31

"*W*hy so glum, Miss Baine?" Garrett asked as I stared back at Garai's receding coastline. We were aboard the Voyager once more, the ship now fully repaired, and the salty sea breeze tugged at my hair as the winds pushed us further out to sea, toward home. "If I didn't know better, I'd say you were sad to be leaving."

"I am," I admitted, still looking at the coastline. We had traveled all the way back to Maral port, and were now finally embarking on the long sea voyage home. Just a little further down the rails, Director Chen stood next to Liu, conversing in Garaian. The little girl seemed much more excited to be on her way than I was, even though she was leaving her homeland behind. "I wish we could have spent more time exploring Garai, instead of standing around at receptions with stuffy politicians. To be honest, I had a lot more fun on our mission, despite the danger."

Or rather, because *of the danger,* I didn't say aloud.

"I can empathize with that. Those long weeks of diplomacy were enough even for me," Garrett said dryly. "Very worth it, in light of our success, but I agree it would have been nice to see more of the country."

"You two are free to do that on your own dime," the Minister said drolly. I turned to see him approaching us, Iannis at his side. "You can console yourselves with our upcoming stop at the Calinian Islands, which is costing us three extra days." The Minister didn't seem pleased about the delay, and I had to suppress a smirk. He could be a grump about it all he wanted—I was very much looking forward to exploring the volcanic island kingdom, which Iannis had said was spectacular.

"The Captain was quite adamant that we could not afford to bypass the Islands," the Minister went on. "It makes a man wonder whether or not it is a necessary stop, or if he simply wishes to sample the island's pleasures." The annoyance in his voice grew. "I do not have time for such frivolities, with so many important matters awaiting me back in Dara. The Resistance has still left many messes for us to clean up."

"Of course, sir," Garrett said. "I too have much work to do, as I'm sure Lord Iannis does as well." His tone turned slightly less welcoming as he turned toward Iannis.

"Most definitely," Iannis agreed slowly, holding Garrett's gaze. "After all these weeks away from Solantha, I could use a break in between missions, so that I might attend to Canalo's affairs. I do not have the luxury of working solely for the Minister's office, as you do."

"I'm well aware of that," the Minister said, and Iannis and Garrett finally turned to look at him. "And will take that into account when assigning future missions. But until the Resistance is vanquished, that must be our top priority."

"Understood," Iannis said, and I stifled a sigh. I *really* hoped that we wouldn't get roped into another mission any time soon. Weren't there any other mages in the Federation capable of dealing with the Resistance?

"I doubt we will have any problem squashing them like the vermin they are, not at this stage of the game," the Minister went on. "But in case they do manage to get to me again, I will need to nominate a successor." Garrett straightened at that, like a bloodhound catching the scent of prey. "I have decided that it will be either you, Garrett, or Lord Iannis, depending on your respective performance between now and the next Convention." The Minister looked from one to the other with a self-satisfied expression, as though expecting a show of gratitude.

"That's very flattering, Minister," Iannis said, sounding almost bored. It was clear from his expression and voice that he was indifferent, and didn't really take the announcement seriously.

"An honor," Garrett said, his hazel eyes bright with challenge. "I will perform my duties outstandingly, Minister, as I have always done."

"See to it that you do," the Minister said, narrowing his eyes briefly. Garrett's cheeks flushed, and I figured they were both thinking about his previous fall from grace. "I will be in my cabin if anyone needs me," he finally said, then turned away.

Garrett gave Iannis a long, cool look, then stalked away as well. I sucked on my teeth as I leaned against the railing, doing my best to bury my frustration at the whole thing. I was getting really tired of the constant pissing contests between Garrett and Iannis, and now on top of it, the Minister wanted to name Iannis as his successor?

"How the hell am I ever going to finish my apprenticeship if the Minister keeps piling more and more duties on you?" I grumbled as Iannis leaned against the railing next to me. "Or if, Magorah forbid, you become the next Minister. We'd have to move to Dara." I shuddered at the prospect of living in a place so prejudiced against shifters.

"I very much doubt that will ever happen," Iannis said as he casually looped an arm around my shoulders. "The Minister is unlikely to step down any time soon. I suspect he is just trying to make us work harder to curry his favor. I'll believe his offer is sincere when he makes good on it, not a moment before. Anyway, Garrett is welcome to the position. I doubt he will want to give me any more responsibilities than he can help, given his animosity toward me, so if he does get it, you'll have me all to yourself. Relatively speaking," he added with a wink.

"I sure will. And in less than a year, you'll be all mine." Leaning into him a little, I wrapped myself up in his warmth and allowed my worries to be carried away by the ocean breeze.

THE CALINIAN ISLES were as spectacular as Iannis had promised, and then some. I fell in love with them the moment we stepped foot on the island, where we were received by a group of adorable boys and girls who placed flower garlands around our necks. The majority of our party, Iannis included, immediately went to visit the local Northian consul, eager to hear whatever news he might have from home. I, on the other hand, was thoroughly sick of meetings, so I whisked Liu away with me to explore the small port town where our steamer was moored.

"This is very pretty," Liu said, her dark eyes sparkling as she gazed upon a mother-of-pearl necklace. She'd dragged me into the very first jewelry shop we'd passed, and though I wasn't much for baubles myself, I was more than happy to let her flit around the shop, oohing and ahhing at the display cases and charming the shopkeeper and his wife.

"It is," I agreed. The chain was gold, and the mother-of-pearl pendant, shaped into a plumeria, seemed to glow a soft white in the late morning sun. "Why don't you try it on? Maybe we'll buy it."

Liu's eyes widened. "Really?" she squealed, bouncing up and down on the balls of her feet. Her braided hair bounced with her—Director Chen had taken care dressing her this morning in pink and white silk. "But this is too expensive for me."

"Don't be silly," I said as the shopkeeper's wife opened up the case. "One has to splurge every once in a while on vacation, or what's the point?"

The necklace looked lovely against Liu's ivory skin, so I bought it for her, as well as another necklace for Tinari. As we were about to leave, I remembered Com's daughter, and paid for a third. It was a novel experience, pulling out my full purse to pay for expensive trinkets without having to worry if I could afford it. In Garai, we hadn't been allowed to pay for anything, except when we were in Leniang Port, so my purse was still pretty hefty.

Liu wore the pendant out of the shop, and we spent the rest of the morning indulging in a glorious bout of shopping fever. With Liu's enthusiastic help, I quickly found presents for Com and Elania, Rylan, Fenris, Janta, Annia, and even Nelia, my social secretary. We might have been weighed down with packages, but my heart was lighter than it had been in weeks. A sunny day of shopping on a friendly island could do that to a girl.

An hour later, Iannis found us just as we were hunting for a place to rest. He quickly hired a minion to take our packages back to the steamer, then led us to a beachside bistro. Sitting outside on a charming wooden patio shaded by palm fronds, I ordered a huge cup of fruit and ice cream for myself, and a smaller one for Liu. Iannis ordered a local drink, some kind of colorful liquid with a tiny umbrella in it. Liu had never tried ice cream before, but she was hooked after her first bite of the cold, creamy dessert, and, within minutes, was already asking for more.

"So, what news was there from Solantha?" I asked as Liu dug into her second cup. She was still very thin, so I didn't see the harm in indulging her. "You seem a little down." I'd noticed the shadow in his eyes immediately, but had decided not to say anything until we were settled.

Iannis leaned in a little closer, the skin around his eyes tightening. "Dara Federal Prison burned down while we were in Leniang," he said.

"*What*?" My stomach dropped. "What happened to Thorgana, then? Did she survive the fire?" And what about all the other prisoners? There must have been hundreds in the facility.

"Her fate is unclear. Many of the prisoners were either injured or killed, and a good dozen or so went missing. Thorgana's body has yet to be identified amongst the dead... but many of the bodies were burned beyond recognition, so it's possible she did not survive."

I put my ice cream spoon down, my appetite gone now. "It would be a relief if she'd died in that fire," I said, as horrible a thought as it was, "but we can't assume that. She could be at large even as we speak." Suddenly, the sun was too bright, the bird calls too harsh, the waves too violent as they crashed against the surf only yards away. If Thorgana was alive, she would unleash hell upon the Federation in retaliation for all that we'd done to her. I was sure of it.

"Yes," Iannis agreed. "The humans are also becoming very restive. Not the Resistance so much, but the religious fanatics who follow Father Calmias. They are still demanding that he be freed."

"Ugh." I rolled my eyes. "Well, if Thorgana is on the loose, now would be the worst time to free that genocidal bastard." My lip curled at the memory of him standing in the Ur-God temple, calling for his congregation to unite against mages and shifters. He might be an old man, but I would never forget the power and charisma he exuded, and the way he used it to drive his audience toward bigotry and hatred.

"I agree. We will have to deal with him when we return to Solantha. And speaking of which...." He reached into his sleeve and pulled out a blue envelope. "A letter arrived for you. From your bodyguard."

"Really?" I blinked in surprise as I took the letter, gazing down at the familiar script on the front of it, addressed to me. It was Rylan's, all right. He'd rarely contacted me during his years in the Resistance, so if he was sending me a letter, it must be important. Impatient, I tore open the envelope, then unfolded the stationary inside.

"*Dear Sunaya,*" I read aloud, Rylan's voice echoing in my head. "*I hope you are enjoying your trip abroad. Your pesky parrot seems to miss you as much as I do, and has permanently attached himself to me. We both agree that I make a poor substitute for you, and hope you'll come back soon.*"

Iannis and I laughed at that. "So it *is* still alive," I exclaimed. Was alive even the right word? Existing? Perpetuating? Pain-in-the-ass-ing?

"It would seem so," Iannis agreed. "How very curious. I should like to study your pet when we return."

"*In the meantime, F. and I have decided to name it Trouble,*" I read on. "*Amazingly, it's responding to the name, so I think you're stuck with it. Serves you right for not naming it yourself.*"

I snorted at that. "I probably would have picked that name myself," I admitted with a shake of my head.

"It is quite suitable," Iannis agreed.

"*The children we interviewed are all doing well, and are being taken care of. Your friend Janta has taken an interest in Tinari, and is looking into adopting her.*"

"An excellent choice," Iannis said. "Janta will make a great mother for her."

"I agree!" My heart lightened at the thought that Tinari had finally found a new home. Glancing at Liu, who was humming a song as she worked on her ice cream, completely tuning us out, I wondered if the two little girls could become friends. Liu didn't have magic, but the two girls were close in age. And besides, I was proof that one could socialize outside of one's own race.

"Unfortunately, not all the news I bring is good." My heart sank at that. *"There have been several earthquake tremors recently, more frequent than usual for Solantha. And someone has put out a contract on your head for ten thousand pieces of gold."*

"Shit," I growled, my fingers tightening around the letter. "Are these assassination attempts never going to end?"

"That is a very large sum, especially for humans," Iannis observed. His eyes glittered with restrained fury, though in general he was much calmer than I'd expected. "It seems far too coincidental that a contract was put out on you so soon after Thorgana went missing."

"Yeah." I licked my lips. "But it could also be Father Calmias. His followers blame me for his incarceration, after all. They might have raised funds to take me out."

"Either way, we'll need to be very careful," Iannis warned. He reached for my hand and squeezed it tightly. "I will send word ahead to have Palace security increased."

I bit back a sigh. What else was new? *"Your friend Comenius and his daughter have returned from Pernia. The wedding has been postponed, and they haven't set a new date yet as far as I know. F. and I have been busy, so I haven't had a chance to ask Comenius in person about what happened. But I thought you might want to know."*

"Damn it," I groaned, lowering the letter. "I was afraid this might happen... but I really hoped it wouldn't. Com shouldn't let his daughter drive him and Elania apart. They're so good together!"

"Things might not be as bad as they sound," Iannis said. "It is possible Comenius has simply postponed the wedding because his daughter needs the time and space to settle in."

"I guess we'll find out when we get back." And if there was a rift between Com and Elania, hopefully I could help sort it out. Comenius deserved to be happy.

"By the way, F. has been getting grumpier by the day. Guess he doesn't like being separated from Lord Iannis. He's asked me to urge you to come home as quickly as possible, and I have to agree. You've been gone too long! Just don't forget to bring something back for your favorite cousin, who has to live vicariously through you now that he's retired.

"Love, Lanyr."

I grinned a little at that, but my smile faded as I noticed the serious look on Iannis's face. "I suspect that last bit from Fenris is more serious than it appears," he said, rubbing his triangular chin. "There is something he wishes to discuss that is dire enough he felt he could not allude to it even in a private letter."

"Any idea what it could be?" I asked. He knew Fenris a lot better than I did.

"No," Iannis said, his expression suddenly lightening. He sat back in his chair, then picked up his glass and took a long drink from it. "And since there is nothing we can do about it now, we'll simply have to put it out of our minds until we get home. We're scheduled to meet with the Queen this afternoon, but I'll take you up on that volcano tomorrow. I've booked a secluded lodge on the beach, just for the two of us."

"Oh?" I lifted my eyebrows as warmth began to slowly spread through me. "So your solution is to frolic on the beach, then?"

"I have a little more than frolicking in mind," he purred in mindspeak, his violet eyes gleaming. Heat pooled in my lower belly, and I had to remind myself that Liu was sitting right next to us before I gave into the urge to grab his face and pull his mouth against mine.

"*I'm sure you do*," I responded with a grin. A warm breeze laced with magic licked against the nape of my neck, and I shivered in anticipation. Finished with our ice cream, we paid for our drinks, then left, my left hand in Iannis's and my right hand in Liu's.

There might be problems lurking on the horizon, but I knew there always would be. Life had not dealt me an easy hand—it had dealt me cards full of danger and excitement, and I wouldn't have it any other way. Those hard times only made bright, sunny days like this even sweeter, and I wouldn't let anyone stop me from enjoying them for all they were worth.

To be continued...

Sunaya's journey will continue in Scorched by Magic, Book 7 of the Baine Chronicles! There are more books coming, so make sure you subscribe to Jasmine's newsletter so you don'

Want to keep up with Jasmine on social media? You can find her on Facebook, follow her on Twitter @jasmine_writes, and follow her on Instagram @jasmine.walt. You can also email her at jasmine@jasminewalt.com if you have questions or just want to say hi. She loves hearing from her fans!

GLOSSARY

Annia: see under Melcott, Annia.

Ancestral Spirits: according to Shifter belief, once a being is done with reincarnation, they may become ancestral spirits.

ar': suffix in mages' family names, that denotes they are of noble birth, and can trace their descent to one of Resinah's twelve disciples.

Baine, Sunaya: a half-panther shifter, half-mage who used to hate mages and has a passion for justice. Because magic is forbidden to all but the mage families, Sunaya was forced to keep her abilities a secret until she accidentally used them to defend herself in front of witnesses. Rather than condemn her to death, the Chief Mage, Iannis ar'Sannin, chose to take her on as his apprentice, and eventually his fiancée. She struggles to balance her shifter and mage heritage.

Baine, Melantha: Sunaya's cousin, and daughter to the Jaguar Clan's Chieftain.

Baine, Mafiela: Chieftain of the Jaguar Clan and Sunaya's aunt.

Baine, Mika: a young jaguar shifter, daughter of Melantha Baine.

Baine, Rylan: one of Chieftain Baine's least favored children, and Sunaya's cousin. An active member of the Resistance, with the rank of Captain, he was captured and imprisoned during the uprising in Solantha. His sentence was commuted and he is currently serving it out as Sunaya's bodyguard.

Ballos, Jonias: a reclusive, elderly mage living in the Mages Quarter of Solantha. Sunaya's father studied under him while he was in Solantha.

Benefactor: the name the Resistance called their anonymous, principal source of financial support, before Sunaya unmasked her.

The Black Curtain: shop owned by Elania Tarrignal in Witches' End, where under-the-table hexes can be discreetly obtained.

Canalo: one of the fifty states making up the Northia Federation, located on the West Coast of the Northia Continent.

Canalo Council, usually just the **Council:** a governmental body composed of eight senior mages, supposed to advise the Chief Mage and substitute for him in case of sudden death or incapacity.

Capitol: building in the capital, Dara, where the Convention of Chief Mages meets every other year to conduct government business.

Chen, Lalia: the current Director of the Canalo Mages Guild in Solantha. She serves as deputy to Iannis ar'Sannin, the Chief Mage.

Chartis, Argon: former Director of the Canalo Mages Guild, dismissed by the Chief Mage for insubordination and attempts to undermine the Chief Mage's authority. He subsequently joined forces with the Benefactor to avenge his dismissal.

Chieftain: a title used to distinguish the head of a shifter clan.

Calmias, Father Monor: a charismatic preacher in Ur-God temples, with many followers all over Northia.

Castalis: a country and peninsula at the southwestern edge of the Central Continent, ruled by Sunaya's father, the High Mage.

Central Continent: the largest of the continents on Recca, spanning from Garai in the east to Castalis in the west.

Comenius Genhard: a hedgewitch from Pernia, owner of the shop Over the Hedge at Witches' End. Close friend of Sunaya Baine, employer of Noria Melcott, and lover of the witch Elania.

Creator: the ultimate deity, worshipped by all three races under different names.

Dira: mage, one of the secretaries at the Mages Guild.

Dara: capital of the Northia Federation, located on the east coast of the Northia Continent.

Elania Tarrignal: Comenius's fiancée; a witch specializing in potions, with a shop in Witches' End.

Elnos: see under Ragga, Elnos.

Enforcer: a bounty hunter employed by the government to seek out and capture wanted criminals. They operate under strict rules and are paid bounties for each head. While the majority are human, there is a strong minority of shifters, and even the occasional mage.

Enforcers' Guild: the administrative organization in charge of the enforcers. Also, the building from which the various enforcer crews work under their respective foremen.

Faonus: one of the three founding mages of the Federation.

Fenris: formerly known as Polar ar'Tollis, the Chief Mage of Nebara. To escape execution for committing treason against the Federation, he allowed Iannis to change him into a wolf shifter. He now goes by Fenris, and lives in Solantha Palace as a close friend and confidante of the Canalo Chief Mage.

Firegate Bridge: Solantha's best-known structure, a large red bridge spanning the length of Solantha Bay. It is accessible via Firegate Road.

Captain Galling: the human captain of the Enforcer's Guild in Solantha City, appointed by the former Chief Mage and Council.

Garai: the largest and most populated country on the Eastern Continent. Garaians are known for slanted eyes and ivory skin as well as their complicated, rune-like alphabet.

Garidano, Cirin: The Finance Secretary of the State of Canalo. He is loyal to Iannis, but also very ambitious.

Graning, Zavian: the Minister of the Northia Federation. Elected by the Convention for an indefinite term, he is charged with coordination of governmental business and particularly foreign affairs, between the biannual Convention sessions that he prepares and presides.

Great Accord: a treaty struck by the ruling mages centuries ago which brought an end to a devastating war known as the Conflict. It is still the basis upon which mages rule their countries and territories. All new laws must be in accordance with the provisions of the Great Accord.

Gulaya: a star-shaped charm, usually made of metal, that is anchored to a specific location and can take its wearer back there at need. They are rare, and difficult to recharge.

Haman ar'Rhea: High Mage of Castalis, a country in the south-west of the Central Continent, and Sunaya's long-lost father.

Iannis ar'Sannin: Chief Mage of Canalo. He resides in the capital city of Solantha, from which he runs Canalo as well as the Mages Guild with the help of his deputy and Secretaries. He is originally a native of Manuc, a country located across the Eastern Sea.

Isana ar'Rhea: daughter of the High Mage of Castalis and Sunaya's half-sister.

Incidium: a powerful illegal drug that produces euphoria.

Janta Urama: mage and scholar, head librarian in the Solantha Mages Guild.

Lanyr Goldrin: The pseudonym Rylan Baine uses in his tiger-shifter bodyguard guise.

Leniang Port: a lawless port city on the south coast of Garai.

Loranian: the difficult, secret language of magic that all mages are required to master.

Mages Guild: the governmental organization that rules the mages in Canalo, and supervises the other races. The headquarters are in Solantha Palace. They are subordinate to the Chief Mage.

Magi-tech: devices that are powered by both magic and technology.

Manuc: an island country off the west coast of the Central Continent.

Magorah: the god of the shifters, associated with the moon.

Melcott, Annia: a human enforcer. She is a close friend of Sunaya's, and Noria's older sister.

Melcott, Noria: Annia Melcott's younger sister. A gifted inventor, who used to work part-time in the shop Over the Hedge, belonging to Comenius Genhard, and has a mage boyfriend, Elnos. She passionately believes in equality between all races, and supports the Resistance, which she eventually joined. She is currently serving out a five-year sentence in the salt mines.

Micara: one of the mages who made up the Founding Trio of the Federation, together with Faonus and Jeremidah.

Mills, Thorgana: the Benefactor's true identity. On the surface, Thorgana appears to be nothing but a human socialite, content to let others run the media empire she inherited from her late father. In actuality, she is a bloodthirsty half-shifter, half-human hybrid who hates shifters and mages with a passion, and will stop at nothing to ensure they are wiped from the face of Recca. After being exposed as the Benefactor, her companies were seized and auctioned off, and she was imprisoned in Dara.

Minister: the mage who presides over the Convention of Chief Mages, and coordinates the affairs of the Northia Federation between sessions, particularly foreign relations. Technically the Northia Federation's head of state, though the full Convention of Chief Mages outranks him. The office is currently held by Zavian Graning.

Miyanta: daughter and disciple of the First Mage Resinah, from whom the ar'Rhea family traces its descent.

Noria: see under Melcott, Noria.

Northia Federation: a federation consisting of fifty states that cover the entire northern half and middle of the Western Continent. Canalo is part of this federation.

Osero: one of the fifty states of the Northia Federation, located north of Canalo on the continent's west coast.

Over the Hedge: a shop at Witches' End selling magical charms and herbal remedies, belonging to Comenius Genhard.

Pandanum: a base metal used, inter alia, for less valuable coins.

Pernia: The home country of Comenius Genhard, located in the northwestern area of the Central Continent.

Polar ar'Tollis: the former Chief Mage of Nebara, now known as Fenris. He was condemned to death by the Federation after helping a human family escape execution.

Prison Isle: an island in the middle of Solantha Bay that serves as a prison for Canalo's worst criminals.

Ragga, Elnos: Noria Melcott's former boyfriend. He is a student at Solantha academy and one of the few mages who believes in equality amongst the races. He and Noria worked together to develop new magi-tech devices.

Ragir, Lady Aria: wife to the High Mage of Castalis and First

Lady of that country (since her marriage, styled Lady Aria Ragir ar'Rhea).

Recca: the planet and world in which the Baine Chronicles takes place.

Residah: the mages' book of scripture that holds Resinah's teachings.

Resinah: also known as the First Mage, whose teachings are of paramount spiritual importance for the mages. Her statue can be found in the mage temples, which are off-limits to non-mages and magically hidden from outsiders.

Resistance: a movement of revolutionaries planning to over-throw the mages and take control of the Northia Federation, financially backed by the Benefactor. Over time, they became bolder and more aggressive, using terrorist attacks with civilian casualties, as well as assassination. They even tried to take over Solantha, when the government was in disarray after they had engineered the Chief Mage's disappearance. Sunaya's discovery that the Benefactor and the human leaders of the Resistance were planning to turn against the shifters once the mages were defeated dealt a blow to the unity of the movement, but its human component is far from completely defeated, and working on "secret weapons."

ar'Rhea: family name of a noble Castalian family of mages, who trace their descent to the first mage Resinah through her daughter Miyanta.

Rowanville: the only neighborhood of Solantha where all three races mix.

Sandia: a large country (and subcontinent) of the Central Continent, populated by many different peoples.

Serapha charms: paired charms that allow two people, usually a couple, to find each other via twinned stones imbued with a small part of their essence. Normally, only the wearer can take a serapha charm off.

Shifter: a human who can change into animal form and back by magic; they originally resulted from illegal experiments by mages on ordinary humans.

Shiftertown: the part of Solantha where the official shifter clans live.

Solantha: the capital of Canalo State, a port city on the west coast of the Northia continent.

Solantha Palace: the seat of power in Canalo, where both the Chief Mage and the Mages Guild reside. It is located near the coast of Solantha Bay.

Thrase, Nelia: a young human woman who serves as Sunaya's social secretary.

Tillmore, Roanas: the former Shiftertown Inspector and father figure/mentor to Sunaya. He was poisoned while digging into the silver murders, prompting Sunaya to take over the investigation.

Tua: a legendary and highly dangerous race of very long-lived beings with powerful magic, who sometimes cross from their own world into Recca, most frequently in Manuc.

Ur-God: the humans' version of the Creator. According to their scriptures, the Ur-God favors humans over all other races.

Vanderheim, Curian: Thorgana Mills's husband, a human millionaire and businessman. He went underground after Thorgana was imprisoned.

Witches' End: a pier in Solantha City, part of the Port, where immigrant magic users sell their wares and services.

Zavian Graning: see under Graning, Zavian.

ACKNOWLEDGMENTS

Thank you very much to my beta readers, particularly Victoria, Lenka, and Heather, for reading the early draft of Deceived by Magic and giving such helpful feedback. As usual, my beta readers always help turn my books from simply 'good' to 'freaking awesome'. <3

I'd also like to give a BIG thank you to my writing partner, Mary, for all the hard work you've done on this book. Your personal knowledge and travel experience in Asia really helped bring the setting for this story to life.

Another thank you is owed to Cynthia Shepp, my copy-editor. It's fantastic to have someone who's not only reliable, but flexible and willing to accommodate my crazy schedule! The fact that you like my books is also a nice plus. ;)

I'd also like to thank my author BFFs, Michael-Scott Earle and J.A. Cipriano, for making me laugh on a regular basis and being my comrades-in-arms, even if only behind the curtain. This is a crazy business we're in, and I'm glad to have you guys on my side.

And of course, I'd like to thank my AMAZING readers, who

have stuck with me on this wild ride since day one. Sunaya's journey has been crazy fun to write, and I'm glad you're enjoying her story as much as I am!

ABOUT THE AUTHOR

Jasmine Walt is obsessed with books, chocolate, and sharp objects. Somehow, those three things melded together in her head and transformed into a desire to write, usually fantastical stuff with a healthy dose of action and romance. Her characters are a little (okay, a lot) on the snarky side, and they swear, but they mean well. Even the villains sometimes.

When Jasmine isn't chained to her keyboard, you can find her practicing her triangle choke on the jujitsu mat, spending time with her family, or binge-watching superhero shows on Netflix.

Want to connect with Jasmine? You can find her on Twitter at @jasmine_writes, on Instagram @jasmine.walt, on Facebook, or at www.jasminewalt.com. You can also shoot her an email at jasmine@jasminwalt.com.

ALSO BY JASMINE WALT

The Baine Chronicles Series:

Burned by Magic

Bound by Magic

Hunted by Magic

Marked by Magic

Betrayed by Magic

Deceived by Magic

Scorched by Magic

Tested by Magic (Novella)

Forsaken by Magic (Novella)

The Nia Rivers Adventures

Dragon Bones

Demeter's Tablet

Templar Scrolls

Serpent Mound

Eden's Garden

The Gatekeeper Chronicles

Marked by Sin

Hunted by Sin

Claimed by Sin

The Dragon's Gift Trilogy

Dragon's Gift

Dragon's Blood

Dragon's Curse

The Legend of Tariel

Kingdom of Storms

Den of Thieves

Empire of Magic